A STUDY IN GOLD

A STUDY IN GOLD

An Oxford Dogwalkers' Mystery

Annie Dalton

This first world edition published 2017
in Great Britain and the USA by
SEVERN HOUSE PUBLISHERS LTD of
Eardley House, 4 Uxbridge Street, London W8 7SY.
Trade paperback edition first published
in Great Britain and the USA 2018 by
SEVERN HOUSE PUBLISHERS LTD

British Library Cataloguing in Publication Data
A CIP catalogue record for this title is available from the British Library.

ISBN-13: 978-0-7278-8717-7 (cased)
ISBN-13: 978-1-84751-824-8 (trade paper)
ISBN-13: 978-1-78010-892-6 (e-book)

Typeset by Palimpsest Book Production Ltd.,
Falkirk, Stirlingshire, Scotland.

PROLOGUE

'Tadadadada da DA!'

Lili suspected she'd hear this mindless song repeated in her nightmares till the day she died. Firmly sandwiched between two of her extremely good-humoured kidnappers (she guessed there must be at least twenty in total), she was forced to inhale their alcohol fumes, not to mention the odours from their clothes, which could have benefited from a dry cleaner. The overly-excited revellers seemed benign but they were also very, *very* drunk and it had become a point of honour to hang on to Lili for the duration of their stupid dance, however long that turned out to be.

She made smiling attempts to extricate herself. 'I need to go and find my boyfriend. I'm not used to these silly shoes! I'll break something!' But her protests only made them more determined.

'Pretty little thing like you,' slurred the soldier, who was gripping her firmly by the waist. 'If Ginger Rogers can dance backwards in heels, I'm sure you can manage it forwards!'

The last thing Lili wanted was to give anyone a reason to remember the girl in the red dress, the girl who didn't even have a ticket for the ball. So, she pasted on her best party girl smile, sang 'Tadadadada da DA!' from a dry mouth and wondered what the hell she was supposed to do now. Why hadn't he come to meet her as they'd arranged? Had he set her up after all? Terror made all the tiny hairs prickle on the back of her neck; maybe she was being watched at this moment . . .

'We have to dance in and out of every door on the ground floor!' the young woman in front yelled to Lili over her shoulder. 'Except the bathroom obviously!' She let out a shriek of laughter.

Still out of breath from running, Lili felt herself perspiring through her dress. She'd have to get it professionally cleaned before she took it back. She hoped no-one had noticed that she'd already ruined her expensive silk stockings, not to mention badly scratching up her hands. *It couldn't be helped*, she told herself. She'd simply made the best of a bad job. But her prayer that she'd be able to re-enter and leave the house undetected had not been granted. Everyone was supposed to be in the ballroom by this time, jitterbugging, throwing streamers, celebrating the end of the war to end all wars. Lili hadn't anticipated a drunken conga emerging from the billiards room, which she was almost certain hadn't been on her floor plan and triumphantly intercepting her just as she reached the bottom of the staircase. She certainly hadn't bargained on a sandy-haired man in a British army uniform seizing her by the elbows and whirling her away in the opposite direction.

She had been helplessly pushed and pulled along what felt like miles of shadowy corridors, turning left and right apparently at random, like being trapped on some lurching runaway train. She stumbled along, her stockinged feet sliding about inside her too-large high heels, the unpleasant sensation adding to her fear that everything was spiralling out of her control.

People can't tell, she tried to comfort herself. *They can't tell from looking at me.* Rationally Lili knew that the chilling sensation of being watched was due to high levels of adrenaline racing around her body, but this didn't help when every nerve-ending was shrieking at her to kick off her borrowed shoes and run. To top it all, she could feel that vile elasticated garter belt stretching and tightening under her dress with every tiny movement. She could kick off her high-heels if she had to, but she doubted she could run far in this hateful corset-like garment.

A moment later, Lili caught a glimpse of herself as they passed a tarnished old wall mirror. She was surprised and gratified to see how convincing she looked. Her glossy dark hair had been swept up in its Victory roll, her mouth was slick with red lipstick and the shimmering scarlet silk clung to every one of her curves. Yes, her eyes were too bright and her cheeks had flushed to a hectic pink. But in the mirror, her wide-eyed expression just looked like the result of too many gins combined with the general post-war euphoria. The worst of Lili's panic ebbed away. She had thought on her feet and she had come up with a temporary solution. It should be safe for the next forty-eight hours or so. Then, somehow, she'd find a way to retrieve it.

Without warning, she collided with the girl in front, causing the soldier behind her to barge into Lili. Everyone had straggled to an ungraceful halt. Lili heard helpless giggles coming from the front of the line. The dancers had been confronted with a flight of shallow steps. After a brief consultation, people half stumbled, half fell down the three or four stairs, generating more giggles and a lot of swearing.

'What a shower of incompetents! This is a complete and utter shambles!' the soldier yelled in her ear.

Then a commanding male voice shouted, 'on three. One, two THREE!' and the dancing and moronic 'Tada-ing,' started up again.

They were in an older part of the house now. The ceilings were higher and the floors tiled. Lili found herself being jostled through a heavy, oak-panelled door into what she saw, with relief, was the library. Disorientated by all the switches of direction she'd lost her bearings. Now she realized that the line of dancers was laboriously looping back to the ballroom it had presumably started out from. Her floor plan had showed the ballroom as having doors opening on to the terrace. If all the other guests were as drunk and jolly as this lot, she should have no problem slipping out unnoticed.

'Tadadadada da DA,' she sang happily with the others and pretended not to notice the soldier giving her an appreciative squeeze.

Once around the library and then out again. A smart right turn led into the sadly faded dining room; it was probably grand, once. Then an immediate left took them into the Victorian conservatory, where potted palms cast ghostly shadows over arrangements of dilapidated wicker chairs. Out in the corridor again and,after a few more raucous 'Tadadadas,' they were within sight of the ballroom. The warm brassy sound of a big band had been gradually growing louder and now Lili could hear a tenor voice caressingly singing, 'As Time Goes By'. As the big band music swelled, the dancers decided to drop their mindless chant in favour of singing along.

'You must remember this; a kiss is just a kiss.'

Inside the ballroom, Lili pretended to stumble and stooped down as if to examine her shoe, but this ruse wasn't necessary. Now they'd achieved their goal of dragging Lili the length and breadth of the old manor house, her kidnappers appeared to lose interest and simply melted away.

She began unobtrusively making her way towards the far side of the room. After the gloomy maze of corridors, the ballroom was painfully bright, lit with the crystal glitter of dozens of chandeliers. All around, she could hear the muted scuffling of couples slow-dancing over the polished wooden floor. She edged past a sailor and his girl, gazing into each other's eyes, their expressions rapt. 'The world will always welcome lovers,' sang the tenor. Lili now saw the band, up on their raised platform. The musicians' brass instruments glittered under the lights as they played well-loved favourites, which had helped to keep everyone sane during the war. Home-made banners hung over their heads proclaiming VICTORY and WELCOME HOME TO OUR BRAVE TROOPS and PEACE IN OUR TIME in patriotic red, white and blue. All around the ballroom, little Union Jacks had been strung up for bunting.

Putting all her trust in her floor plan and its theoretical but crucial French doors, Lili continued to make her way through the crush. It was then that the band swung exuberantly into 'In the Mood' and the energy levels in the ballroom went through the roof. Couples started wild jitterbugging and swing dancing. Trying to avoid the jabbing elbows and knees, Lili failed to see the man in the Scots Guards uniform closing in until it was too late.

'Don't give me the brush-off, darling,' he coaxed in his Glaswegian accent, 'this is a historic day and I'm in urgent need of a beautiful girl to dance with!'

'I can't help you, I'm afraid,' she said politely. 'I'm, I'm looking for somebody.'

'I'm somebody, won't I do?' He caught at her hands, smiling into her eyes, very sure of his charms. 'I only want to dance, darling! Just a dance. Nothing sinister.'

'I told you, I *can't*!' Frantic now, she shook him off.

She felt a soft breath of air against her neck and cheek. *Thank God*! The floor plan had been right after all. There were French doors leading out on to a terrace, which were, mercifully, standing open. Lili fled, forgetting the unsuitable shoes and the corset-like garter belt, just letting the night-scented breeze tell her where to go.

Outside, the May evening was blissfully cool and fresh after the heat and noise of the ballroom. Couples had drifted outside to dance, smoke a crafty cigarette or just kiss in the shadows. One man sat slumped on a low wall, obviously the worse for alcohol. Around the terrace, flaming torches gave out a ruddy light.

Heart beating, Lili glanced around, but didn't see anyone obviously watching and carefully descended the stone steps leading down into the garden. The music, laughter and talk began to fade behind her. Just a short way along a gravel path and she was plunged into pitch darkness. One of her stockings caught on something. A bramble. But by this time Lili's silk stockings were a lost cause and she recklessly tore herself free.

Earlier, in the afterglow of sunset, it had been easier to find her way. She'd forgotten how dark the countryside became when the sun went down. Country darkness was a different and more menacing animal to the city kind. Anything or anyone could be hiding out here, waiting to make their move. *There's no one out here but you, Lili. You're being an idiot.* She made herself take calm, deliberate breaths and felt that infernal garter belt breathing with her. The first thing she was going to do when she got home was rip the damn thing off and throw it out with the rubbish.

In the ballroom, the band started to play 'Land of Hope and Glory'. Its patriotic sentiments seemed to belong to a different world to the one Lili had been born into; a world where wars were just, victories won only by the great and good and happy endings lasted forever.

'But you *did* it,' she whispered to herself. Because of her, it was almost over. Soon she'd put the final full stop to the decades of damage, but, for the time being, she'd concentrate on finding her way back to her car. In an hour or less, she'd be back in her London flat.

'God, who made thee mighty, make thee mightier yet!' voices bellowed from the ballroom.

Lili's heart was beating too fast for comfort, yet she forced herself to keep still a few moments longer, letting her eyes gradually adjust to the night, breathing in the delicate scents of spring.

There was an explosion directly over her head. She jumped as lurid green stars rained down, hissing, from the sky. Simultaneously, the sound of cheers and popping champagne corks came from the terrace. Despite herself she felt compelled to turn and watch.

Another, much louder detonation lit up the garden, turning night briefly into day. Fountains of silver light floated down then dissolved as if they had never been. Subsequent fireworks came so thick and fast that the garden seemed to be pulsing on and off, vanishing then magically reappearing, one moment black, another bleached out gold.

In one of these golden pulses of light, Lili saw someone standing between her and the house and felt herself turn cold. Everyone else on the terrace was looking up at the sky watching the fireworks, but this unknown person was looking deliberately and directly at Lili. The outpouring of light from the ballroom made it impossible to identify features or tell if they were male or female. Not that it mattered, she thought numbly. They'd found her.

Then her fight or flight instincts kicked in. She could run right at them, take them by surprise, kick out at their kneecaps and scream for help. Somehow she'd get past them, back to the light and warmth and hide herself in the crowd. She'd dance that ridiculous conga all night long, if it would keep her alive. But even as her mind wildly calculated and made bargains, the figure was suddenly in front of her, cutting off her escape, not speaking or threatening, just breathing softly and steadily. Waiting.

The garden dimmed and brightened then dimmed again. Lili didn't have a choice. She had to go further into the dark. She ran, willing the fireworks to stop so she could simply melt into the ink-black night like the terrified animal she'd become.

She felt a heel give way, stumbled and fell. She had time to register hundreds of tiny sharp stones cutting into her knees and palms, then strong hands seized her by the shoulders, dragging her backwards across the gravel. If anyone on the terrace was to turn and look out into the garden, they'd see. But no one did.

Lili screamed then, although she knew no one could hear her through the music, the fireworks and the cheers and laughter. Then she screamed again, because the first scream had unleashed so much raw terror that she was physically incapable of stopping.

Before she could open her mouth in a third visceral scream, her skull was being smashed against a cold hard surface. Lili's head filled with unbearably bright white points of light and after that something must have happened to her hearing, because the bangs of the fireworks,the distant strains of 'Land of Hope and Glory' and even the sound of the breeze stirring the leaves overhead, were simultaneously silenced.

Next minute she was forcibly plunged under water. Cold, rank, weed-smelling water filled her nostrils, her mouth and throat, her lungs. She struggled, not because she was strong or brave, but because she couldn't not struggle. Lili's body wanted to live and so she fought and fought against this terrible thing that was being done to her, but the hands were too strong.

Towards the end, Lili's eyes opened for the last time and she thought she could see the reflection of the soundless fireworks in the water. They looked like impossibly beautiful flowers, the kind you might see in a dream. She had one clear thought. *Please God, let it be safe now.*

And then. Nothing.

ONE

'All I can say is that the Baroness must have fallen on very hard times! Ugh, I do so *loathe* the smell of camphor!' Isadora fastidiously draped the moth-eaten fox fur around her neck, then tilted the room's one small mirror on its swivel stand to admire the effect.

Anna gave her a distracted smile. She was texting Jake.

They've put us in the old matron's room. 2 inches max between each bed. Remind me why I said I'd do this again?

She deleted the text. Too whiny.

Isadora plumped herself down on the bed beside Anna. 'You're looking pale, Liebling.'

Anna was amused to notice that she had already assumed a strong German accent.

'Because I am a friendless orphan reliant on the Baroness for my economic survival,' Anna said in a small colourless voice. 'I dare not defy her wishes by wearing make-up or making myself attractive in any way.'

'Ach, the Baroness is a monster,' sighed Isadora, 'if there were any justice in this world, *she* would be the murder victim!'

For the first time, Anna took a good look at her friend in her new incarnation as the Baroness von Rosenbaum.

'You look *amazing* Isadora!'

'I based my impersonation on one of my more frightening Russian aunts,' Isadora said, with one of her dark laughs. 'Apart from the Bavarian accent obviously.'

Isadora's costume consisted of a long, tweed, riding skirt, a fitted jacket which she wore with a pair of her own glossy, leather boots and a military, little hat, which she'd eventually managed (Anna had registered a few hissed expletives) to pin to her cloud of wiry black and silver hair.

The door to the bathroom opened and Tansy emerged, slightly self-conscious, in a silky tea dress patterned with roses in subtle vintage hues. The wide sleeves, with their faint suggestion of butterfly wings, stopped at her elbows, showing her pale golden skin to full advantage. Tansy had painted her lips a startling, pillar box red. Her dark curls were caught up beneath a chic little hat. Her eyes widened at the sight of Isadora. 'Wow, all you need is the whip!' She belatedly registered Isadora's fur with its tiny feral teeth. 'Euw! Isadora, tell me you're not going to wear that minging piece of fur?'

'She's the Baroness now,' Anna reminded her. 'You should probably not describe items of her clothing as "minging". You look gorgeous by the way,' she added warmly. 'I totally believe you are making a film in Berlin.'

Tansy did a little twirl. 'Thank you, Anna! I mean, Miss Smith,' she corrected.

'No, please, call me Evelyn,' Anna said in her Evelyn voice. 'Maybe over time we can become friends? I can darn your silk stockings for you and you can give me your old worn-out dresses.'

Tansy laughed. 'Your costume isn't *that* bad.'

Anna looked down at her dreary, Fair Isle sweater. The colours made her think of congealing school dinners.

'Thank you,' she said politely. 'I knitted it with some wool that no-one else wanted while the Baroness was taking her afternoon nap.'

Isadora gave a disparaging glance around their institutional looking room.

'They could use this as a set for a low-budget production of Jane Eyre.'

'Absolutely no changes needed,' Anna agreed.

'It's better than the dormitory option,' Tansy reminded her.

'There never *was* a dormitory option,' Anna said firmly. She had made that quite clear to Anjali. She had agreed to help her sister-in-law out. After three female participants in Anjali's company's first ever murder mystery weekend had dropped out at the last minute, Anna had even co-opted her friends to help make up the numbers. Yet she'd refused point blank to share one of Mortmead Hall's former dormitories with a bunch of strangers.

'We should probably go,' Isadora said.

Anna stood up with a sigh, pulling down her frumpy tweed skirt.

'No phones, remember,' Isadora said sternly to Tansy, who was quickly checking hers. 'Once we get outside our room it's 1939.'

The former matron's quarters were situated up one of several confusing side corridors. Luckily, Tansy had brought her floor plan. She consulted it for a moment.

'Oh, wow, there's a maze. Oh, but it's off-limits,' she added disappointed.

With the help of her floorplan, Tansy reoriented them towards the front staircase. As the friends descended the wide curving stairs, Anna was surprised by a pang of genuine emotion. *We look like the real deal*, she thought.

At the same moment, Tansy said, 'This is *so* cool! We look like we really belong in the 1930s!'

Hearing her voice, a man appeared through a doorway, wearing the sober clothing of a hotel concierge.

'Guten Morgen, Baroness,' he said to Isadora, clicking his heels. 'I hope your accommodation is satisfactory?'

'Yes, yes,' Isadora said tetchily. 'It will serve, given the unfortunate circumstances.'

'We live in terrible times?' the concierge said, shaking his head. 'But I would like to reassure you that we will do everything in our power to make you and Miss Smith comfortable during your stay with us.'

'I love this guy! I totally believe he's for real,' Tansy whispered to Anna.

They had already met the concierge on their arrival. He was actually one of several professional actors hired to help facilitate the ten different murder mysteries being played out in Mortmead Hall over the weekend. Their mystery was titled 'The Last Train from Munich' and was set just before the outbreak of the Second World War. It featured eight ill-assorted travellers, who found themselves stranded in a Munich hotel after missing the late-night train to Paris. No one, of course, was what they seemed and at least one of the characters was responsible for the murder of an Austrian industrialist, whose body had been found in his bed before the murder mystery properly began.

The concierge gave Tansy a respectful bow. 'Miss Fonteyn! How wonderful to have you with us at the Hotel Aurora.'

Tansy gave him a pleased little grin. 'I'm thankful to be here believe me. For a while I was worried I'd have to spend the night on Munich station!'

Her American accent wasn't bad, Anna thought. She was thankful that her part only required her to trail around being put upon.

'Coffee is being served in the library,' the concierge said. 'If you will please follow me, you can make the acquaintance of your fellow travellers.' He pushed open the panelled doors. Five strangers, clothed in pre-Second World War styles, looked back at them with unreadable expressions. Anna fought down a powerful urge to bolt.

'I shall return shortly,' the concierge murmured and left them to it.

Isadora took charge, sweeping grandly into the room.

'Good day, I am Baroness von Rosenbaum and this is my companion, Miss Smith,' she said gruffly, relieving Anna of the necessity to introduce her character.

'Betsy Fonteyn,' Tansy said with a smile that combined Tansy's genuine warmth with the airy confidence of a true star and she sank gracefully into the nearest seat.

The rules of the game had been explained in advance. Everyone in the group was a potential murder suspect. Predictably, everyone was also hiding secrets – some of them darker than others –and which they had to try hard not to divulge. People could ask each other any number of searching questions. They could also obfuscate and evade, making it hard for their team mates to uncover the truth, but they were not allowed to lie outright. The mysteries all had to be solved by supper time, after which there was to be a grand VE day ball – the weekend's timeline jumping from the era immediately before the declaration of war to the euphoric celebrations at the war's end – Anna presumed so everyone could go out on a high.

In addition to the Baroness, her dowdy, near-silent companion and the famous actress, Betsy Fonteyn, the suspects were: Monty Shine, a salesman in a very loud, ill-fitting suit; Edward Fairly, a brave RAF pilot; Daisy May, a bubbly upper-class girl fresh out of boarding school, ('Yeah right!' Tansy said at lunch); a mysteriously troubled Swiss scientist and Rory, a big game hunter recently returned from South Africa. Over the next few hours, the team members elicited further details about the fictitious characters' lives and movements, in an attempt to shed light on the murder of the poor businessman, who was found dead soon after their arrival at the Hotel Aurora. But who was the dead man really? Was he perhaps after all a spy?

Every half hour or so, the concierge reappeared to help keep their investigation on track with prompts to go to a particular part of the house, where they had to seek out crucial clues. On these excursions, they ran into similarly dressed people from the other groups, intent on solving their own murder mysteries.

Anna seemed to be the only person who found this entire charade excruciating. Eighty or so adults, maintaining the childish fiction that this huge, Victorian house was actually a German hotel or Bletchley Park or whatever the other fictitious wartime venues were, and getting hotly competitive about solving their imaginary murders.

It was especially ironic that Anna had cajoled her friends into taking part in this fictional murder mystery, since the three women had met over the body of a real-life murder victim in Oxford's Port Meadow, while they were out walking their dogs. An unlikely basis for friendship, you'd think, yet they'd been through so much together that Anna felt like they'd known each other forever and Tansy and Isadora obviously felt the same.

'This is actually just Cluedo isn't it,' Tansy hissed to Anna during a welcome coffee break.

'Except Cluedo only takes like, an hour,' Anna said gloomily.

Anjali seriously owes me for this, she thought. Really, she had done it for Tim. He'd phoned her late on Thursday night and she'd heard his colicky new-born screaming in the background throughout the call.

'Anjali's so stressed,' he'd said, sounding extremely stressed himself. 'The baby's not sleeping and the guy who's supposedly running High Table Events – while she's on maternity leave – is having personal problems, so Anjali's basically running things from home. They had everything set. They found an empty country house at a rock bottom rate, they got in a writer to create the mysteries, hired some actors and now all that hard work could go up in smoke. Please Anna, I know it's desperately last minute but is there any chance you could help?'

Anna had only recently discovered that Tim – who had always seemed to her like a younger, far more appealing brother than her real brothers – actually *was* her brother. This discovery had arrived with a certain amount of weird baggage. Nevertheless, Anna welcomed it as a miracle. Out of the traumatic wreckage of her early life, she'd acquired a flesh and blood sibling. *Of course* she'd help him out.

Luckily Tansy and Isadora hadn't needed much persuading and Jake had offered to dog-sit Bonnie. Now, Anna just had to get through the next few hours in this itchy sweater. She gave an unobtrusive glance at her watch and was appalled to realize that there was still a whole hour until lunch.

'Ok, Liebling?' Isadora whispered, 'we're all going to the conservatory now!'

Anna stooped to pick up Isadora's gruesome fox fur, which had slithered to the ground unnoticed.

'Coming, Baroness,' she said in a dutiful voice.

They located the beautiful, if dilapidated, Victorian conservatory and roamed around, peering under wicker chairs and into potted palms, until the handsome RAF officer found the clue.

'He's a sweetie,' Tansy whispered to Anna. 'I've got a feeling he's got a thing for Miss Smith.'

'He wants to rescue you, Liebling!' Isadora said as the Baroness then, in her own voice, she added, 'He looks ridiculously handsome in that flying jacket. It's a shame all the others are so dire.'

The others were indeed dire. Monty the salesman could never remember his character bio. He had to keep fishing the relevant sheets of paper out of his pocket, rereading them to himself with apparent bewilderment.

Rory, the big game hunter, had an alpha male complex and insisted on dominating proceedings. The scientist was not so much troubled as downright creepy and, as Tansy hissed to her friends over lunch, the woman playing Daisy (the girl who was supposedly fresh out of the sixth form) had to be at least thirty years older than her character if she was a day.

'Plus, I'm sure "Daisy's" married to "Rory" IRL,' she added.

'IRL?' said Isadora.

'In Real Life,' Anna explained. 'It's an online thing.'

'Oh,' said Isadora, losing interest.

After lunch, they had to make their way over to the ballroom. 'I hate to think how many servants they needed to run this monstrosity,' Isadora said.

Tansy nodded. 'Imagine those little homesick boarders rattling around in here when Mortmead Hall was a school.'

'Not the most upbeat name for a school,' Isadora said with one of her dark laughs. 'The Mead of Death!'

'I think it's just been auctioned off,' Anna told them. 'It's been on the market for years, ever since the school closed. That's why Anjali got such a good deal. This weekend is like a trial run so her events company can iron out any glitches. If it's a success, she'll be looking for a regular venue.'

The afternoon seemed to pass quite quickly. The concierge kept them busy with timely prompts, small snacks and frequent changes of scene. By the day's end, Betsy Fonteyn had been shockingly exposed as the cold-blooded murderer, who had been employing her acting skills as a double agent. Tansy was thrilled with herself.

'I can't believe nobody rumbled me!' she said as they went to the school dining room where a makeshift bar had been set up. 'Not even you guys!' She darted them a look. 'Of course, I *did* have an excellent role model.' She was referring to her father, a London gangster, (a *retired* gangster he insisted) known as Frankie McVeigh.

'Don't be silly,' said Anna.

'I hope supper is better than our lunch,' Isadora said, plaintively. 'Mine was stone cold.'

'And mine,' Tansy admitted. 'We should feed that back to Anjali.'

'I don't mean to be like the special little snowflake,' Anna said, 'but I'm going to skip supper. I'm a bit peopled out.' The need to be by herself was suddenly overwhelming.

'Me too,' Tansy confessed. 'Unfortunately I'm incapable of missing a meal!'

'Go and have a lie down, Anna,' Isadora said. 'Tansy and I can wander around the grounds till dinner. I could do with some fresh air before we have to face those dreary people over dinner.'

Alone in their room, Anna checked her phone. Jake had left a message.

Bonnie took me and Liam on a long walk, now L and I are watching the Rugby and she's in her usual spot.

He attached a photo of Anna's White Shepherd, her head resting on Jake's bare feet. This time last year Anna had nobody in her life, apart from her beloved grandfather, because of one fateful, summer night . . . She was just sixteen when she had let herself into the family home – reeking of dope and semi-hysterical from her breakup with Max – and discovered her parents and her three siblings had been savagely butchered. The murderers had never been found.

Remembering, Anna's hand instinctively went to the small scar near her navel. She also could have lost her life that night. For a long time, she'd wished she had. Sixteen years had passed, but the horror never lessened and she had believed that she would never find her way back into the world. She had been convinced that she would never trust or love again.

Yet now she had friends, a brother, a new-born niece and a relationship with Jake McCaffrey, who asked absolutely nothing of her except that she should be herself. And she owed all of these things to Bonnie.

Her fairy-tale wolf. That's how Anna privately thought of her White Shepherd. Before Anna found her in the rescue shelter, Bonnie had belonged to Jake, a former Navy SEAL. He had discovered her loyally guarding the body of a little Afghani boy, who had been killed by a roadside bomb. Jake had coaxed the traumatised pup into his jeep and took her back to base, where she'd become a kind of honorary canine marine, accompanying Jake and his men on various ops. When Jake was posted on to the Philippines, rather than abandon Bonnie, he'd sent her to live with his widowed aunt Mimi in Oxford, but when she'd died unexpectedly, Mimi's neighbours had sent Bonnie to the shelter.

Bonnie was how Jake and Anna first came to meet. And a few months ago, after a long period of mutual caution, Jake had finally stayed the night, this time, in Anna's bed.

The next morning, Anna had been amazed to find that the world didn't seem to have suffered any ill effects. The opposite if anything. Though the sky was iron grey and rain fell steadily past the window, (Anna had forgotten to close the old-fashioned wooden shutters the previous night in their haste), everything looked ten times more alive than a wet winter's morning in Oxford was supposed to look. Best of all, she and Jake had not turned back into two strangers, as she had secretly dreaded. She'd seen his face as he drowsily opened his eyes and caught sight of her. She had been raised up on one elbow watching him sleep and she thought, she *hoped*, it was a physical impossibility to fake that kind of sleepy tenderness.

She stretched out on her narrow bed and dozed a little, letting her mind drift and, for the first time, allowing herself to daydream of a future with Jake. After a while, she heard Isadora and Tansy's voices. There was a discreet knock and Anna hastily sat up. 'I'm decent. Come in!'

'I know I sound like a broken record,' Isadora said, fighting her way between their Dickensian iron bedsteads. 'But God, those people are tedious! Why go to something like this if you have next to no social skills!'

'We brought you a couple of starters and a pudding in case you were hungry after your sleep,' Tansy said. She wafted two small parcels wrapped in paper napkins temptingly under Anna's nose. 'The mains were harder to transport.'

'Tansy was all for making a Mallory Towers midnight raid on the kitchens later,' Isadora said with a little snort. 'That's before she saw the chef.'

Tansy kicked off her shoes, collapsing on to her own bed which emitted a metallic jangle of protest. 'He looked exactly like an ex-con who used to do a bit of this and that for my dad,' she explained. 'He's probably as gentle as a little puppy, but I don't think I'll risk it!'

Isadora switched on her phone and began laboriously texting. 'Just checking Hero is OK,' she explained. Hero was Isadora's Tibetan spaniel cross. Isadora's lodger, Sabina, who had become a kind of surrogate grand-daughter, was taking care of her for the weekend.

'I'm quite looking forward to this ball,' Tansy said.

'So am I!' Isadora glanced up from her phone. 'I heard someone saying it's open to all kinds of people, academic historians, local history buffs, Second World War re-enactment types.'

Anjali's company, High Table, had supplied them with vintage evening clothes as well as daywear. Anna was secretly thrilled with her dress. It was a flattering shade of green that reminded her of willows in spring. The bodice, draped and fitted above a cinched in waist, had short, split sleeves and a skirt that fell to the floor in a swirl of pleats – as though designed for dancing. 'Things obviously looked up for Evelyn by the war's end!' Anna joked to Tansy. The moment she stepped into her dress, Anna felt, possibly for the first time in her life, utterly and confidently feminine. It must have shown in her face, because Tansy said, 'You're feeling it now, aren't you? You're channelling the sassy, 1940s spirit!'

Anna had hoped to ignore the gauzy little piece of nonsense which she was supposed to pin on to her hair, but Tansy and Isadora insisted.

They made their way down to the ballroom, which was decked out like a glitzy 1940s movie. Anjali's company might have scrimped on accommodation, but they'd gone overboard on this VE Night ball, Anna thought, as she took in the crystal chandeliers and the stage, where a Glenn Miller-type tribute band was playing an old wartime favourite. The dance floor was already crowded and Anna felt a pang of nostalgia for a time she'd never actually known. They looked so *real*. The women with their glossy rolled up hair and slinky satin gowns. A few men wore period suits and black ties, but the majority wore the dress uniforms of the British or American services. Isadora was gazing at the patriotic banners hanging from the walls.

'Oh, dear, Peace in our Time,' she said, a little wistfully, 'if only that were true.' Then the band launched into 'Little Brown Jug' and her face lit up. 'Oh, how *heavenly*! Do either of you know how to jitterbug? No? Then I'll show you!'

They quickly attracted a crowd of admirers, some of whom attempted to copy Isadora's moves with varying degrees of success.

'Did your parents teach you?' Tansy said, when they eventually stopped to catch their breath. Like Anna, she'd thought of Isadora as a strictly 1960s girl.

Isadora shook her head. 'My parents weren't the dancing kind. One of our lodgers taught me. Every Sunday evening, we'd roll back the rug and dance to Victor Sylvester on the wireless. Dorothy taught me the waltz, the quickstep, the fox trot and how to jitter bug. I was six years old and, for the few months that she was living with us, Sunday was the happiest night of my week!'

The band switched to an old Cole Porter number. The RAF officer from their group came up to ask Isadora to dance. Freshly shaved and showered, he was as handsome in his dress uniform – with its medals and festoons of gold braid – as he had been in his flying jacket.

Tansy whipped out her phone to take a photo of them, to the annoyance of Rory who came striding towards them, red-faced.

'Mobile phones are against the rules! This kind of thing ruins the mood!'

'She's not ruining my mood, darling,' Isadora called over her partner's shoulder. 'This moment will never come again! I intend to seize the day and I advise you to do the same!'

Later people drifted out on to the terrace to watch the fireworks. It seemed that Tansy had started a trend and Anna spotted discreet flashes as guests snapped photos of their friends. The band struck up with 'String of Pearls', a tune which Anna's grandmother had especially loved. She had secretly dreaded this weekend but, at that moment, Anna realized that she was perfectly content to be here with her friends, letting the evening unfold.

When they eventually returned to the old matron's quarters in the small hours, Anna brushed her teeth, tried in vain to get comfortable on her lumpy mattress and decided there was no way she'd get a wink of sleep. Then, suddenly, rooks and wood pigeons were performing deafening bird karaoke in the trees outside their window and it was morning.

Anna and Tansy had hoped to miss out the communal buffet breakfast, but Isadora, visibly hung-over, said she couldn't function without several cups of coffee. When they walked into the dining hall, Anna was thrown to see everyone wearing their normal 21st century clothes, even though she, Tansy and Isadora had made the same transition.

For some reason, all of their group had opted to sit together. It seemed a peculiarly British kind of solidarity, everyone grimly working their way through pallid fried eggs and limp rashers of bacon, making strained conversation with people they hoped fervently never to meet again. Judging from the way that they avoided eye contact, 'Daisy' and 'Rory' had fallen out.

Isadora helped herself to coffee. Tansy, a former vegan, looked queasily at the food on offer. 'I'll just stick with some of that anaemic fruit salad,' she started to say, when a harrowing scream came from outside. Everyone looked up with identically uncertain expressions. After a weekend of pretence, no one quite believed that raw, animal-like sound could be for real.

It was Tansy who moved first, wrenching open a side door. Anna followed. They raced out into the dew-wet grounds and down uneven stone steps to where a young woman stood beside a large, ornamental pond. She was just a teenager really, in a green overall, clutching her unlit cigarette, her round unformed face blank with shock.

A woman's lifeless body floated in the water, her limbs blue-white in the sunshine, her eyes staring emptily at the sky, her red silk dress darkened almost to black.

TWO

Needing something normal to do while they waited for the police, Anna and her friends packed their overnight bags, carried them downstairs and stowed them in the back of Anna's car.

'If I'd stayed a minute longer, I'd have smacked that Daisy around the face,' Tansy said, when they were out of earshot. 'Did you hear her phoning all her mates? *Boasting* that her and Rory's murder mystery weekend ended with someone actually *dying*? Obviously it's the most thrilling thing that's happened to her in years.'

Having disposed of their luggage, they went to sit out on the terrace with fresh cups of coffee. It was a beautiful May morning. Anna could smell the faint scent of wallflowers wafting from the garden. Most of the guests had opted to remain indoors, instinctively keeping their distance from the corpse. But Anna couldn't have borne to go back into that dining room, with its breakfast smells and everyone feverishly speculating about what had happened. Fortunately, Isadora and Tansy felt the same.

Anna had phoned Tim at once. She'd heard him hastily relay the news and Anjali yelling, 'if this is a joke, it's bloody bad taste!'

Then she'd phoned Jake to explain why she'd be home late. Tansy had already called Liam; her boyfriend was with the Thames Valley Police and he'd said he and Inspector Chaudhari were on their way.

Wincing from the bright, spring sunlight, Isadora ripped into a third – or possibly fourth – sachet of bone-white sugar, turning her coffee into black syrup. Shock, combined with a fierce hangover, made her look haggard and old, hardly recognisable as the vibrant woman who had taught them to jitterbug the night before.

'What *is* it with us?' she said in an undertone. 'People go their whole lives without seeing a corpse, but we trip over dead bodies almost every time we turn around.'

'This isn't like those other times though.' Tansy said.

'Isn't it?' Isadora said.

'No! There was some serious drinking going on last night. When we left at two or whenever it was, there was a woman throwing up her heart in the bushes and a guy was passed out on the terrace. There's no proper, security lighting in the garden if you noticed, and Anna, those steps are lethal, aren't they?'

Anna nodded, privately thinking how much Tansy suddenly sounded like her police sergeant boyfriend.

'And that was in daylight,' Tansy said earnestly, 'but in pitch darkness, for anyone who wasn't one hundred percent sober, it was basically an accident waiting to happen.'

Isadora didn't seem to be listening.

'It's just so awful,' she said almost to herself. 'That poor woman. Last night she put on her dress and did her makeup and now . . . it's the *randomness* I can't bear.'

Anna nodded. 'Sometimes it feels like the Angel of Death flew over, crooked his bony finger and decided, "I'm taking so and so tonight," and you spend the rest of your life trying to figure out why it was them and not you.'

Isadora gave a tight nod. 'Exactly that,' she said tersely and Anna guessed she was thinking of her unknown half-siblings, who'd died in a concentration camp before Isadora was born.

Anna knew all about survivors' guilt. For years, she'd believed that she was somehow to blame for her family's murders; if she had not been such a selfish little bitch, if she'd come home in time for her sister Lottie's sixth birthday party like her mother had asked, somehow, Anna could have miraculously prevented the carnage.

Anna's emotional scars had now healed sufficiently that she no longer felt personally responsible for each and every misfortune that happened in her vicinity. But the image of some impervious angel brushing her yet again with its icy wings was hard to shake off. Anna couldn't help feeling that this inexplicable new death must mean something, that it was significant in some way she couldn't yet understand.

A brief wail of sirens floated across the grounds from the main road, then cut off in a kind of electronic chirp, as the first police cars turned in through the gates of Mortmead Hall.

'Liam said he'll come to find us,' Tansy said. 'He's not allowed to interview us, obviously, but he'll try to get us processed quickly so we can go home ASAP.'

'What a thoughtful soul he is,' said Isadora.

'He is incredibly thoughtful,' Tansy agreed. 'Though . . .' she let her sentence tail off, then realized Anna and Isadora were looking at her expectantly. '. . . Oh, he's not quite his normal self, that's all.' She gave an unhappy little shrug. 'I think it's just stress.'

Isadora downed the last of her coffee. 'He's picked a stressful profession.'

Tansy nodded. 'Once he gets made Inspector that will only get worse.'

A few minutes later, Liam Goodhart emerged from the house with his boss, Inspector Chaudhari, plus a tubby, tired-looking man in a boiler suit, who Anna presumed to be the duty medical examiner, and an agitated woman from Housekeeping.

Liam spotted them and came over, looking concerned.

'Tans are you OK?'

She nodded. 'Just a bit shocked.'

'Not surprised,' Liam said, with feeling. 'They're setting up an interview room in the old ballroom. I've asked Sergeant Mellors if he'll interview you guys. He's a decent bloke, even if he did go to the wrong university.' He flashed Isadora a grin. 'Hopefully he won't keep you too long.' He hurried to catch up with his boss.

Anna was the first of the three of them to be interviewed. The ballroom had been set up for multiple interviews, since there were so many guests to question. Anna took a seat opposite Sergeant Mellors. He had flame red-hair, sharp Slavic cheekbones under almost luminously pale skin and if he knew her family history, he was far too diplomatic to let it show.

'I understand you and Ms Lavelle found the body?'

'One of the staff actually found her,' Anna said. 'She screamed and Tansy and I rushed out to see what was wrong.'

'And you were attending this murder mystery weekend?'

'Yes. My sister-in-law runs the events company. They had some people drop out, so I asked two of my friends to help make up the numbers.'

'Did you see the deceased woman at any point during the weekend?'

Anna shook her head. 'Not sure. She wasn't in my group. I might have passed her without knowing when we were sent off to hunt for clues.'

She saw Sergeant Mellors trying to keep a straight face.

'I know it's embarrassingly Famous Five,' she said apologetically. 'I suppose she could have been at the ball.'

'Was there anything about the weekend that stands out for you? Anything that could help us to identify her?'

From a nearby table, Anna heard a frustrated male voice grumble 'I keep telling you, the ball was open to outsiders. You didn't have to sign up for the murder mystery weekend to attend. For instance, there was one big, beefy guy wandering around like Braveheart. He definitely wasn't in any of the groups.'

A memory tickled the back of Anna's mind, a stocky man dressed in the full regalia of some Scottish army regiment. She didn't recall him as big and beefy, but in his kilt, knee-high socks and cap, with its jaunty regimental feather, he'd had a definite presence. She had a vague impression of him waylaying a young woman in a red dress.

'I'm not a hundred percent sure, but I might have seen her,' she said tentatively. She gave him as many physical details as she could remember: black hair striking against her white skin, dark eyes, possibly mid-thirties and that clinging, red, silk dress.

'And you think she wasn't keen on this man's attentions?' Sergeant Mellors asked.

'No, definitely not,' Anna said.

'Did she seem scared of him?'

Anna shook her head. 'It was more like he was an irritant, just getting in her way. I don't want to make too much of it. I don't really know what I saw. It was all over in a flash.'

Somewhere close by, Rory was being taken through the same questions.

'A rather *foreign* looking woman, I would describe her as,' he said in the strident tone that had become unpleasantly familiar over the weekend. 'I noticed her because she was on the dance floor, but she seemed to be on her own. I thought she must be looking for someone.'

It soon became obvious that Anna had nothing else to tell Sergeant Mellors. As she left the ballroom, she heard a woman saying, 'I think I saw the young woman you mean! She was dancing the conga, having the time of her life! Oh my God, is that who they found in the pond?'

It was late afternoon by the time they got back to Oxford. Anna dropped Tansy and Isadora off in Summertown. She'd offered to run Tansy home, but she said she'd get the bus back to St Clements, where she and Liam had rented a small garden flat.

'I need to get some shopping,' she said. 'I want to cook Liam something nice for when he gets home. Cheer him up.'

This was the second reference Tansy had made to her boyfriend's state of mind. They'd only just moved in together. Could that be part of what was stressing Liam? Had it happened too fast? Was he feeling suffocated now that the two of them were living in that tiny little flat? Anna wasn't sure if these were questions she was entitled to ask. She watched Tansy set off towards the bus stop, carrying her overnight bag and had to fight the impulse to call her back, so she could do or say something comforting.

Anna had intended to go straight home to Jake, but as she drove off down the Banbury Road, she spotted the familiar left turn for Bramley Lodge. It was the retirement home where her grandfather lived and the urge to check on him overpowered every other thought.

Though George Ottaway seemed happy and enviably at peace with himself, he had recently had his ninetieth birthday and she couldn't expect him to live for ever. Anna didn't believe in God or karma, yet she had felt the icy brush of those impervious wings and she needed to see him, to hug him and make sure he was still OK.

As always, her grandfather's room smelled of oil paints, turpentine and his favourite blend of Darjeeling and Lapsang. For once, he was not painting when she arrived, but sitting in his armchair, listening to Billie Holiday singing 'The Very Thought of You'. He wore one of his beloved, old, checked shirts and his white hair was sticking up at odd angles, as if he'd taken a nap since the last time he'd combed it.

'What a wonderful surprise!' he said warmly. 'I was just thinking about making a pot of tea. Will you join me?'

'I'll make it.' Anna hugged him, inhaling his familiar Penhaligon aftershave. Her grandfather had never been a man to put on weight, but these days he felt disturbingly slight in her arms. 'I remember Granny singing this when she was washing up,' she said, releasing him.

'It was her favourite song,' he said.

She went into the tiny, galley kitchen and filled the kettle.

'How funny that you should be playing it just now. The band played this exact song last night at the ball!'

'Was the singer as good as Billie?'

'Obviously not, but he wasn't bad,' Anna said, spooning tea leaves into the old brown pot, one of the few things he'd brought from the house in Park Town. By the time she had everything arranged on the tray, the song had finished and her grandfather had turned the music down to a bluesy murmur.

She set the tray down between them and made herself comfortable on the old sofa, mentally noting a new still life propped against a wooden chest. A tumble of cool blue crockery and a white jug, with blood-red tulips, was on a dazzling sunlit cloth. He must have painted this one since her last visit. George Ottaway had been a soldier, a businessman, a devoted husband, father and grandfather. Then, widowed in his eighties, he had discovered that he was also an artist, though he refused to dignify himself with that title. 'I'm just a dabbler, my dear,' he'd said to Tansy, when she tried to persuade him to exhibit his paintings at the gallery where she worked. 'I should only embarrass us both.'

Anna looked up from pouring his tea to see her grandfather watching her expectantly.

'So you went to your murder mystery weekend despite your misgivings,' he prompted. 'Was it worth the effort?'

Anna had taken great care over the years, or so she'd imagined, to conceal the grimmer details of her life from her grandfather. But it was very slowly dawning on her that he possibly understood her better than she knew herself. She remembered how he'd applauded each tentative step out of her self-made prison: deciding to get a dog, allowing Tansy and Isadora into her life. When she'd finally introduced him to Jake he couldn't disguise his delight. Had he pictured Anna turning into an old woman, her hair in greasy elf locks, eating cold beans from the can, as she obsessively trawled the dark net for clues? All this time, she thought, her grandfather had been secretly desperate for her to be happy, to have a life, fun and friends.

Even so, out of habit, Anna found herself giving him a highly-edited version of her weekend; mischievous character sketches of the people in her group and incidents that she hoped might amuse him.

'So, it wasn't really your cup of tea,' George Ottaway chuckled after she'd described Daisy inexplicably channelling the young Princess Elizabeth for her innocent school girl.

'To begin with, I thought it was utterly ridiculous, all these supposed adults rushing around like extras in Miss Marple.'

'You never were much of a joiner,' her grandfather said with a grin. 'I remember taking you to see Peter Pan. You can't have been more than three years old. When they begged the audience to clap their hands to show they all believed in fairies, you literally *sat* on your hands, clenching your little jaws together as if resisting torture!'

Anna stared at him open-mouthed. 'I *refused* to save Tinkerbell? What a horrible child I must have been!'

'Not at all,' her grandfather said at once. 'You were genuinely concerned for Tinkerbell. You just refused to succumb to mass hysteria. Quite rightly in my opinion. I was rather proud of you!'

Anna hastily looked away. She didn't remember the pantomime, but her mother had always given the impression that Anna was a stroppy, distrustful, little girl. This new interpretation of her character touched her to the point of tears.

'Well, anyway,' she said, taking refuge in briskness, 'believe it or not, by the end of the day I had almost suspended all my disbelief!'

'Honestly? You felt as if you had genuinely slipped back in time?' She nodded. 'At the ball, especially. Anjali and her team really went to town on the details. Plus, we'd spent all day immersed in various wartime scenarios, so it wasn't hard to imagine that we'd all come through that terrible war and were ready to celebrate like crazy.' She smiled at her grandfather. 'Was it like that in real life?'

'I'm sure it must have been.' For some reason he avoided her eyes, taking the lid from the teapot to see if it needed topping up, and pouring in – it seemed to Anna – completely unnecessary hot water.

Aware that she'd said something to disturb him; she tried to turn it into a joke. 'So – did you go crazy on VE Day? Jump into fountains? Kiss beautiful strangers?'

'I'm afraid not. It sounds rather wonderful.' He attempted a smile.

'So what –?' she started.

'I was with the men who liberated Bergen Belsen.' Her grandfather's voice came out with unusual force. 'That sounds extremely grand but it was actually more distressing and shameful than celebratory.'

Anna set down her cup. 'I had no idea. Mum never said.'

'She didn't know. I never talked about it. I couldn't. I think I briefly alluded to it to your grandmother once.'

'It must have been horrible.' Anna pulled a face. 'Sorry, that's a grossly inadequate thing to say.'

'There are no adequate words,' her grandfather said, very quietly. He rubbed his hand across his face as if to banish some unspeakable image. 'I still dream about it. The smell. The – the bodies.' He took a breath. 'Sorry.'

'No, I'm sorry,' Anna said. 'I didn't mean to make you feel so . . .'

She'd have given anything to take back her careless words, anything to spare him the memories of such horror. Not knowing what else to do, she poured them both fresh tea so they could both regroup.

'Well—' George Ottaway said, with a slightly shaky laugh, '—to return to the present day. Your weekend was good in parts? Like the curate's egg?'

'Actually, it took rather a grim turn,' she admitted. After what he'd just told her Anna felt she owed her grandfather the truth. 'Last night, a woman had too much to drink, wandered off into the grounds, fell into a pond and drowned. Or so we think.' She had an unwanted flashback to the dead woman floating amongst the budding water lilies.

'These things happen.' Her grandfather sounded uncharacteristically brusque. 'That's one thing I learned in the army. If some drunken idiot is bent on self-destruction there's isn't a thing you can do to prevent it.'

Anna was taken aback. 'To be fair, we don't know for sure if she was drunk or self-destructive.' But George Ottaway wasn't listening. He seemed distracted, as if he was wondering how to broach some unpleasant subject. She heard him take a steadying breath.

'Talking of drunken idiots, I gather Dominic Scott-Neville is back in the country.'

Anna felt a sudden dark buzzing inside her head.

'No doubt he's back to fritter away the family fortune,' her grandfather said, apparently oblivious to her distress, 'after he's danced on his father's grave. Not that I'd blame him. Ralph was a – well, we all know what Ralph was,' he finished grimly.

Despite the hothouse warmth of Bramley Lodge, Anna felt herself go freezing cold to her core. For a moment, she was back on that college rooftop on New Year's Eve, hearing Alec Faber gasp, 'If you think I'm a monster . . .' She couldn't seem to breathe.

Her grandfather started talking again. 'Don't look so shocked, darling. Your grandmother and I weren't so old and out of touch that we didn't know what was going on. We knew Dominic was part of that crowd you ran with. We knew about the drink and drugs.'

But Anna was still on that terrifying rooftop, as Alec's dry calloused hands frantically tried to pull away from hers. 'Just let go!' he'd begged hoarsely. 'Can't you see I want to die?'

'I had no idea you even knew Dominic's name,' she said faintly. Somewhere beneath the inrush of unwelcome memories, she was aware of a feeling of suffocating shame.

'I knew it all right,' he said grimly. 'And all his other entitled friends. That ghastly boyfriend of yours. Max, wasn't it?

You were worth ten of any one of them, but you just couldn't see it.'

He saw Anna's stricken face and his voice softened. 'On the other hand, if you hadn't been out running wild every night, you might have been home when . . .' He shot an inadvertent glance at the family photograph on the table behind him. 'There've been times when I've thought I should thank the little bastard.' His voice suddenly cracked.

Her grandfather didn't know everything then, Anna thought. He didn't know what she'd suspected for so many years and driven herself to the edge of madness trying to prove.

'Your father worried about you too obviously,' he went on. 'But by that time, he was too entwined with the Scott-Neville family to be able to take a stand.'

His words jolted her back to the present. She stared at him. 'What do you mean, "entwined"?'

'Because of all the money Scott-Neville Senior poured into your father's auction house.'

'I didn't know about that!' Anna said, appalled.

'It was just after Will was born,' her grandfather said. 'Hempels had hit a bad patch. I never knew the details. All I know is that Ralph Scott-Neville conveniently stepped in to save the day. Just as a silent partner, but it meant your father felt his hands were tied.'

Anna felt her known world tilting on its axis. Julian might not have been her biological father but, in her heart, he was still her dad. It was unthinkable that he'd been mixed up with the Scott-Nevilles, the same family that had spawned Dominic. *If you think I'm a monster . . .*

'Your father wasn't the easiest man to get along with,' her grandfather said. 'But he wasn't a bad person. If anything, he cared about you all too much. He wanted his family to have the best of everything.'

I wasn't his family though. Anna felt a guilty pang. She still hadn't told her grandfather about Tim's discovery that he and Anna were brother and sister. How could she tell him that her mother, his daughter, once had an affair with Chris Freemantle, her father's best friend?

She saw George Ottaway pass his hand shakily over his face. 'I don't know how this conversation got so dark. All this talking about the war. It's opened up a whole can of worms. Tactless old man that I am. And now I've upset you.'

Anna insisted that he hadn't, but as they said their goodbyes her grandfather seemed subdued and she knew he wasn't convinced.

As she drove back to Park Town, she kept helplessly flashing back to New Year's Eve, when she had fought to save Alec Faber from falling to his death. Alec Faber, who had betrayed the trust of his superiors at the Foreign Office and been callously betrayed in his turn. Professionally disgraced and cast out by his family, he had lost everything except an unquenchable thirst for revenge. But his last words, ground out through gritted teeth, still reverberated through Anna, like a dark riddle that had the ring of a malign prophesy. *Dominic Scott-Neville was my brother's godchild. And if you think I'm a monster, Dominic is the devil!*

She let herself in through her front door and was immediately, rapturously greeted by Bonnie. Anna knelt in her hallway and wrapped her arms gratefully around her White Shepherd.

'I have *missed* you,' she said.

'She's missed you too,' Jake called. 'Kept going upstairs to look for you.'

She found him in her bedroom and was childishly disappointed to see him packing his bags.

'Hi, stranger,' he said.

She walked into his arms. *Home*, she thought, closing her eyes. In novels, female characters always went on about how their men smelled of lemons, mint or some other homely-yet-manly kitchen ingredient. Jake, however, just smelled uniquely and appealingly of Jake.

'I'm sorry it's taken so long to get back,' she said into his shoulder. 'I did an unscheduled detour via Bramley Lodge.'

'To check on George? I thought you would.'

'How does it feel to live with an obsessive?' she asked him forlornly.

'He's ninety,' Jake said. 'He's incredibly precious to you.'

'But so are *you* precious to me! And I've just wasted an entire weekend of you being here.'

He tightened his arms around her. 'Sweetheart, I'm a rough, tough boy from South Carolina and I intend to stick around to annoy you for aeons yet. So, don't you fret about some little bitty weekend. How was George anyway?'

Anna would have trusted Jake with her life, but she still felt too raw to share what her grandfather had told her, so she just said casually, 'He was OK.'

He gave her one of his searching looks. He knew something was up, but being Jake he wouldn't push it. So he said equally casually, 'Mind passing me those shirts?'

She picked up the pile of identical, flawlessly-pressed cotton shirts.

'Wow,' she said in awe. 'One day I must get you to teach me to iron like a marine!' She handed them over, careful not to disturb Jake's pristine folds.

'You know, it's a funny thing.' Jake's southern drawl was suddenly as thick as honey. 'People have this mistaken idea that getting into the marines has something to do with how well you handle fire arms or how many sit-ups you can do in sixty seconds. When it's actually all about the ironing!'

She laughed, relieved. Jake knew she needed him to keep it light. They continued in the same light jokey vein, until his taxi came to take him to the airport.

She and Bonnie watched from her front step, as the taxi performed a neat U-turn in front of the lovely, old, Georgian terrace.Then they went back indoors and down the stairs to her basement kitchen. Despite everything that had happened there, this was the room she instinctively retreated to for comfort.

After Anna's grandfather had signed over the house to her, she'd had it converted into three flats, two of which she rented out. She'd also got the builder to open up the kitchen to bring in more light. Now, French doors looked out onto a leafy courtyard with her herb pots and bird-feeders. She opened the doors and went outside, Bonnie following at her heels. With hopeful eyes, Bonnie brought Anna one of several old tennis balls that were littered around the garden and Anna threw it for her for a while, trying to take both their minds off Jake's absence.

She decided she needed something to eat. She soaked slices of bread in beaten egg and milk with a spritz of vanilla – she had Jake to thank for this last addition. Then she smeared oil on one of her grandmother's heavy-bottomed pans and set it to heat on the stove. Anna had inherited all her grandmother's pans, along with the Limoges crockery that she had secretly coveted ever since she was a little girl. She still caught herself looking for those perfect, translucent cups and saucers on her dresser shelves, even though she'd seen them smashed to smithereens by someone who was trying to kill her and Bonnie. The dresser had remained bare for months, except for a single cup which Tansy had painstakingly repaired for her. Then, for her birthday, Tansy and Isadora had taken Anna to a local department store and bought her a set of kitchen crockery by Littala. Designed in Finland, the mugs, bowls and plates all featured glowing fairy-tale designs against a rich midnight blue.

When Anna had cooked her French toast to the right degree of puffy goldenness, she drizzled on maple syrup, shamelessly eating it straight out of the pan. As she ate, she could still feel the shock-waves from her grandfather's revelation.

Her own father mixed up with the Scott-Nevilles. How had things at Hempels got so bad? And how come Anna hadn't known? The auction house had been in her father's family for more than three generations. Her dad had both passionately loved and resented it, like an endearing, yet excessively demanding, elderly relative.

When she was small, Anna had been similarly passionate about Hempels. Then, in high school, she'd made new friends whose fathers were film directors, TV presenters and music producers. In her supercilious teenage world-view, a boring auction house couldn't compete; something she'd made eye-wateringly clear, she remembered, to her everlasting shame.

Seriously, how hard would it have been, to try to take an interest in the business that meant so much to him? The same business that kept Anna and her siblings comfortably fed and clothed. She wished – she immediately checked herself. *Don't go there, Anna.*

She washed the pan, dried it, hung it on its steel rod next to the others and heard the faint *ding* as it knocked briefly against the others. She realized she was vividly picturing the elegant, old, Georgian building in South Kensington and felt a confused longing.

It's not too late, she told herself. Hempels had not died with her father. In fact, under its new owner, its reputation seemed to be going from strength to strength.

A normal person would just jump on a train and pay them a visit. With a pang of shame, Anna admitted to herself that she would probably never again be that person. Since the murders, too many places had become fraught with painful associations. Oxford, her beloved city, was full of such hidden minefields.

But going to Hempels, her father's auction house, would completely undo her.

THREE

S urfacing from a confused dream, Anna reached for Jake then, with a sensation like missing a step, remembered that he was on the other side of the English Channel.

He'd sent her a text.

Here I am in Paris and I'm spending it with a bunch of international security geeks. P.S. Don't go getting into mischief now you're a lady of leisure.
P.P.S Bet I know where Bonnie slept the night!

Anna would swear she hadn't made even the tiniest sound, yet she could feel Bonnie on high alert in her basket, only just containing her longing to start the day.

Peering over the edge of the bed, she saw dark-rimmed eyes hopefully looking up at her. 'How do you know the exact minute I wake up?' Bonnie wagged her tail. 'Classified info, huh?'

Anna threw on some old clothes and a pair of trainers that had seen better days, grabbed an energy bar and took Bonnie for a long walk in Port Meadow, because, as Jake had pointed out, there was currently nowhere else she had to be.

After much soul-searching, Anna had handed in her notice at Walsingham College. She'd taken the job share as a means of keeping herself grounded, whilst she pursued what she'd thought of as her real occupation; following up any lead that might help her to find her family's killers. Then, after her near-death experience on New Year's Eve, it became a matter of urgency for Anna to reassess her life. *Well, it was the first time I'd had a life to re-assess,* she thought with a flicker of humour.

She glanced down at Bonnie, as she stopped to sniff some compelling, springtime scent that had sprung up since their last visit. Trotting through the shiny, young buttercups, she looked exactly like a white wolf; the magical wolf who had changed Anna's life.

It was just weeks after she'd brought Bonnie back from the rescue shelter, that Anna had found herself involved in a murder investigation along with fellow dog walkers, Tansy and Isadora. Inexplicably, this traumatic experience had helped Anna begin to heal from her own trauma. It wasn't the most obvious cure, she thought, just as stumbling across the body of a murder victim wasn't the obvious basis for lasting friendships, but by the time the case had been resolved, these two very different women had become indispensable to her well-being.

So now that she'd finally got a life, Anna had decided to do something with it, something worthwhile. She had no idea what this might be, but giving in her notice had seemed like a crucial first step. Her admin job had started feeling too much like another place to hide. *A holding pattern,* she thought, remembering a phrase her therapist, Miriam, had used. The repetitive tasks of university admin were supposed to keep Anna safe and sane. But life *wasn't* safe, tidy, or remotely controllable, as Anna had good reason to know.

Bonnie had wandered off to investigate a mole hill. Like her owner, she was enjoying not being squeezed into a timetable.

'Barney – *Barney!*' someone yelled, followed by a couple of blasts on a whistle. A leggy, young spaniel, brown and glossy as a horse chestnut, came bounding up to Bonnie, long ears flying. Anna's White Shepherd endured his antics until he tried to lick her face and then she calmly knocked him flat on his back where he remained, with a surprised, faintly goofy expression.

'I'm so sorry!' A man came racing up. 'Right, you little thug, you're going back on the lead!' He grabbed the pup by the collar, hastily attaching a smart, red lead. 'Barney's still only nine months so he's a bit full-on. Plus, he's our first dog. All training tips welcomed!'

Anna shook her head, laughing. 'I can't help you there. Bonnie came pre-trained by American marines!'

She was still smiling to herself as she and her dog went on their way. Barney's owner had assumed that Anna was a seasoned dog owner equipped to pass on useful tips, when it was really the other way around. *It was Bonnie who trained me*, she thought. She wandered along the familiar trails over the ancient commons, with Bonnie bounding on ahead. As she walked, she was aware of birdsong, the slightly overpowering scents of hawthorn and flowering cow parsley, but she was thinking about Ralph Scott-Neville She'd met him of course. Once she'd been accepted into Dominic Scott-Neville's circle, it was inevitable she'd run into his father. He'd been at Dominic's eighteenth, obviously, and she'd encountered him at mealtimes when she and her friend Natalie joined the Dominic's family's annual skiing holiday. Anna tried to remember if her father had expressed dismay at her heading off to St Moritz with the Scott-Nevilles, but could only recall a last minute row with her mother.

Anna had never felt comfortable with Ralph. He had, what her grandmother would have described as, an *unfortunate* face, unfortunate for the century he'd been born into, that is. In the court of Henry VIII, dressed in doublet, hose and snowy ruff, Ralph Scott-Neville's beady-eyed, sharp-nosed, narrow-chinned features would have blended right in with all the other back-stabbers and conspirators.

Anna had also met Dominic's grandfather, Bertie, after Dom sweet-talked her and Natalie into showing their faces at the old man's 90th birthday celebration.

'Won't your parents mind us gate-crashing?' Anna had asked.

'Oh, they'll *mind*,' he'd said, as if she was an idiot. 'But if you're there, they won't feel they can kick up a fuss. Besides, my grandfather loves pretty girls,' he'd added with a leer.

She and Natalie had been disgusted because Bertie's third wife was at least thirty years younger than the shrivelled vulpine old man. Anna seemed to remember she was originally from Venezuela. All the Scott-Neville women claimed some exotic provenance and, so far as she'd seen, spent their days grooming themselves like so many indolent cats. Dom's mother had been an Argentinian heiress and now Dominic himself had married an American model and socialite.

As she walked beside frothy, cow parsley, Anna was disturbed to find that she could perfectly recall Ralph Scott-Neville's unnerv-ingly inexpressive face. Yet, behind those blandly empty features, she'd been aware of a cold cunning. Anna shivered. She wished she could travel back through time and plead with her father to take care. Let Hempels go to hell, anything rather than become financially 'entwined' with that cold, cruel man.

A little way off, a group of dog-walkers had stopped to chat, their dogs impatiently milling around them. Anna hastily veered off down a different trail.

The growing need to reopen her investigations into her family's murders was like a gravitational pull. But if she gave into it this time, there was no guarantee she'd be any more successful than before – and now she had so much more to lose.

Don't go getting yourself into trouble.

Jake had known something was eating at her.

'There's a look you get,' he'd told her once, when they'd been lying and talking in the dark. 'When I see it, I know you've gone some place I can't follow.' He'd said it completely without judg-ment, simply stating a fact.

'What do you do then?' she'd asked, feeling her heart beating in her throat.

'I wait,' he said, very quietly. 'I wait till you come back.'

This conversation had pierced Anna to the quick. How she must hurt him when she withdrew into that unreachable place. She was terrified that she might be sucked back into the black hole of her old obsessions. She didn't want to be that crazy Anna ever again.

Just one month. If she hadn't turned anything up in that time she'd stop. She'd be able to control it now. She caught herself mentally bargaining with – she wasn't sure who – her old therapist? Like an alcoholic insisting she could control her drinking, she thought. *One month*, she thought again. *Then I'll give it up I swear.*

She went home with Bonnie, made herself a strong cup of coffee and drank it while she checked her emails.

She wished she could have told Jake about her conversation with her grandfather but, even if he hadn't just been leaving to catch a plane, she knew she'd have found it too painful. Jake had never known her dad. He only knew the confused little bits and pieces she'd told him; more confused than ever now that she knew Julian wasn't her biological father. If she'd passed on her grandfather's bombshell to Jake, he might think less of Julian and she couldn't bear that. She couldn't bear the thought that her dad might have been somehow tainted by his involvement with Ralph Scott-Neville,

Julian and Julia Hopkins. Near-identical names for two very different people. Her father had been a detached, prickly, a stoical workaholic. Her mother was given to short-lived enthusiasms, debilitating headaches and emotional outbursts. And adultery, apparently. Despite the jokey comments provoked by the similarity in their names, her oddly-matched parents stalwartly remained Julian and Julia. Never Jools, Jude or Julie.

She didn't dare to let herself miss them. After how she'd behaved when they were alive, she didn't feel she had the right. For sixteen years, there had been an aching space where her mother and father should have been.

But I've got Tim, she thought. *I can talk to Tim.*

She reached for her mobile and pulled up her brother's number, then just sat staring at her phone, her fingers hovering over the icons. Until recently, Tim had worked as an investigative journalist. Now he planned on being a stay-at-home dad for a while, free-lancing for one of the broadsheets, while Anjali built her company. Would it be selfish to tell Tim what she'd discovered about Julian? Given that Anjali's first murder mystery weekend had ended with a real corpse, weren't he and Anjali under enough pressure?

Tim's a grownup, she reminded herself. *If he's too busy or too stressed, he can tell you!*

She swiped her finger over the call icon. Tim picked up almost at once. To Anna's relief he sounded like his cheerful, pre-baby self. He interrupted her garbled apology.

'I know this sounds brutal, Anna, but it's true what all those vile PR moguls say. There truly is no such thing as bad publicity.'

'You mean this poor woman's death is going to be good for business?' Anna asked. 'Not that I don't want Anjali's business to be successful but . . .'

'I knew what you meant,' he said quickly. 'But the fact is people are going to remember her company now. And it's not like High Table will be using Mortmead Hall for future events. It's just been sold.'

'Yes, I heard,' Anna said.

'Someone bought it as a gift for his bored little wife, who'll probably turn it into another *chichi* boutique hotel, just what Oxford needs. So, what's up?' he asked in a different tone. 'You sound frazzled.'

'I just found out my dad might have been in bed with the devil,' she blurted out. 'God, sorry! I sound like such a drama queen!'

There was a pause, then Tim said calmly, 'Just a bit. Plus, I might need some clarification on the devil thing.'

Typical laid-back Tim, she thought gratefully.

'I went to see my grandfather last night,' she explained, 'and he told me that around the time Will was born, dad's auction house almost went bust and Ralph Scott-Neville stepped in to save the day. He – my grandfather – thinks that's why Dad felt he couldn't object to me running around with Dominic and his—'

'Anna, slow down,' Tim interrupted. 'I *know* you, remember! Now you're wondering if this had anything to do with your family's murders.'

'Well, yes. Does that sound paranoid?'

She heard him sighing down the phone. 'No, because I've been guilty of making the same leap. To be honest, Anna, this is kind of old news.'

'You *knew*! You knew my dad got mixed up with Scott-Neville?' Anna was beginning to realize just how big a part her family's murders had played in Tim's decision to become an investigative journalist. Like Anna, he'd made his own investigations into the tragedy.

'I'd heard a rumour,' Tim said. 'And I had the same reaction as you. Then, every time I tried to investigate, I found myself mysteriously stone-walled.'

'By the Scott-Nevilles?'

'By the Scott-Nevilles and their cronies. But, as you know, Ralph's and Dominic's alibis for that night were water-tight.'

'I know,' she said irritably. 'Some big family party at Woodstock.'

'With hundreds of witnesses,' Tim said. Anna heard him take a breath. 'I do think it's *quite* interesting that, despite Dominic's water-tight alibi and umpteen witnesses, the Scott-Nevilles obviously felt their son needed serious reining in and packed him off to learn about his uncle's wine business in Argentina, rather than going to Oxbridge as originally planned.'

'Reining him in, but also keeping him well out of the public eye? So will you help me do some digging around?' she asked Tim.

'I'll do some low-key digging,' he agreed. 'See if there's any chatter about the other Scott-Nevilles.' Anna heard his baby daughter let out a thin wail of protest. 'I can't give this too much time for reasons you can probably hear,' he said humorously.

'Tim, I'm just grateful that I can talk to you,' she said. 'Anything else is icing on the cake, believe me.'

She hung up and found she was suddenly buzzing with nervous energy. When Anna was still in therapy, her therapist used to talk a lot about 'closure'. Anna had tried and failed to imagine how that miraculous and, so far, elusive condition might feel. How was closure even possible, she'd thought, when she still couldn't walk down the street where her old house used to stand or walk past her brothers' school without feeling that her heart was breaking.

Or revisit my father's auction house. She instantly felt her stomach clench as if her body had already reached a decision. *I wouldn't have to go inside. I could walk up the street and take a look, then go straight back home.* It would be one small but significant step towards banishing her old shadows. Who might she be without them? For the first time, Anna thought she knew. *Free*, she thought. *I'd be free.*

Next morning, Anna caught the bus to the station. But when she arrived on the platform, the train to Paddington was running late. A laconic Oxfordshire voice gave "Beasts on the line", as the probable cause. As a child, Anna had hopefully pictured dragons or griffins and had been deeply disappointed when her parents explained that it was most likely sheep.

She bought herself a cup of coffee, found an empty bench and waited for the beast problem to be resolved. Last night, unable to sleep, Anna had checked the Hempels' website. After her father's death, the auction house had been bought by a Swiss business man, but had kept the old name. Though smaller than Sotheby's or Christie's, Hempels had an international reputation for a certain kind of fine art, gaining the respect – and envy – of the bigger auction houses and agencies.

Anna had been touched to see a tribute to her father on the website. In Julian's bio, he was lauded for his unparalleled expertise, his ethics and his insistence on ensuring the provenance of art objects. Though the man himself had gone, his scrupulously high standards remained as the benchmark of good practice.

Having read this, Anna had felt very slightly reassured. Her father's involvement with Ralph Scott-Neville still troubled her. But she felt – she *hoped* – that the man they'd described was the same upright, honourable man that she'd known for sixteen years.

She was just wondering whether she should have driven to London after all, when her train arrived, half an hour late. As she took her seat, she had a rare childhood memory of one of the few times she'd gone into work with her dad. Julia had been pregnant then with Dan. She was coming up to town later the same day and they were taking Anna to see The Nutcracker.

All the seats on the train were either occupied or had been reserved so Anna had had to sit on her dad's lap. She remembered being thrilled to be going into work with her daddy like a grown-up girl. A Tsarina's crown was being auctioned and the prospect of seeing a real, Russian princess's crown had been almost too exciting to bear.

In present time, Anna felt the train slowing to a crawl. It shuddered to a standstill with a great squeal of brakes, leaving Anna with a view over some allotments, where a woman was busy weeding. Inside the carriage, people rustled papers and played with their phones. No explanation was given. No conductor appeared. Everyone just waited in a very British silence. The woman emptied her barrowful of weeds onto her compost heap, locked her barrow and tools inside her shed, and walked away. This left Anna with nothing to look at.

After almost twenty minutes, the train gave a sudden lurch and they were off again, though at a much-reduced speed. Anna eventually arrived at Paddington an hour later than she'd planned.

When she described these minor delays and everything that followed to Tansy later, Tansy said with conviction, 'It was *meant to be*. Anna, if you'd arrived any earlier, you never would have known!'

Passing a sushi stand on the station, Anna havered, then finally decided against it and hurried down to the stale air of the Underground. To her relief, there were no delays on the Circle

Line and she soon emerged into the sunlight and traffic in South Kensington. It was more than sixteen years since she'd been to her dad's auction house, but her feet unerringly took her to the right street.

And suddenly there it was on the corner, with its elegant iron railings, the white painted portico and its three supporting columns. When she saw the familiar name above the heavy double doors, Anna felt an inner jolt, as if she'd gone back in time. For a moment, she almost believed that she'd find her father inside at his desk, humming tunelessly, his glasses perched on the end of his nose.

Not giving herself time to think, Anna hurried up the short flight of steps and was surprised when the doors swung open at her touch. Things were more relaxed in her father's time, obviously, but surely everyone was security conscious now? She'd expected at least an intercom, so she could announce herself and be buzzed in. Feeling uncomfortably like an intruder, she walked cautiously into the foyer, expecting that faintly musty scent of old furniture, but found herself breathing smells of fresh paint and beeswax. The walls had been repainted a soft, Georgian yellow. The scuffed, wooden floors had been stripped and polished to a honey-coloured glow. The effect was sunny and golden. It would have been welcoming, if there had been anyone there to greet her.

There was a receptionist's desk, with phones and a computer, but the computer was still covered and the receptionist nowhere to be seen. Anna looked around for someone to tell her where she should go. She thought she could hear voices coming from downstairs. Her father's office had been on the lower-ground floor, next door to the valuation room.

She made her way downstairs and saw two porters blocking her view of her father's old office. With their backs to Anna they stood, immobile as waxworks, on either side of the partially-open door. *Like gun dogs*, she thought, every nerve-ending focused on the loudly audible quarrel that was taking place inside.

'It never belonged to you! You people had no right!' A man on the verge of hysteria cried out, then a second voice, calm but authoritative.

'Please try to calm down, Sir, or I'll have no choice but to have you removed. I can only repeat what my colleagues have already told you many times. The painting you describe does not exist. Believe me, if it existed Hempels would know about it.'

'That's a lie and you know it! My father saw it in his grand-parents' dining room every Friday night, when they all celebrated *shabbas* together.'

'Mr Fischer, much as I dislike sounding like a broken record, I can only reiterate that the painting you describe has never been mentioned in any catalogue of any auction house. Now I'm afraid I must ask you to leave.' The calm sounding man must have been gradually edging his furious visitor closer to the door, because Anna finally caught a glimpse of someone, who reminded her of a dishevelled male version of Isadora. He had a shock of long, white, wiry hair with one startling streak of jet black. His crumpled, old clothes seemed thrown on; a scarecrow, who had assembled himself in a high wind. In contrast, the tall, beautifully-dressed man, who was calmly but inexorably shepherding him from the office, looked like a Hollywood matinee idol from the nineteen-forties. The older man almost stumbled out into the hall, his eyes filled with tears. He was probably only in his sixties, Anna thought, but he looked grey with strain.

The porters immediately unfroze, silently moving one to each side of him.

'Come on, sir,' one said. 'You've had your five minutes. Excuse us, miss,' he added politely to Anna.

The porters escorted the distraught man up the flight of stairs that led to the street. They didn't jostle or manhandle him. Again, Anna had the image of well-trained gun dogs.

'The Mafia has better ethics than you people! You should be ashamed!' She heard the man shouting down the stairs.

'Now, now, Mr Fischer,' one of the porters said wearily. 'Don't make this any harder than it needs to be.'

Then Anna heard Fischer scream, 'Julian Hopkins *knew* we were telling the truth! He *told* me he believed me! You haven't heard the last of this. I'm never giving up!'

Anna heard the soft thud of the doors closing. Then her head filled with white noise.

FOUR

Anna took a sip from the heavy, ice-cold goblet that had been pressed solicitously into her hand, so cold the water hurt her teeth. She still felt that ominous buzzing in her ears. She hadn't blacked out, but she'd come close. The matinee idol man had swiftly helped her to a chair inside his office, then brought her the water. Alexei somebody, he'd said he was, but she'd still been too shocked to take in his last name. She must have blurted out something, because he'd murmured something about it being 'a very great honour to have Julian Hopkins' daughter here at Hempels'.

Anna had a strange sense of being back in her own home and wondered if it was just because of the wooden shutters. Once upon a time, when she was very small, Hempels had been like her second home. Alexei's vast desk hadn't been there in her father's time, she was almost sure. Polished to a silky sheen, there was nothing on it except a telephone and a framed picture or photograph, though of what or whom she couldn't see from her chair.

The walls had been repainted here too in some no doubt authentic Georgian red. A few exquisite objects were displayed here and there and she was surprised. She couldn't remember later what any of them were, only her surprise that they weren't locked inside a glass case, but kept out in the open, as though this was some opulent private apartment.

The office even *smelled* opulently of beeswax, good coffee and *money*, she thought. Alexei continued to hover, concerned.

'Would you like me to refill your glass?'

Anna could see a flawlessly folded silk handkerchief in his top pocket. It was an ox-blood red, like the walls, and brought out an identical dark crimson fleck in the tweed of his Savile Row suit. *He has kind eyes*, she thought, wishing she could summon up his last name.

'More water would be lovely,' she said, 'though I'm feeling much better, thank you. It was just the shock.'

'I can imagine,' he said sympathetically, 'I am so sorry that you had to witness such a distressing scene. Unfortunately, Ms Carmody, our receptionist, is off sick. She normally fields unwelcome intrusions such as Mr Fischer's.' He refilled her glass and she noticed his wedding ring, a wide gold band with a pleasing geometrical pattern etched into it.

Anna took another sip from the heavy, glass goblet.

'Who *is* he?' she asked. 'And why would he drag my father into this?'

Alexei gave her a reassuring smile, 'Hempels is small but it has acquired a certain cachet. Unfortunately, some people believe everything they read online and they associate us with astronomical sums of money changing hands. We have one lady who calls us up from Hereford wanting us to verify yet another priceless Old Master she bought in a car boot sale. Mr Fischer comes here every few months and vents his feelings about his imaginary Vermeer. It goes with the territory, I'm afraid. It's extremely regrettable that your visit and his happened to coincide.'

Anna felt a frisson of shock. It had never occurred to her – why would it? – that Fischer had been talking about a lost Vermeer. Such a painting would be priceless.

'But he was talking as if he'd had personal dealings with my dad,' she said, bewildered. Julian had been dead for over sixteen years, yet Fischer's disappointment seemed so fresh. Before her conversation with her grandfather, she might have been less suspicious. But now she knew her father had been involved with the Scott-Nevilles, all kinds of alarm bells were ringing.

Alexei shrugged. 'Your father was well respected in the art world. In this age of the internet, it wouldn't be too hard to come up with his name. He is mentioned in our website after all.' He gave another faintly foreign shrug.

'I suppose.' She longed to believe that this matter-of-fact explanation was the true one.

'I don't doubt that Mr Fischer himself fully believes what he's saying,' Alexei seated himself on the edge of his beautiful empty desk. 'But . . .' He shook his head. '. . . He is deluded, I'm afraid.'

'His painting really doesn't exist?'

He shook his head. 'Inside his tortured mind only.'

But Anna could still hear Fischer raging, 'Julian Hopkins *knew* we were telling the truth. He *told* me he believed me!' He'd made it sound as if her father had let him down in the worst way. She felt she couldn't bear it, if Fischer's assessment of her father was true. Wild and strange as he had seemed, he hadn't struck her as mad. Yet sixteen years later, he was still trying to track down his imaginary painting.

Alexei's kind, blue-grey eyes briefly met hers.

'I knew your father,' he said quietly. 'I learned the business from him and I admired him more than I can say. You won't remember seeing me at his funeral, but . . .' He made a sorrowful gesture. 'It was a terrible time for all of us at Hempels. As for you, Anna – may I please call you Anna? I cannot bear to imagine the loss.'

A young woman appeared at Alexei's door wearing a white shirt and charcoal grey trousers. Alexei smiled at her.

'Ah yes, Caroline. Any word from the agency?' Caroline quickly crossed the space between them and murmured in his ear.

'Not till tomorrow?' Alexei made an irritated tisking sound. 'Then do you think you and Sophia could sort something out between you, just for today? We must have someone on the front desk.'

Anna bent to pick up her bag, embarrassed. 'I've come at a bad time.'

'Not at all.' Alexei took a breath. 'As it happens a client has just cancelled. If you are fully recovered, would you like me to show you around, so you can see some small changes we have implemented since you were last here?'

'I would love that, thank you,' Anna said, 'that's so kind.'

'It is my pleasure! Come, I will take you on a tour.'

They made their way upstairs and through a set of double doors into the long high-ceilinged hallway, familiar to Anna from her childhood visits. But, as they walked into the first showroom, all familiarity fled. In her father's time, the building had been a ramshackle warren filled with wonders. This was a different, polished, more orderly world, full of light and space; *so much space*, she marvelled. The effect was to make the widely-dispersed objects on display appear more priceless still. Burnished wooden floors stretched on for miles. Tall, columnar vases, filled with fresh flowers, were placed at perfectly judged intervals. This new version of Hempels resembled nothing so much as a prestigious art gallery.

Anna had a sudden vivid image of her six-year-old self, sturdy
Clarks shoes echoing on scuffed floorboards as her father took her
to see her favourite thing in Hempels; a stuffed zebra which she
had secretly longed to take home.

What's that word? She thought suddenly. *Palimpsest?* The filmy
layers of the present through which you occasionally discerned
ghostly traces of what had been here before. That's what Hempels
felt like to her now.

They walked along an avenue formed between immense Chinese
vases – the kind the six-year-old Anna had imagined hiding inside,
like Ali Baba and his forty thieves – and into a room which
displayed only antique porcelain. Her eye was instantly drawn to
a Limoges tea-set; the impossibly delicate cups seeming to glow,
as if giving off their own inner light.

'How beautiful.' Anna swiftly pushed away a memory of dresser
shelves crashing down.

'Is this strange for you, being back here?' Alexei asked.

'In a way,' Anna said. 'But lovely too.'

'You feel close to your father here?'

She nodded. 'He loved this place. It meant everything to him.'

'You must come again,' Alexei said.

As they walked from showroom to showroom, he told her how
he had come to work in the UK.

'I was born in Soviet Russia. My mother defected during the
late 1960s. I was just a toddler then, so still quite portable.' He
smiled. 'It was a big scandal. My mother was a well-known opera
singer. The Soviets were not happy to lose her.'

Alexei was older than he looked, Anna thought, and less foreign
than he seemed, if he'd grown up and been educated in the UK.
Perhaps he'd found being a professional Russian émigré a useful
persona in his line of work? Or maybe Alexei had spent all his
childhood listening to other Russian exiles and now this was just
who he was?

They looked into several, dimly-lit rooms, where paintings by
famous artists hung against walls the colour of wet slate.

'Is that a Turner?' Anna asked, hoping Alexei couldn't hear her
stomach rumble.

'Yes, yes! Well done. Your father taught you well!'

They entered a room where glass cases glittered with jewels

and Anna told Alexei about the Tsarina's crown. They wandered past chairs, tables and inlaid cabinets, while Alexei helpfully murmured names; Sheraton, Chippendale, Adam Hepplewhite. Anna could feel her blood-sugar dropping. She should have stopped for sushi after all.

And then.

'The *zebra*!' Anna said, astonished. 'He's still here!'

'But of course! He is Hempels' lucky mascot,' Alexei said, smiling. 'We have had him repaired here and there and now he is as good as new! Oh, but now you look sad, Anna. Something has upset you?'

'I was genuinely so pleased to see him,' she said apologetically, 'but I can't seem to feel quite the same about him as I did when I was a little girl. I didn't worry about animals becoming extinct in those days. I think I just saw him as an especially wonderful kind of stuffed toy.'

'Then we will quickly move on,' Alexei said. 'This tour was not intended to make you feel guilty or sad.'

'So when your mother defected did she bring you to London?' she asked, to make up for her reaction to the zebra.

'Yes, yes. She established herself very quickly at the Royal Opera House. It was around the same time that many Russian performers, including Nureyev, had defected. There was this feeling that London was the place where exiles would always find a warm welcome.' Anna pictured him as a little boy, in a room filled with the smell of Russian cigarettes, someone playing Rachmaninov or Stravinsky on a grand piano, passionate political discussions and tears for the country they'd left behind.

'Not such a warm welcome now unfortunately,' Anna said, thinking of recent items on the news.

'No, not nearly so warm. My mother and I came here as refugees and now . . .' Alexei gestured smilingly to their surroundings. 'These days it's not so easy, I think.' He took a breath. 'Anna, if I have not worn you out, I want to show you something very beautiful before you leave.'

Anna was beginning to feel dazed, but he had been so kind that she didn't feel she could refuse. Alexei led her to a room devoted to antique rugs and hangings. She followed him through a blur of colour and pattern. She heard him murmuring Arabic-sounding

names that slipped away from her like water, as soon they were
spoken. *Concentrate*, she told herself, feeling her palms growing
damp, longing now to be back home with Bonnie.

At last, Alexei stopped and she saw his gaze come to rest on a
rectangular carpet, densely patterned in the profound blue and
violet hues of a twilit garden.

'Pure silk,' Alexei said in a reverent voice. 'From Isfahan in
central Persia. Four hundred years old. Yet look at these wonderful
blues, scarcely faded.' It was true; against the chalky pallor of the
wall the colours seemed astonishingly fresh and bright.

'And these stylised little birds look! Can you make them out?
The ratio of knots per square inch is so high it can't even be counted.'

'That makes it especially precious doesn't it,' Anna said, remembering her father enthusing in similar language.

He nodded. 'We expect it to fetch up to five million pounds.'

What stories this carpet could tell, Anna thought. She imagined
tall date palms casting long shadows against the brilliance of the
desert and women's hands, some gnarled with age, deftly knotting
those cooling garden colours in the dust and heat, the call to prayer
drifting from the mosque.

'Isfahan was larger than London four hundred years ago,' Alexei
said. 'It was more cosmopolitan than Paris.'

'And now?'

He shook his head. 'Now it is mostly known for a highly conten-
tious nuclear facility.'

They went back into the wide shining hallway, just as someone
emerged through a door, talking and gesturing to an elegant, young
woman, who was busily entering notes into her tablet. Her simple,
shift dress looked as if it had been knitted from expensive designer
moss. Her hair was twisted into a silky, nut-brown coil on the
back of her neck. She didn't appear to register either Anna or
Alexei; all her attention was focused on the stocky, silver-haired
man beside her.

'Oh, here is my boss, Herr Kirchmann, who owns Hempels
now,' Alexei said in an undertone. 'He is with Alice Jinks, his PA.
I must introduce you.' He waited until Herr Kirchmann and Alice
had finished their discussion, then stepped forward smiling.

'Thomas, if you have a moment, I have someone special for
you to meet.'

To Anna's astonishment Thomas Kirchmann smiled at her in delighted recognition.

'But I know you, don't I? You are Julian's eldest daughter. How wonderful that you've come to visit us. Has Alexei been showing you around?'

'Yes, he has.' Anna hoped she didn't look as disconcerted as she felt. 'I feel rather guilty at taking up so much of his time.'

'Not at all. This is a momentous occasion for us. Have you had lunch, Anna?' Before she could reply, Herr Kirchmann frowned at his watch. 'But I think it is too late now for lunch?' His face cleared. 'In which case, we must go out for afternoon tea!'

'No, no, really,' Anna said. 'I turned up completely unannounced. I couldn't possibly . . .' This was not at all how she'd envisaged her visit to Hempels turning out.

'I won't take no for an answer,' he said cheerfully. Hempels' new owner was already gently steering her by the elbow. 'Alexei, you will come with us,' he added, including him with a gesture that was part welcoming, part command. 'And Alice of course.'

A tiny crease appeared in Alice's smooth forehead. 'But Herr Kirchmann, your diary—'

'*Nonsense!*' Thomas Kirchmann interrupted and Anna felt the hidden steel beneath the jolly, German uncle exterior. 'We can always make time for old friends. We shall all go to Pfeffers. It is the only place in London where they know how to make good coffee!' he added to Anna.

'I'm not sure if that is strictly true, you know,' she said laughing, resigning herself to catching a much later train. Bonnie had a dog flap, so she could access the garden any time she needed to. All the same, Anna didn't like to leave her for so long.

'Alexei knows I am right, don't you, Alexei? Every time I take him, he buys their special strudel for his wife. They are absolute perfection, believe me! Alice, you will call ahead, please and reserve us a table.'

Anna found herself feeling sorry for Alice, as she was dispatched to clear Thomas Kirchmann's diary, reserve a table at the perfect coffee house with the perfect apple strudel and call a town car to take them there. At last, all the arrangements had been made and their little group of four emerged from the auction house. Above the rooftops, the London skies were growing hazy, threatening rain.

'You know I was once a client of your father's?' Herr Kirchmann said. 'He always had a photograph of you on his desk.'

'Yes, he did.' Anna felt herself doing a belated double-take. 'Surely that can't be how you recognised me?'

'Thomas never forgets a face,' Alexei explained. 'Not even one he's glimpsed in a photograph.'

'Seriously?' Anna said. 'That's virtually a super-power!'

Herr Kirchmann spread his hands. 'But, Anna, you have not *changed*!'

She laughed. 'I think I have.' A gleaming Jaguar drew up.

'In essence you are exactly the same,' Kirchmann insisted. 'And now I think this is our car! You really haven't been to Pfeffers before?'

'Never,' she said.

'Then I can assure you that you have a treat in store.'

Reluctant to get into the back with the others, Anna smilingly climbed in beside the driver before Alexei or Alice could pre-empt her. They drove off and Anna heard faint beeps from Alice's tablet as Kirchmann's PA valiantly continued to send and receive messages, squeezed in between her boss and Alexei.

She heard Alexei say, 'David Fischer was here when Anna arrived.' Then he dropped his voice but Anna caught the word, 'distressed.'

'I am extremely sorry to hear that,' the older man said heavily, but as Anna wasn't sure if he was addressing her or Alexei she didn't respond.

Herr Kirchmann abruptly leaned forward addressing the driver. 'Where are you from, young man? Afghanistan?'

The driver looked as startled as Anna had felt when Kirchmann identified her from a childhood photo.

'Yes, I am from Kabul. You have been there?' He sounded understandably cautious, Anna thought, not knowing what his passengers' prejudices might be.

'I have been to Kabul but a long, long time ago,' Herr Kirchmann said.

Kirchmann and the Afghani driver were soon chatting amicably. Free to think her own thoughts, Anna stared out of the window, aware of the stale breeze stirring her hair. In a few moments, they'd be passing Harvey Nichols. When she was sixteen, she and Natalie would come up to London just to wander from floor to floor of this flagship Knightsbridge store, deciding what they'd buy when they were grown up and free from all adult constraints. Afterwards they'd go to *Patisserie Valerie* for coffee and a slice of incredible lemon tart, which they'd divide scrupulously between them.

A black, lycra-clad courier zipped past on his bike, barely making it through the lights. The driver made a disparaging comment and Herr Kirchmann said, 'Not as bad as in Kabul, surely,' and they both laughed. Airbrakes hissed. Buses exhaled diesel fumes. The traffic came to a standstill and Anna found herself outside her old Temple of Delights, looking into a window which resembled a set for some glorious extra-terrestrial production of The Magic Flute. It was impossible to tell, from inside the car, what the glittering fantasy forest populated with peasants, princesses, fairy-tale birds and animals was supposed to be promoting, but it was so charming that she didn't care.

'Quite soon there is a left turn,' Thomas Kirchmann said at last.

'Yes, let us out here, please. Thank you.'

He led them past a magisterial Victorian building that could have given Mortmead Hall a run for its money, and then they had arrived at Pfeffers. Outside, striped blue and white awnings were hung and the name Pfeffers stencilled in gold across the windows. From the street, Anna caught a glimpse of brass lamps, dark wood and sparkling glass, everything expensively gleaming. She followed the others inside. Heady scents of strong coffee, melted chocolate, cinnamon and vanilla reminded her that it was hours since she'd eaten. The sounds of clinking crockery and the hiss of frothing milk competed with a grand piano, where a young man bent languidly over the keys. A waiter, with a pristine, white apron tied around his waist, showed them to their table and Anna sank gratefully into her squashy leather chair. Nearby, newspapers, in several European languages, hung from a wooden rack. On the dark panelled walls, sepia photographs of street scenes in old Vienna added to her feeling that she had crossed into a different time and country. She wouldn't have been completely surprised to catch the masculine whiff of a cigar.

Herr Kirchmann smilingly waved away the menus.

'Just bring us a little of everything.'

A little of everything turned out to be quite a lot: tiny sandwiches on sourdough rye bread, raspberry and poppy-seed cake, the famous perfect strudel in a brittle, wafer-thin pastry, Sachertorte and a blueberry and lemon Gugelhupf. Their waiter softly breathed their names, as he set down each exquisitely presented item. A pink-cheeked waitress brought coffee and hot milk in steaming silver pots.

Anna reached hungrily for a sandwich, only to have Alice lay a discreet finger on her sleeve.

'Only if you like liver,' she said so softly that no one else could possibly have heard.

'Oh, no. Thank you,' Anna said equally softly and took a smoked salmon sandwich instead.

Alice ordered mint tea and nibbled at a tiny tartlet, or rather reduced it to microscopic crumbs, whilst continuing to send and receive a steady flow of emails.

'So what made you want to take over my father's business?' Anna asked Herr Kirchmann.

'Well, as I said, I used to be a regular client, but after Julian's death there was a time when Hempels' future seemed—' he hesitated '—uncertain,' he finished at last. 'Oh, there was no shortage of potential buyers, but Hempels has a tradition of excellence that goes back for over a hundred and fifty years. I found that I could not bear for that thread to be broken.' Thomas Kirchmann gave her a quick smile and Anna was shocked to see tears standing in his eyes. 'Can you understand that?'

For a moment, Anna couldn't find words. Herr Kirchmann's obvious concern for her father's legacy touched her more than she knew how to express. *I should have known all this*, she thought. Why had she not known?

'Please, you must try the strudel,' he said, the courteous host. 'It is out of this world.'

Anna tried it and it was.

'Yes?' he said. 'Aren't you glad I brought you?'

Isadora would love Pfeffers, she thought. Not just because she had a sweet tooth, but because her parents came from a world where coffee houses like Pfeffers could once be found on every street corner.

'Excuse me,' Alexei said. 'I must go and buy some strudel for my wife.' She watched him make his way among the tables to the counter. He was different here, she thought, quieter, deferring to his larger than life boss.

She became aware that Thomas Kirchmann was still explaining himself. 'My father, my biological father, used to own a little gallery in Kerzenstaendergasse, in Innsbruck.' He smiled at her. 'In English that means Candlestick Lane. Innsbruck is full of such medieval streets even now. One day, my mother came into his gallery and my father fell in love with her. She was much younger, which caused some talk, but they were very happy, until – well, I'm sure you know what happened in Austria in the 1930s?'

'I'm guessing something to do with the start of the Second World War?' she said.

He nodded. 'Have you heard about the Entartete Kunst?'

Anna tried to remember her high-school German.

'Is that something to do with culture?'

'Literally it means "degenerate art". Did you know the Nazis held public burnings of paintings they judged too degenerate or seditious to exist?'

Anna shook her head. She had only known of the book burnings.

'The Nazis had a special military unit department known as the Kunstschutz,' Herr Kirchmann said. 'Literally the name means "art protection", though in fact it was anything but. The Kunstschutz was devoted to tracking down and confiscating all artworks, specifically, but not exclusively, works of modern art.' He deliberately met her gaze. 'Over a thousand paintings and sculptures. Almost four thousand water colours and prints.' He shook his head.

Had her father ever mentioned these acts of barbarism by the Third Reich, Anna wondered?

Alice had finally put away her tablet. She sipped at her second cup of mint tea with an expression of polite interest, careful not to intrude herself into this conversation. Yet she sat as alert as a cat, Anna felt, for the slightest sign that her services might be needed

Thomas Kirchmann poured more coffee for himself and Anna.

'It was all a cynical propaganda exercise,' he said soberly. 'The Nazis calculated that art experts from all over Europe would come running, with their cheque books, to save these priceless works of art. They had found the perfect way to fund their war machine. They continued to loot artworks from every country that they occupied; paintings, ceramics, jewellery and religious treasures. Of course, first and foremost, they plundered the homes of wealthy Jews.'

Anna suddenly found she had lost all interest in her delicious strudel.

'They were selling off stolen items to raise money for guns and planes?'

Herr Kirchmann nodded.

'And I suspect as future security for Hitler and his cronies, in case the unthinkable happened and they lost the war.' He took a breath. 'Well, when my father understood what was going on, he let it be known that his gallery had a basement in which he would hide artworks belonging to Austrian Jews, until the danger had passed.'

'Your family is Jewish?'

Kirchmann smiled.

'No, my father was just a good man, what Jews call "a righteous gentile". But, inevitably, in those dark times, someone betrayed him to the Gestapo. By this time, my father had managed to send my mother and me to Switzerland. Sad to say, my father was executed outside his gallery by a Nazi firing squad. The gallery was ransacked and every one of the paintings he had died to protect was spirited away by the Kunstschutz.'

Alexei had returned to their table, with his beribboned box of pastries, in time to hear the end of Herr Kirchmann's story.

'So you never really knew your father?' he said.

'No. I was just a baby when we left.'

Thomas Kirchmann told them that, like so many people after the war, he and his mother had lived in poverty for several years. Then his mother, still only in her thirties, had met and married a wealthy Swiss entrepreneur.

'Did you like him?' Anna said.

'Very much. Like my mother, he made a point of telling me of my father's bravery, his determination to do what was right. I think, over the years, my father's story soaked into my bones. I wanted to make him proud of me. I wanted to be just like him and defy the Nazis. But these were different times, and possibly I was not as brave, so eventually I trained to be a lawyer.'

'I didn't know that,' said Alexei, surprised.

'In my spare time, I continued to dabble in the art world, which is how I eventually came to know Julian.' He smiled at Anna. 'But then some years ago, I had – you would call it – a kind of crisis. I realized that I had to do something to honour my father's legacy. And then, when I saw that Julian's beloved Hempels was on the market . . .' he sighed and gestured. 'I was so sorry, Anna, I can't tell you how sorry, but I also felt that here was my chance.'

Anna looked across the table crowded with silver coffee pots and plates of elegant patisserie, in which they had scarcely made a dent, and found herself looking into his candid blue eyes. *I like him*, she thought. *I'm glad he was the one who bought Hempels.*

'I apologise for making it such a long story,' he said.

'No,' she said. 'I'm glad you told me.' She thought she would always remember how he'd said: *I found that I could not bear for that thread to be broken.*

Alexei and Thomas began to discuss the difficulties involved in restitution, locating and returning artworks looted during times of armed conflict, to their rightful owners.

Anna knew she should try to join in, but by this time she was all talked out. She caught Alice watching her with her cool little half-smile.

'Do you live in London, Anna?' she asked.

'Oxford,' Anna said. Just at that moment, even Paddington Station seemed as remote as the moon.

'What time is your train?' Alice said in an undertone. 'If you like I could call you a cab?'

'Do you know, that would be wonderful,' Anna said gratefully.

Once she was on the homeward train with raindrops spattering on the dirty window, Anna began to revive. Alexei had given her his card. Anna slipped it out of her wallet. *Alexei Lenkov. Hempels Auction House* it said, in charcoal script, on stiff cream card and it supplied his contact details. She would call him soon. Now that they'd broken the ice it would feel easier to ask Alexei if he'd ever heard anything about Ralph Scott-Neville putting money into Hempels.

She was suddenly ridiculously thrilled with herself. She had allowed herself to be swept off to a Viennese coffee house by Hempels' exuberant new owner. She'd spent the afternoon with

three complete strangers and survived. Even a few months ago
this would have felt impossible. Anna sent a buoyant text to Jake.
Just back from 1920s Vienna. Wish you'd been there.
A moment later her phone pinged. Anna assumed it was Jake
responding to her text but it was Tansy.
Have u seen Oxford Mail?
Puzzled, Anna replied.
No. Been consuming yummy cakes in London. Why?
Tansy's reply drove everything else out of Anna's head.
That woman in the pond, she was murdered.

FIVE

Anna only went home to shower and change her clothes.
Bonnie was overdue for a walk, so they walked over to
Summertown through shining, rain-washed streets.

Isadora came to let her in, her little dog Hero dancing at
her heels.

She just said, 'Oh, darling girl,' then wordlessly led the way
back down the long gloomy corridor.

In the kitchen, tall arched windows that would have been at
home in a college chapel stood open, letting in light and birdsong.
Hearing them come in, Tansy looked up from her chopping board
and Anna saw a few curling strands escaping from her usual messy
pony tail. She gave Anna a subdued version of her usual, warm
smile, obviously shaken by the news.

'I'm glad you could come,' she said, then went back to chopping mint and parsley at the kitchen counter.

Isadora hurried over to her cooker and bent to peer at something
under her grill. Her feet were bare under a long, floaty purple skirt
that had lost most of its sequins.

'What can I do?' Anna asked.

'Your usual thankless task?' Tansy suggested.

'Oh, shush,' said Isadora without looking up. '"A tidy house is
a sign of a wasted life."'

With an inward sigh, Anna looked down at her friend's kitchen table which had disappeared yet again under a familiar detritus of bills, scribbled coffee-stained notes, and copies of arcane medieval manuscripts in English and French, probably research materials for Isadora's overdue book on Courtly Love.

Outside, a gnarled, old apple tree was in blossom. Bluebells flowered amongst spring nettles, which looked almost luminously green in the evening light. Since she'd got Tansy's message, Anna had felt as if all her senses were operating at higher than normal intensity. The piercing calls of the birds, the brilliant spring light after the rain, the horror of yet another violent death.

She glanced over at Tansy, who was chopping olives, radishes and cherry tomatoes for some elaborate kind of salad. Around one fine-boned wrist, she wore a tiny jade Buddha threaded on to a thin strip of leather. The tips of her fingernails were coated with rose pink gels, thickly sprinkled with silver. Tansy looked nothing like you'd imagine the daughter of an infamous, London gangster ought to look.

A few months ago, Tansy had briefly been homeless and Anna had offered to let her stay in her spare room. It was the first time since her teens that Anna had willingly shared her space and she'd been surprised and pleased at how well they'd got on.

'I'm going to miss you so much,' Tansy had said, the night before she left to move in with Liam. 'You're like my sister from another mister!'

At this precise moment, though, Tansy seemed a little too focussed, Anna thought, concentrating all her energies on her salad. Anna wondered if it was just the murder that was upsetting her or something closer to home.

She began the laborious process of transferring Isadora's books and papers up to the far end of the long wooden refectory-style table, attempting to keep everything in some kind of order, all the while knowing that the next time they ate in Isadora's kitchen, she'd have it all to do again. On top of the fourth and final pile, she laid the folded copy of today's Oxford Mail, but couldn't yet bear to read it.

Isadora moved the chicken pieces around on their rack with her tongs, making sure they were all cooked through. The kitchen was full of the fragrance of hot spicy chicken. Both dogs closely watched these proceedings, nostrils working overtime.

The door opened and Isadora's lodger, Sabina came in with a canvas book bag slung over one shoulder and a bicycle helmet under her arm.

'Wow, that smells amazing!'

Isadora pulled out the spitting, bubbling pan of almost-blackened chicken, turning off the heat, then turned around to smile at her.

'We'll save you some, darling. Sabina has to babysit tonight,' she explained.

'And do some studying, I hope, if little Aubrey and Orlando will just stay in their cots!' Sabina laughed, tossing back her long, squeaky-clean blonde hair as hundreds of thousands of pretty female undergraduates had done before her. 'It's amazing more of them don't get whiplash,' Isadora had commented once.

Tansy looked up from mixing tiny bites of toasted flatbread into her salad.

'Twin boys! That sounds like a tough gig!'

'Tell me about it,' Sabina said with a grin. Last year, Isadora had taken in two lodgers, to help pay for the upkeep on her rambling, North Oxford house. One had gone back to Korea after only two terms but, after a somewhat sticky start, Sabina had stayed on and was now very much at home. In many ways, Anna thought, she was the granddaughter Isadora had never had. Anna saw Sabina's eyes look for and find the copy of the Oxford Mail.

'I was so sorry to hear about that woman,' she said awkwardly.

'Awful,' Tansy said. 'I still can't get my head around it.'

Sabina went off to babysit. Isadora heaped the aromatic chicken pieces on a platter and brought it to the newly-cleared table. Tansy set the large blue salad bowl beside it. Anna fetched plates and cutlery. Isadora brought more toasted flatbread, with tiny bowls of ground spices and olive oil to dip it in, and they sat down to eat.

In dark times, Isadora's instinctive need to feed the people she loved became an overpowering compulsion. Like Anna, Isadora Salzman had survived when others close to her had died. Now someone had been murdered, a few hundred metres from where they'd been dancing and drinking champagne. But Isadora and her friends were still living, so she had brought them together to mourn and honour this dead woman and also, Anna suspected, to fortify herself against the unknowable mystery of death itself.

Anna dipped a fragment of hot crisp flat-bread into the oil and then into some pungent middle-eastern spice. It was only when she put the piece of bread into her mouth that she realised she was ravenous.

Isadora was suddenly anxious. 'I hope Tansy doesn't mind that this isn't vegan?'

Tansy laughed. 'I lost my vegan credentials months ago – the first time Liam made me a bacon sandwich!'

Isadora tutted irritably. 'I *knew* that! What a forgetful old bat! I can't think why I have this fixation that you're still vegan?'

'Probably because you have such a horror of tofu!' Tansy teased her. 'But seriously, this is all lovely, Isadora. I'm really glad we're all here tonight.'

'It didn't seem right for us to be in our separate houses and all thinking about her.' She turned to Anna. 'She had such a pretty name. Lili. Lili Rossetti.'

Hearing the name said out loud, it felt as if some invisible essence of Lili Rossetti herself had come into the room and Anna felt a little shiver go down her spine.

Isadora lifted her glass of sparkling water. 'To Lili Rossetti. *Shalom.* We never knew you, my dear, but may you rest in peace.'

Her name made her real, Anna thought, someone with a story, not just an anonymous victim.

'What do we know about Lili? Sorry,' she said aloud, then added hastily, 'maybe you'd rather wait until we've finished our meal?'

Isadora shook her head. 'Not at all.'

'I couldn't get hold of Liam for the latest info,' Tansy said, 'not that he'd tell me anything anyway. But the Mail said she wasn't local. And – I thought this was quite weird – not only had she *not* signed up for the murder mystery weekend, but her name wasn't on the guest list for the ball.'

'That is weird,' Anna said. 'She was dressed up to the nines 1940s style when I saw her – if that was Lili I saw.'

'You saw her?' Tansy said.

'I think so. It was just a glimpse,' Anna said. 'And she obviously looked very different after . . .'

'You never said you'd seen her.' Tansy sounded slightly accusing.

'I didn't realize I had,' Anna explained, 'until someone else interrupted my interview and, like I said, it was just a glimpse. Some guy in a kilt was trying to chat her up and she shook him off and hurried outside. What else did it say in the Mail?'

'That the police have been trying to trace Lili's ex-husband, who was recently hauled up for stalking her, apparently.'

'Might he have been the persistent man in the kilt?' Isadora asked.

'I suppose,' Anna said doubtfully. 'I didn't get the impression that she knew him though. He was just a guy who fancied his chances, that's what I thought.'

'I suppose it will turn out to be the stalkery ex-husband,' Tansy said.

'That seems highly probable,' Isadora agreed.

Anna nodded. Everyone knew that most murders were committed by close family members.

Odd though, Anna thought, that Lili's former husband should have felt driven to murder her in the gardens of a once-grand house while a ball was in progress. A ball Lili had seemingly dressed up to attend, but for which she'd never actually bought a ticket.

Deprived of chicken, Bonnie had come to lie across her feet. Anna would need to move her before she got pins and needles.

'The Mail published a photo.' Tansy unfolded the paper, opening it to the inside page so Anna could see. A dark-haired woman in evening dress and pearls smiled up at them. She was raising a champagne flute as though making a toast at some kind of smart black tie do.

'Does that look like the woman you saw?'

Anna tried to imagine the woman in the photo, with glossy scarlet lipstick, her dark hair put up in a 1940s Victory Roll.

'I'm almost sure that's her,' she decided at last.

'She looks like an interesting person,' Tansy said. 'Don't you think?'

Anna studied Lili Rossetti's small vivid face. *Interesting, intelligent, complicated*, she thought. *What a stupid waste.* She folded up the paper, returning it to the pile.

When nothing was left on their plates except for chicken bones and the odd shred of cardamom pod, Anna helped Tansy rinse the plates and stack them in Isadora's dishwasher.

'I would love to have the recipe for that dish,' Anna said.

Isadora gave her a gratified smile.

'A friend discovered this wonderful company that sells spice kits online. It's almost as good as foreign travel!' She fixed Anna with the pouncing expression that must have terrorised generations of undergraduates. 'Talking of foreign travel, Tansy told me you spent your afternoon in London eating Sachertorte and strudel. Yet for some reason you didn't invite me!'

Anna knew Isadora was just teasing but she felt a sudden wave of fatigue.

'Oh, that is quite a story,' she said. 'I'm not sure I should go into it now.'

'Well, we disagree, don't we Isadora!' Tansy said. 'Now you've made it sound so damn intriguing!'

'I went to visit Hempels,' she confessed.

Tansy's eyes went wide. 'Your dad's auction house?'

Anna nodded. 'I met the new owner and he insisted on taking me out to this amazing Viennese coffee house.'

'But – what made you go to Hempels in the first place?' Tansy asked. 'Isn't that the first time you've been there since—?'

'Yes. The very first time.' Anna went to drink from her glass, found it empty and poured herself more mineral water. 'After I dropped you guys off on Sunday, I felt like I needed to see my grandfather and make sure he was all right.'

Isadora briefly touched her hand. 'And I phoned my son and told him how much I loved him,' she said. 'This is what death does to us.'

Anna took a breath. 'So, I told my grandfather an edited version of the murder mystery weekend.'

'Playing up the fun parts and missing out the drowned woman?' said Tansy.

'Yes, and I asked him where he was on VE Day and he admitted, with obvious reluctance, that he was with the troops that liberated Bergen-Belsen.'

Isadora's hand went to her mouth. 'You never knew?'

Anna shook her head. 'After he'd told me, I felt I should tell him what really happened at Mortmead Hall instead of, you know, treating him like a feeble old man, who might keel over from the smallest shock. And somehow this led on to him . . .'

Anna took a calming breath and started again. 'He told me that my father had been worried about some people I was mixing with that summer. Particularly someone called Dominic Scott-Neville.'

'Wasn't he—?' Tansy started.

'The boy whose family took out a restraining order against me when I went nuts? Yes.' Even now Anna felt herself go hot with shame. 'My grandfather said my dad didn't feel able to intervene because he was – well, apparently at some point, Dominic's father, Ralph, had saved my father's auction house from going under.'

Tansy reached for the bottle of mineral water and refilled her own glass.

'And you never knew any of this?'

'I had no idea that my dad had any contact of any kind with the Scott-Nevilles. It's such a horrifying thought, that now I almost feel like I didn't know him at all.'

'So you went to the auction house to see what you could find out?' Isadora said.

Anna nodded. 'Unfortunately, I got there just after some wild-looking guy was ranting about some painting, a Vermeer, that he is convinced my dad knew about. Alexei said it couldn't be true, that the guy was just deluded but . . .'

'Who is Alexei?' Isadora interrupted.

'Alexei Lenkov. He is a director at Hempels. He said my father had too much integrity to ever do anything underhand and I really want to believe him. But then I think; why would someone of such integrity ever involve himself with Dominic's dad?'

'You knew him?' Isadora said.

'I didn't exactly *know* him,' Anna said, 'but Nat and Max and I hung out with his son, so I ran into him now and then.'

'You didn't take to him,' Isadora said.

'There's something very wrong with that whole family. I think I knew it even then. I just didn't want to see.' *If you think I'm a monster, Dominic is the devil.* 'Then, around the time my family . . .' She had to stop to gather her thoughts. 'Barely a fortnight later, if what I heard was true, Dominic's father whisked him off to his wife's relatives in Argentina, allegedly to learn about the wine trade.'

'You don't think Dominic might have had something to do with their deaths?' Isadora said.

'Sometimes I do,' Anna said. 'After it happened, I was seeing evil conspiracies coming out of the walls.'

'Oh, *Anna*.' Isadora's voice held so much compassion, that Anna suddenly found herself dangerously close to tears.

'I was off my head,' Anna said, being brutal because her other option was to lay her head down on the table and weep. She quickly gulped more water from her glass. 'Anyway, the reason this all got stirred up is that Dominic's dad died last year and so Dominic has come back to take over his father's estate.'

'That's got to suck,' Tansy said.

Anna gave a tight nod. 'It does. Especially now I know my dad had got mixed up with his family in some unknown way.'

'Keep talking,' Isadora said, getting up. 'I need to put finishing touches to our pudding.'

'Ok, but can we please talk about something else?' Anna reached down to stroke her White Shepherd, who came to lean against Anna's knees, instinctively sensing Anna's distress. Just why this was so comforting, Anna could never have explained to anyone except to Jake. She simply accepted now that her most private feelings were an open book to her dog.

'Well, personally,' Tansy said, diplomatically taking her cue, 'I need to know about this super-smart coffee house you were telling us about. Just *please* tell me it wasn't Pfeffers?'

'It was Pfeffers,' Anna said apologetically.

'That is *so* unfair! I have *always* wanted to go there!'

'Seriously? But Pfeffers is like an anti-vegan shrine – it's all meringues, cream and chocolate – and more cream!'

Tansy nodded vehemently. 'Believe me, I *know*!'

'Oh, my God, it must have been *so* hard for you being vegan,' Anna said with real sympathy.

'Not at the time,' Tansy said. 'But when I stopped – I was like the Cookie Monster! I was like: "Universe, give me EVERYTHING you've got!"'

Isadora set down three mismatched, but pretty, china dishes, each one holding a moist dark square of some dense, chocolatey confection. If Tansy was Anna's sister from another mister, Isadora was her eccentric aunt, Anna thought, given to force-feeding everyone who came through her door.

'Tansy, I will treat you and Anna to coffee and cakes at Pfeffers,'

Isadora said. 'Perhaps for my birthday? But just now I feel I need to know more about this man and his imaginary Vermeer.' She reached for her laptop. 'What did you say his name was?'

'His name was David Fischer,' she said, remembering Alexei and Thomas Kirchmann murmuring together in the back of the car.

The three women hitched their chairs closer together so they could all see the screen.

'You type. Your fingers are faster,' Isadora told Tansy.

Tansy was too kind to mention that a three-year old child's fingers were faster on a keyboard than Isadora's.

Google offered them an artisan cheesemaker, an American astrophysicist and an experienced practitioner of Five Elements Acupuncture in Nottingham. After it had offered them four or five times, Isadora said, 'I'm so stupid. Try the German spelling. "Fischer" with a "c".'

Tansy typed the new spelling into the search engine.

'And put in "Vermeer",' Anna said.

'Ooh.' Tansy sat up straight. 'This could be his website. It's got a link to Vermeer's paintings.'

'Click on "About",' Anna said.

Tansy clicked and they read in silence for a few moments.

'Wow!' Tansy turned to Anna. 'This is like the speech you heard at Hempels, word for word.'

Anna felt her stomach clench as she read what amounted to David Fischer's mission statement.

> *For the last forty years, my life has been dedicated to the restitution of the Vermeer. It once hung in my grandparents' dining room, in Vienna, and my father saw it as a young boy, every Friday night, when the family came together for shabbas. Every one of those aunts, uncles and cousins, who ate and prayed together in that peaceful candlelit room, was murdered in Hitler's death camps. Every one, except for my father. This priceless painting, (it was previously thought that Johannes Vermeer produced only twenty-five in his lifetime) along with everything else of value in my grandparents' house, was looted by the Kunstschutz.*
>
> *Against all odds, my father survived the camps. He met and married my mother and eventually they came here to*

England. He lived well into his eighties, despite suffering serious ill health as a result of his time in the camp, but his mind remained needle-sharp to the end. He was able to exactly describe the painting, which had the title A Study in Gold.

I have been to all the major auction houses and art galleries and renowned art historians, and they all tell me, 'David, nobody has ever heard of this painting. It's like the unicorn. It is a fairy-tale, a myth, a delusion.' But my father was the most honourable man I ever met. He detested all liars and fantasists and, up to the day he died, he had such perfect recall of every object in his grandparents' apartment, he even drew me a detailed plan. So, despite everything the so-called experts tell me, I have no choice but to believe that my father was telling the truth.

Fischer went on to describe unsuccessful attempts to get to the bottom of this mystery. In the early 1980s, he was approached by one of Hempels' porters, who claimed to have seen a painting in the office of Charles Hopkins, Anna's grandfather. This painting matched the description of one of the three stolen paintings mentioned by Fischer senior. The porter remembered it because: 'Mr Hopkins, was usually such a gentleman, but on this occasion, he practically threw me out. So I had a feeling something wasn't quite right.'

Anna pushed back her chair.

'I'm not buying this. Thomas Kirchmann would never have bought Hempels if there had been any hint of corruption.'

'He was the man who took you out to Pfeffers?' Isadora asked.

'Yes.' Anna told them how Herr Kirchmann's father had hidden the forbidden paintings from the Kunstschutz and that Thomas Kirchmann was now also involved in helping to return stolen artworks to their rightful owners.

Isadora listened nodding.

'I have heard many stories of this kind,' she said. 'Thousands of precious artworks were looted from Jewish families which have never been found.'

'Thousands,' Tansy echoed. 'Seriously?'

'Thousands upon thousands,' Isadora repeated sombrely. 'But Anna, even if this porter was right and Fischer's Vermeer had somehow come into your grandfather's possession, that doesn't mean he was involved in buying, selling or nefariously profiting from it.'

'Doesn't it?' Anna felt a spark of hope.

'There could be any number of perfectly legitimate reasons for this painting to be in his office.'

'But he virtually threw the porter out. Allegedly,' Anna added.

Isadora shrugged. 'Perhaps your grandfather thought it was better for the porter not to know about something that could put him in harm's way?'

Tansy stared at her. 'You mean it could have put him in danger?'

'Yes, that's what I mean.' Isadora picked up Hero, cuddling her and the little dog immediately tried to lick her ear. 'Anna, if you want – and only if you want – I could ask my friend Geraldine, who knows everyone in the art world, to look into it. In case she's heard anything about your David Fischer and his quest.'

Tansy made tea for them all and the conversation moved on to other things. A friend of Tansy's had just started up a company running tours of Vietnamese street food and that had made Tansy restless.

'Working at Gudrun's art gallery is not really that different to being a waitress. I'm scared I'm going to get stuck in a rut.' Tansy tugged at a loose strand of her hair. 'I'm still young, I should be having adventures. Ideally, adventures that don't involve anyone's violent death,' she added with a grimace.

'I'll go along with that,' Anna said wryly.

Tansy's smile faded. 'It doesn't help that Liam is permanently stressing these days. We're like two pacing lions in a cage.'

'Why is Liam stressing?' Isadora asked.

'I don't know. He's gone into his man-cave. He says if I want to talk about anything touchy-feely I should talk to my girlfriends.' She made an impatient gesture.

'That doesn't sound like Liam,' Anna said.

'Not the old Liam, no,' Tansy said gloomily. 'Maybe I shouldn't have moved in with him so soon? But at the time it felt so right.'

Isadora gently scratched her little dog between her ears. 'It's probably just spring fever.'

'Is spring fever an actual thing?' Tansy asked hopefully.

'Absolutely!' Isadora assured her. 'It makes everyone restless and discontented. The same force that drives the green fuse through the flower or whatever that Dylan Thomas quote is, makes us hideously aware that we are not immortal.' She flashed them an enigmatic smile. 'In other – not unrelated – news, I heard from an old friend, the other day, completely out of the blue.'

'An old friend or an old lover?' Tansy said at once.

'Is there any reason it can't be both?' Isadora gave her one of her undergraduate-quelling looks.

'No reason at all,' Tansy said laughing.

'It wasn't Valentin?' Anna said, remembering a conversation she'd had with Isadora soon after they'd met. Valentin had been the love of Isadora's life at an age when she'd given up all hope.

Isadora shot her a startled look. 'You have an alarmingly good memory.'

'It *was* Valentin?' Tansy was instantly intrigued.

'Yes, it *was* Valentin,' Isadora said irritably. 'He wants me to visit him in Prague, help him with a book he's writing!' She gave one of her dark hoots of laughter. 'Quite ridiculous after all this time. Anyway, I couldn't possibly put Hero into kennels.'

'No, Isadora, you *must* go!' Tansy said eagerly. 'Seize the day, seriously! You can take Hero on the train, get her a doggie passport. Anna's got one for Bonnie, haven't you?'

She nodded. 'Jake made me.'

'Hero will be happy wherever you are,' Tansy insisted.

'Well, I have *no* plans to leave Oxford,' Anna said, adding jokingly, 'you two go off, have adventures and me and Bonnie will solve all the crimes on our own!'

Isadora dropped Anna off in Park Town on the way to taking Tansy back to St Clements.

It was late and Anna was stupidly tired after her day, yet, against her better judgment, she found herself opening her laptop. With a cup of camomile tea steaming at her elbow and peaceful snores coming from Bonnie's basket, she did another search for David Fischer, but this time she just trawled through images.

'David Hasselhoff?' she muttered under her breath. '*Really?*' She scrolled on past a host of equally random Davids. It was hopeless, yet she kept futilely scrolling. What was that motivational quote? *How you spend your days is how you spend your life?*

Give it up, Anna, she advised, then found her attention being pulled back to a small pixelated photo. She zoomed in. Then she went to fetch a magnifying glass, but still couldn't believe what she was seeing. The photograph belonged to the archives of the Wennekes Institute for Preserving Art in Times of War and it showed a dishevelled David Fischer standing next to a dark-haired woman, with a vivid, intelligent face.

'Lili Rossetti,' she whispered.

SIX

It was not the first time that Anna had stayed up, obsessively entering names into Google, when she should have been asleep in bed. But at this point, stopping seemed too much like giving up. And so it was that Anna typed Lili Rossetti's name into the search engine and made an unwelcome discovery.

She immediately closed her laptop, as if that might keep this alarming information from spilling out. She was dimly aware that her kitchen had grown cold and that she was very thirsty. She poured herself a glass of water, but instead of drinking, she carefully set the glass down on the counter, because doing things carefully meant she still had some self-control, and then she started up the stairs to her study.

She got as far as opening the door, but for the first time she hesitated. The light shining from the hallway picked out familiar details: the lamp on her desk, her metal filing cabinet, her running machine. Everything had been squashed into one corner to make space for the ominous cupboard that dominated the room. Jake had never asked her why she kept her super-sized, antique armoire in her study and she'd never explained. She'd found it in a street market, falling in love with its hand-painted patterns, though in places only the faintest blue and gold stippling remained. She hadn't intended to use it for her personal Pandora's Box, a repository for all her nightmares. But, for a time, the cupboard had seemed like the only way she could keep her madness from overflowing into the rest of her life.

Still she didn't move, just stood in the doorway, trying to calm her breathing. She mentally reviewed the macabre contents that she now knew by heart: newspaper clippings, curling photographs, witness statements, printouts of floor plans, scrawled-on Post-its, all connected by crazy spiders' webs of taut criss-crossed strings. Anna wondered if she would ever tell Jake, share these horrors with him and exorcise them from her life forever. She had a recurring fantasy, where he helped her to chop this monstrous piece of furniture into pieces, and then they took the broken-up cupboard and its contents into the garden and burned everything down to ash. And in this fantasy she was no longer ashamed.

Anna heard the soft click of Bonnie's claws on the wooden stairs. A cold wet nose pushed itself forcefully into her hand. Exhausted gratitude washed over her. *I'm not alone.*

'You're right,' she told her dog. Her voice sounded small and far away. 'I'll call him.'

She pulled her mobile out of her back pocket. Jake answered on the third ring.

'Hi, sweetheart, you just caught me in the shower. Hold on!'

She held on, literally gripping the phone for dear life. 'I was worried I'd wake you.'

'No, I only just got in.'

She closed her eyes, felt herself gradually returning to her body. She heard herself ask. 'The conference goes on this late?'

'God no!' Jake sounded horrified. 'Just couldn't sleep. Too much sitting and too much talk. These security geeks make you lose the will to live. I went out for a walk around the city, trying to tire myself out.'

He described his walk around the Fifth Arrondissement, where Ernest Hemingway and his friends had hung out in the 1920s.

'I've wanted to go there ever since I read *A Moveable Feast.* Ever read that book? I was scared it would have changed, but it's beautiful.'

He told her about a French Canadian he'd met in a bar; an ex-soldier who'd served in Iraq, and who was in the process of setting up a charity to rescue and rehome dogs, like Bonnie, from war zones.

'Not, of course, that there are any dogs like Bonnie,' he added.

'None,' Anna said.

While she and Jake had been talking, Anna and Bonnie had

migrated to her bedroom. She perched on the edge of her bed and pulled a woollen throw around her shoulders. Bonnie sat at her feet, with her pure white ears pricked, occasionally tilting her head and looking puzzled, as if she could detect Jake's voice coming through the phone.

Jake didn't ask why Anna had called. He knew she'd tell him when she was able. He just chatted to her about his evening. He and the ex-soldier had eventually left the bar and found a small café, where they ate *cassoulet* and talked about the stupidity of war and the crazy wisdom of dogs.

Though she had cleverly concealed this knowledge even from herself, Anna had fallen in love with the sound of Jake's voice some weeks before she'd met him in person. The first time he'd said her name she'd almost passed out with longing.

'You shouldn't be in security, Jake McCaffrey,' she told him now, pulling her throw more closely around her. 'You should be on late night radio.'

'I'm not entirely sure that's flattering.' Jake sounded amused. 'We have some pretty extreme late night stations in the US.'

'Like?' Anna settled back upon her pillows, allowing herself to be lulled.

'Well, there's a few that cater to preppers.'

'You're going to have to explain preppers.'

'People who are preparing for the coming apocalypse.'

'Like survivalists?'

'Kind of an offshoot. Then there's all the evangelical stations obviously. Plus, there's one widely syndicated station that focuses on the weird and wacky: near-death experiences, alien abductions, crop circles, Big Foot sightings, the Hollow Earth theory . . .'

'Is that what it sounds like?'

'The Hollow Earth theory? Ah, well, very few people know this, but this planet contains unlimited interior space, which is lucky as they're gonna need plenty of room for all those roaming herds of mammoth down there.'

'Sounds like you've listened to this station a lot,' she commented.

'Never missed a night.' Jake laughed and she felt a spreading warmth behind her ribs.

'In the UK, late-night talk radio is designed to soothe insomniacs, like the radio version of hot milk and honey,' she said.

'Happy to be your late-night radio host any time,' he said.

Anna pictured him in his hotel room: the battered kit bag containing his few requirements for the trip, his leather jacket slung on the back of a chair, the photo Tansy had taken of him and Anna with Bonnie.

She took a breath and told him. She told him all of it from the dead woman they'd found in the pond, to David Fischer and his allegations about the missing Vermeer. Yet this time she told him what she'd previously held back, that she was terrified her dad had become mixed up with something morally dubious, especially now she'd understood how Lili Rossetti and Fischer must be connected.

'You know how you should stop googling, because you're so tired but you just can't?'

'No, darlin',' he said with affection, 'but I know how you can't.'

And because there was no trace of condescension in Jake's voice, Anna felt able to struggle to the end of her confession.

'I did a search for Lili Rossetti and I found out what she did. She was a fine art restorer.'

The first time that Anna had experienced one of Jake's long telephone silences, she'd wondered if his phone had run out of charge or if he'd simply got fed up and cut her off. Now she knew he was simply absorbing what she'd told him.

'That's quite a coincidence,' he said at last.

'Yes. I hate coincidences like this. They make me think I'm going crazy again. Connecting up dots that don't exist outside my own head.'

'You're not crazy,' he said with quiet certainty. 'So what are you going to do now?' Jake knew her so well, Anna thought. He knew she'd have to follow this up.

'First, I need to get a closer look at that photo,' she said. 'Make sure I'm not just spooking at things that aren't there.'

They talked for a while of other things, then Jake said, 'Think you can sleep now, darlin'?'

'Yes,' she said, softly. 'I think I probably can.'

'This is one of my favourite views,' Isadora said as they drove down Long Wall Street and over Magdalen Bridge.

'Mine too,' Anna agreed.

The loveliness of the May morning made the craziness of the previous night seem like a fever dream. Spring sunshine fell on ancient honey-gold stone, the trees were in full blossom and rows of bright-coloured bikes were padlocked to any convenient railing. Anna loved her city in all its moods and seasons but, this morning, Oxford was at its picture postcard best.

'I'm so glad you asked me to come!' Isadora sounded as if Anna had offered her a huge treat, instead of a day trip to Reading.

'The Institute isn't actually *in* Reading,' Anna said. 'It's on the outskirts somewhere.' She overtook a young woman pedalling hard on her bike, a short academic gown billowing out behind her.

She had called the Wennekes Institute first thing, asking if they could email her a better photo than the one she'd found online, but the woman she spoke to said the photo Anna had seen was ten years old. They only had a hard copy in their archives. The woman offered to post her a copy, if Anna would send them a stamped addressed envelope, but Anna couldn't wait that long. She needed to know now.

She heard Hero whining in her travel crate.

'Shush!' Isadora told her sharply. They turned into the Iffley Road, where stately Victorian houses were interspersed with occasional curry houses, a rare book shop and a bicycle repair business. Anna kept catching glimpses of an alert and interested Bonnie in her rear-view mirror.

'I'm guessing you didn't get much sleep?' Isadora said.

'No,' Anna said.

Before she could explain her latest worry, Isadora said, 'Nor did I. I sat up emailing my friend in Prague, then Geraldine – my friend in the art world who I told you about – and then I did some online research into Vermeer.'

Anna shot her an astonished glance. Tansy used to crack jokes about them being the dog-walking version of Charlie's Angels but, at some point, it had apparently ceased to be a joke and they'd actually *become* the dog-walking detectives.

The usual traffic congestion on the Iffley road needed most of Anna's concentration, making it hard for her to absorb Isadora's enthusiastic potted bio of Johannes Vermeer. Like so many famous artists, he'd died in poverty leaving eleven fatherless children after the art market had mysteriously collapsed. This possibly had something to do with a war in France but Anna might have blanked on that part.

'Most experts agree that he only painted twenty-five paintings at most in his lifetime which contradicts what Fischer says on his website. Oh, I'm *so sorry*!' Isadora had set Anna's indicator flashing with one of her expansive gestures. 'I'm hoping Geraldine can help us figure out where your Mr Fischer's Vermeer – if it exists – might have fitted in the chronology.'

Anna privately thought of the Old Masters as belonging to a dead-and-gone past, more suited to a museum. She had an additional difficulty, though, with Vermeer.

'I've never really liked Vermeer's paintings,' she admitted.

'No?' Isadora seemed astonished.

Anna shook her head. 'They're so static.'

'*Still*, maybe, surely not static,' Isadora suggested, sounding rather as if she was giving a tutorial.

'And his women all have those scrubbed wholesome faces,' Anna said. 'You can just imagine them turning on anyone who is less wholesome than themselves and – I don't know – *denouncing* them to the church elders or something.'

'My goodness,' said Isadora. 'That *is* a powerful response!'

Anna stopped at some lights.

'I could be prejudiced,' she admitted. 'My first psych ward had two Vermeer prints; the Lace Maker and the Milkmaid. Not the ideal way to be introduced to his work!'

'I should think it's enough to put you off for life!' Isadora said.

'Could have been worse,' Anna said, straight-faced. 'Could have been The Scream.' She slid a glance at Isadora. 'Last night, after I found that photo, I did some more online sleuthing. I found out what Lili Rossetti did for a living; she was a fine art restorer.'

Isadora looked startled.

'That is an extremely strange coincidence.'

'That's what Jake said.'

'I distrust coincidences,' Isadora said.

'So do I.'

It took a while to locate the Institute, which was not in some mellow, Berkshire, country house as Anna had been picturing, but sandwiched between The Fun House Soft Play and Party World and a firm of mortgage brokers, in a business park so close to the M4 that they could hear the steady whoosh-whoosh of traffic like ocean waves.

'One doesn't expect somewhere dedicated to preserving the arts to look so corporate,' Isadora remarked in a low voice as they walked in.

The inside was as bland and sterile as the outside. On the wall, behind the receptionist's desk, glossy blown-up photographs were juxtaposed with slabs of text relating to the work of the institute. Anna had time to register grim-faced men with guns, in the smoking wreckage of a modern city, before the receptionist looked up from her keyboard and asked if she could help. Since she wasn't the person Anna had spoken to earlier, Anna had to explain for a second time what was starting to seem like a peculiar mission even to her.

'I'm sorry but I can't leave the desk,' the receptionist said. 'I'll have to get one of our volunteers to take you to our archives.'

She picked up the phone. 'Oh, Anthea, it's you,' she said without enthusiasm. 'I've got two ladies here wanting to see a photograph. Could you come and help?' She replaced the handset and gave them a smile that failed to reach her eyes. A door opened, then closed with a muted thud, and a woman (Anthea, Anna assumed) appeared. Her openly resentful expression suggested that she'd been interrupted and forced away from some far more important activity.

Her hair was pulled back into a single greying twist that hung almost to her waist. She was dressed in floating, and – in places – visibly fraying layers, all of them black. As she drew closer, Anna saw that the roses in her cheeks were actually tiny broken veins.

'*So* sorry to keep you waiting,' Anthea said in a raised, utterly insincere voice, which Anna sensed was possibly for the benefit of the receptionist. 'Now *how* may I help you?'

She took them through to the Institute's archives; it was a windowless room lined with floor to ceiling shelves, all crammed with box files.

Anthea asked what year the photo had been taken and Anna told her.

'It's of someone called David Fischer,' she explained. Anthea gave an irritated huff. 'Oh, *him*.'

Isadora looked at her with interest. 'You don't like him.'

'He's a nightmare.' Anthea said with venom. 'Acts as if the Institute was set up for his personal use. Turning up whenever the fancy takes him, harping on about his precious painting that never existed outside of his father's imagination.'

She started hunting along the shelves and eventually disappeared around a corner. Though they couldn't see her, they could still hear her huffing to herself. Isadora and Anna exchanged glances.

'Diplomacy maybe not her strong suit?' Isadora whispered.

Eventually, Anthea returned with the file.

'It's taken us a while to get into the digital age, I'm afraid.' She hovered, not attempting to disguise her curiosity, as Anna began leafing through the photos.

She quickly found the original of the one she'd seen online. As she'd hoped, it was much sharper and clearly showed David Fischer and Lili Rossetti side by side, at what seemed to be a fund-raiser of some kind.

'May I?' Anna quickly snapped a picture on her mobile, before Anthea could tell her not to. Unlike Anna, Anthea didn't appear to have hang-ups about personal space. She immediately came to peer over Anna's shoulder at the photo. She'd been sucking peppermints; Anna could feel and smell her minty breath.

'Oh yes, *that's* David. You can't mistake that hair! Poor Lili, I saw in the papers she'd been murdered. She was another funny one. Clever, though, in her own way.'

Even her compliments had a spiteful edge, Anna thought.

'What did Lili actually do?' she asked, surreptitiously moving away.

'Oh, she was *very* sought after. Lili worked for all the big London galleries and auction houses.'

Why don't these places ever have windows? Anna could feel herself starting to perspire. 'Well, thank you so much for your help,' she said, this having been her late grandmother's favourite stratagem for bringing unwanted conversations firmly to a close.

Instead of taking her cue, Anthea not only stepped back into Anna's space, she actually took hold of her jacket sleeve.

'They seemed to spend a *lot* of time together, I must say,' she confided, 'though I doubt they were a couple in *that* sense.' She gave them a meaningful look. 'Lili was such a pretty little thing and David was *so* much older, and that *hair* – like a fright wig! I always call him the Reading Rasputin!' Anthea laughed, her eyes bright with malice.

'Reading?' Anna said, startled. 'David Fischer lives in Reading?'

'Yes, he runs a second-hand bookshop in the Harris Arcade, down near the station.' Anthea gave them her terrifying fake smile. 'Now is there anything else I can do for you ladies while you're here?'

'So now I assume we're going to drop in on David Fischer?' Isadora said as they walked back to Anna's car.

Anna felt a flicker of panic. She needed to talk to him, but did she really want to hear what he had to say?

'We should probably let the dogs out somewhere, first,' Isadora said.

Fortunately, she remembered the way to some public gardens. They parked nearby, put the dogs on their leashes and wandered along the paths in the sunshine.

'There used to be an abbey here in medieval times,' Isadora said. She gave one of her hoots of laughter. 'In fact, the last abbot was hanged, not far from this spot. Hung, drawn *and* quartered, poor man.' Isadora related further gruesome snippets of local history, before she realized that Anna wasn't taking it in.

'Something's upset you,' she said. 'Was it that awful volunteer woman?'

Anna swallowed.

'She said Lili worked for the major London auction houses. What if she worked for Hempels?' As soon as Anthea had said it, Anna had had a dreary feeling of inevitability. She didn't know how or why, but somehow everything went back to Hempels and her father's involvement with the Scott-Nevilles.

'It's highly possible that she did,' Isadora said. 'But that doesn't—'

'What if David Fischer isn't just a sad fantasist like everyone seems to want to believe?' Anna interrupted. 'And my father really did fail him in some unforgivable way?'

'Anna, even if Lili did work as a consultant for Hempels, why would that implicate your father?'

'I don't *know*. You'd think learning that Julian wasn't really my dad means I'd feel less freaked out, but it seems to make everything a hundred times worse! I feel like I can't bear to . . .' She stopped, then burst out, 'there have already been *so* many lies. I mean, do you ever really know somebody, Isadora?'

'From my own experience? I would have to say not.' Isadora gave a wry smile and Anna could have kicked herself. She belatedly remembered the charismatic intelligence agent, who had approached Isadora in her first year at Oxford, and for whom she'd said she'd have willingly walked through fire for.

'This is going to sound like a really bad soap,' Anna said, when she felt reasonably sure she wouldn't burst into tears.

'As life so often does,' Isadora said with a world-weary sigh.

'Not this bad.' Anna gave a tearful laugh. 'First, my mum has an illicit affair with Chris Freemantle, my dad's best friend, who, it turns out, is my biological father. And now my dad, who might not be my real dad after all, but is still the man who brought me up and taught us that lying was cowardly and stealing was despicable—'

'You're thinking he was maybe guilty of both?'

Anna nodded.

They parked in the station car park, left a window cracked open for the dogs and set off to walk the short distance to the Harris arcade.

The pretty Art Deco arcade was home to a wide range of businesses, including a vintage record store, a shop selling traditional Chinese medicines, a cigar shop and a beer, ale and cheese emporium called The Grumpy Goat. The bookshop, Dog-eared Adventures, was sandwiched between a nail bar and a shop specialising in comics.

Dog-eared Adventures fitted perfectly into the ambience of the arcade, Anna thought, surprised. Had David Fischer thought up this oddly endearing name for himself? If so, that implied a sense of humour and that too surprised her.

Through the window, she saw a shabby, yet cosy looking space with squashy, comfortable sofas, shelves stacked with books, books piled on tables and yet more books piled on the stairs. *Fire hazard*, said Anna's inner administrator.

Her dad would have loved it. He'd been physically incapable of passing by a second-hand book shop. It had driven her mother and the adolescent Anna wild with irritation. *Oh, Dad*, she thought, and felt a treacherous prickling behind her eyelids.

Though she felt obliged to keep reminding herself that Julian Hopkins hadn't really been her dad, the truth was, he had, in every way that mattered.

'Come on,' said Isadora and almost propelled Anna inside. It had that familiar, old bookshop smell. She could feel her heart beating as she and Isadora wove their way between the shelves. Dog-eared Adventures mainly seemed to specialise in hard-backed books about art and artists, but it also stocked a range of vintage paperbacks. A young woman, her hair in a bundle of dreadlocks, was standing on a stepladder reorganising a top shelf. The hems of her jeans rose up as she stretched, revealing the silver gleam of an ankle bracelet against blue-black skin.

Anna stopped by a table piled with vintage Penguins. She extracted a paperback from one of the piles and took her find over to the counter.

The woman on the ladder spotted her and called down.

'Do you mind dinging the bell for David while I finish up here?'

Her mouth suddenly dry, Anna dinged the bell. Isadora glanced at Anna's purchase.

'*A Moveable Feast*. A wonderful memoir. Just a shame Hemingway was such an old misogynist. Have you read it?'

'Not yet. Jake said I should.'

Plus, it's my alibi, Anna thought, *for if I lose my nerve.*

At that moment, David Fischer emerged from the back of the shop, wearing spectacles with Buddy Holly-style heavy rims. Here, on his home ground and wearing an old dull red sweater, over an old blue shirt made soft with washing, he looked less like a mad scarecrow and more like the slightly distracted owner of a second-hand bookshop.

He saw Isadora and pushed his spectacles up into his wildly disordered hair, smiling. Then he registered Anna and his smile faltered.

'Do I know you?'

'You don't know me, but you may have known my father. I'm Anna Hopkins and this is my friend, Isadora Salzman.'

She saw Fischer's expression change as he remembered where he'd seen her. She saw him clench and unclench his fist. 'You were at Hempels. You heard me talking to Lenkov.'

'Yes,' she said.

He'd turned very pale.

'You're – you're the child who survived. Everyone died that night except you.'

'Yes.' Anna had an overwhelming urge to run.

'I am sorry, truly sorry, for what you've had to bear.' Again, she saw his knuckles whiten. 'But that doesn't change the fact that your father did something terrible to my family. It was his father who committed the crime, but Julian had the opportunity to put it right and he didn't. He *didn't*,' Fischer repeated and his voice shook.

His assistant quickly came down her ladder.

'Is everything OK?' She shot a reproachful glance at Anna and Isadora.

'Yes, yes, Constance,' Fischer tried to smile. 'Everything is fine.'

By this time nearby customers were giving them intrigued glances.

'You'd better come into my office,' he told Anna.

Isadora shot her a sharp look. *Is this what you want?*

Anna nodded. She had to know.

The office, on the other side of a faded, velvet curtain, was sparsely furnished; just a desk overflowing with papers and a single chair, which Fischer took then immediately hitched closer to the wall. He put his reading glasses back on and fiddled pointlessly with some papers before he said, in a voice gritty with suppressed emotion, 'so, Ms Hopkins, are you here to find out if your father was as much as a bastard as I think he is?'

Anna heard Isadora's intake of breath, but she said coolly, 'no, actually. I already know my father wasn't a bastard.' *Please God don't let him have been a bastard.* 'But I am interested in finding more out about Lili Rossetti.'

Though Fischer's expression didn't alter, she felt the atmosphere shift.

'Lili was on my side,' he said stiffly. 'I believe she was on to something and if her abusive husband hadn't finally followed through with his violent threats, I believe we could have got at the truth.' He nodded to himself. 'Yes, I believe we were that close.'

Anna felt a surge of disgust. How could someone be so callous about a friend? Then she thought; *he's not callous, he's ill. This painting has driven him mad.* Nothing existed for him at this moment except the Vermeer. She'd seen it on the psych ward, when an obsession took someone over body and soul. *Seen it, I've worn the t-shirt*, she thought wearily.

With this in mind, she tried to keep her voice gentle.

'Surely you don't think that a man like Herr Kirchmann would have involved himself with Hempels, if there was the smallest whisper of wrong-doing?'

His face twisted.

'Oh the saintly Michael! I've heard that story so many times and that's what it is, a story. I've been to Innsbruck. I've spoken to people who were there. I know what happened.'

Anna felt her heart thumping as she waited for this tormented man to tell her the thing she most dreaded to hear.

'Michael Kirchmann stole my grandfather's painting. He stole all those paintings he was supposedly protecting for his own personal gain.' Disturbingly owlish in his glasses, Fischer turned his fixed stare on Anna. 'And *your* family profited.'

SEVEN

Anna's first instinct was to turn furiously on the man who had made these accusations. She could feel Isadora watching her, concerned, uncertain about intervening.

Then she flashed back to that windowless interview room at St Aldates police station, as she told her sceptical interviewers who she suspected of murdering the woman, whose body she'd found on Port Meadow. The harder she'd tried to convince them, the more deranged her accusations had seemed. Not to be believed was a kind of hell, enough to make the sanest person mad. They'd come to David Fischer's bookshop to ask questions. She should at least do him the courtesy of listening to his answers.

'That's a big claim,' Anna said, as calmly as she could manage. 'Can you show me some evidence?'

She heard Fischer catch his breath and Anna felt some of the tension leave that bare, little office. He hadn't expected her to meet him half way. He took off his spectacles.

'I know what people say, but I'm not one of those comedy conspiracy theorists. I wish I was!' He gave a bitter laugh. 'It would be so much less disturbing than the truth.' He dropped his spectacles on to his desk, lenses down, and Anna itched to turn them the right way up.

'You've seen my website?' he asked them. 'Well, I should tell you that I didn't put everything I know on it. I daren't. It was too dangerous.' He shot Anna an apologetic glance. 'I know how that makes me sound, but my search has led me into murky waters.' He shook his head. 'So many countries, so many different agendas, so many lives have become entangled with this painting, including prominent families, who will do anything to cover their tracks. *Anything*,' he repeated. Then he stopped, and Anna saw some troubling thought pass behind his eyes before he added, 'I understand that you've got no reason to trust me, but you also asked for evidence. So, if you can spare me a few minutes, I'd like to show you something that might change your mind. You . . .' Fischer swallowed, and started again. 'You're Julian's daughter. Maybe you can put right what your father wouldn't – or couldn't.'

Anna remembered the porters escorting him from the auction house. *Come on, sir, you've had your five minutes.* She wondered how many times this mortifying scenario had been enacted. She saw Fischer quickly replace his spectacles, but not before she'd seen the fearful hope in his eyes.

'We've got time,' she said.

'I'll just tell Constance.' He disappeared through the curtain and they heard him quickly conferring with his assistant. Isadora and Anna had time to exchange looks before he reappeared.

'This way,' he said. They followed him through a second curtained doorway and up another steep flight of stairs, picking their way past yet more piles of books. At the top, a door opened into a small sunny apartment. It was little more than a bedsit, except that bedsits, in Anna's experience, were universally grim. This was unexpectedly charming; a comfortable chaos of books and paintings, sofas heaped with cushions and soft throws. She realized she'd been preparing herself for a sick man's stale-smelling burrow, not this pleasantly crowded sunlit room. A plump, tortoise-shell cat regarded them speculatively from one of the sofa backs, then made her way over to be stroked.

A polished table held a seven-branched candlestick, *a menorah*, Anna remembered, from visits to Jewish friends. There were a few pieces of fine china inside a glass-fronted cabinet; Anna admired a dark red, lustre jug and some delicate white cups and saucers, painted with yellow flowers. The Persian rug laid on top of wooden floorboards was old and worn, but the faded colours were pleasing to the eye. A wall clock with an exquisitely painted ceramic face, ticked away softly.

Then it came to Anna that this was a loving recreation, in miniature, of the Fischer family's apartment in Vienna; a world David Fischer had never actually seen and a world that no longer existed. She felt a sudden wrenching pity for this strange, lonely man. Concerned that her feelings might show on her face, she went across to the window and looked down into the twenty-first-century street below. She watched a woman pushing an off-road buggy, people chatting on mobiles and two men in high-vis gear unloading scaffolding from a truck. From up here, it all seemed muffled and unreal. She had the feeling she often had just before a storm; torn between her longing for her tension to be relieved and her childhood terror of lightning, because there was no way of knowing what, or who, the lightning was going to strike.

She turned to see Isadora murmuring sweet nothings to the cat.

'What velvety fur,' she crooned. 'And such *pretty* colours.' She smiled up at Anna. 'I love tortoiseshells. They're almost always bonkers!'

'Please make yourselves comfortable,' Fischer said.

Anna seated herself next to an alcove filled with framed photographs of people she assumed were his relatives.

'My grandparents,' he said, seeing her interest, 'and my uncles, aunts and cousins. My father was only able to bring two or three photos with him, the others he had to hunt for years to find.' One photograph showed a street view of an apartment block, its imposing stone facade softened by the spreading branches of a lime tree.

'Was that where your father grew up?' she asked.

He nodded. 'His family had the top two floors. My grandparents lived on the floor below.' Anna couldn't see any photos of anyone who might be David's wife or child. She wondered if David

Fischer had ever had a family of his own, or if he'd driven them away with his Vermeer obsession.

He went over to an antiquated-looking safe.

'You will probably think this is paranoid, but experience has taught me that I can't be too careful.' He fished around under his shirt, pulled out a key on a fraying straggle of string, and inserted it in the lock. Keypads and electronic codes had evidently passed him by. Reaching inside the safe, he pulled out a thin, cheap, cardboard file.

Isadora said, 'Mr Fischer, before we start, would it be intrusive of me to make us all a pot of tea? I'm completely parched!'

He flushed, obviously flustered. 'Of course, how rude – I should have – I'm afraid I'm out of the habit of entertaining. I'll make some.'

Isadora shook her head. 'Please, let me do it. I'd like to.'

'At least let me show you where I keep the good cups.' But Isadora had already seen his delicate yellow and white china. 'Absolutely not,' she told him firmly. 'Those are far too precious.'

Anna had felt annoyed with Isadora for delaying the opening of the file with this – as she saw it – totally unnecessary faffing around, hunting for tea things in a strange kitchen. But, as her friend brought over the tray with a large blue teapot and three mismatched mugs, she saw that Fischer was looking – if not more relaxed, at least significantly less edgy. He settled himself in an armchair opposite the two women, holding the file on his knees and gently fending off the cat, who clearly believed she had a prior claim to his lap.

'I made us Earl Grey; I hope that's all right?' Isadora said. She lifted the teapot and filled all three mugs. Anna's was poppy red with the words Dog-eared Adventures above a mischievous cartoon hound with a folded down ear.

Fischer saw her smile. 'Constance commissioned them,' he explained. 'She thinks I should do more to promote the business.' He shot them an unexpectedly sweet smile. 'She's very stern with me, Constance is.' He opened the file, slid out some papers and his smile faded.

'Lili Rossetti is the only person, apart from me, who has seen these.'

Down in the street, a loud metallic crash was greeted with male jeers and laughter. Anna felt her heart thud unevenly against her breastbone.

'First this.' Fischer laid a black and white photograph on the coffee table, turning it around so that they could see.

Anna and Isadora leaned forward. The photograph showed three men lounging on an antique Louis Quatorz sofa, wearing the iconic uniform that Anna knew, without knowing how, had been worn by the German SS.

'See this guy in the middle?' They peered at the well-fed middle-aged man with the wide smile. 'That's Herr Richter,' Fischer said. 'He was very high up in the Kunstschutz, a Nazi unit that—'

'Looted priceless artworks belonging to Jews,' Isadora finished. 'Yes, we know.'

Fischer seemed relieved that he needn't go back to basics.

'Can you see that painting behind his head?' he asked. 'It's not very clear in the picture, I'm afraid, but it's a woodland landscape, by a German artist called Hans Thoma. It used to hang in my grand-parents' apartment, beside a Klimt and my grandfather's Vermeer.' He shot them a glance, trying to gauge their reactions.

'With respect,' Isadora said, slipping into her Oxford tutorial voice, 'this doesn't prove anything. Anyone could point at a painting and say, "That was mine or my family's."'

Fischer levered himself out of his chair and went across to the alcove of photographs. They watched him carefully detach one from its hook and Anna saw that his shirt had come slightly untucked from his jeans. He laid the photograph down on the coffee table so they could see.

'My father in his forties, more than twenty years after he came to England.' He pulled another photograph from his folder and set it beside the framed photo. It showed a laughing boy in the centre of a family group.

'My father as a young man.'

Anna felt a pang. He was just a boy, no more than seventeen or eighteen, mischievous, carefree, but with the same dark, almost almond-shaped eyes and the same unmistakable widow's peak.

'This is my grandfather with his arm around my father's shoulders,' Fischer said. 'Those are three of his aunts. His uncle Saul was behind the camera. Now, can you see this painting behind them?'

'It's the Hans Thoma,' Isadora said with a note of surprise. 'The one in your first picture.'

'Yes. The woodland landscape. Now, off to the left, can you just catch a glimpse of the corner of a gilt frame? That was my grandfather's Vermeer.'

There was a moment's silence. They knew, of course, that this didn't prove anything. The gilt frame could have held anything: a piece of embroidery, an amateur's oil colour. And yet, Vermeer or no Vermeer, the fact remained that David Fischer's father and grandfather had once been in the same room as a valuable painting which was later photographed in a luxurious apartment used by high-up Nazis.

Fischer returned to his chair and took a sip of his tea.

'It eventually became necessary for my father's family to leave Vienna. Obviously, they couldn't take everything with them. My grandfather heard on the grapevine about this man in Innsbruck, who was looking after artworks for families like ours. He contacted him. Michael Kirchmann came to Vienna to collect the paintings, also some valuable family jewellery. My father was at home when he came. He told me that Kirchmann was visibly horrified at the growing Nazi presence in Vienna. He had grown up in Vienna, but his lungs were badly damaged by gas in the First World War and the doctors thought Innsbruck's mountain air would be better for his health. My father liked him very much. He said he seemed physically frail but completely trustworthy and, though he was not a Jew, he showed great sensitivity to our family's plight.'

'A righteous gentile,' Isadora said.

'My father's words exactly.' Fischer shot her a wry smile. The tortoiseshell cat had insinuated herself on to his lap without him noticing. He began stroking her unconsciously, as he talked, his thin knobbly hands soothing the soft fur.

'I won't bore you with the whole story, but my father was able to escape to England by the skin of his teeth, even as the rest of his family was being rounded up to be taken to the camps. At the last minute, I don't know why, some premonition maybe, my grandfather made my father tuck Michael Kirchmann's card into his wallet.

'After the war was over – not immediately – but a year or so later, when he'd scraped up sufficient money, my father made his way tortuously through France and Switzerland to Innsbruck. You probably know that it was still extremely difficult to travel through Europe during this period. By this time, of course, my father knew that he would never see any members of his family again: his parents, his grandparents, his sisters, all the aunts, uncles and little cousins. All dead.'

Anna saw Isadora briefly close her eyes. Fischer took a shaky breath.

'I need you to understand that my father did not go to Innsbruck hoping to sell the family paintings and jewels and return a rich man. He went because these things were all that remained of his life. The only things.' His hand stilled on the cat's fur. 'But when he finally reached Innsbruck, he discovered that Michael Kirchmann had been shot and all the hidden paintings and jewels had disappeared from his secret basement. It is not a big leap to assume that these treasures somehow ended up in the coffers of the Third Reich.'

The cat jumped down and strolled away to the kitchen area where they heard her lapping steadily from her bowl. His throat suddenly dry from talking, Fischer began to cough and he took a long gulp of his tea before he resumed his story.

'I think it's well known now that the Nazis were meticulous, not to say fanatical, record keepers? My father had the idea that it might be possible to use these obsessively kept records to help him find out if his family's paintings had been sold on or given away to some favoured officer. I'm speaking of much later in my father's life,' he explained. 'After he'd established a life for himself in this country, after he had married and Europe had begun to return to some kind of normality. Whenever he could spare the time from his work, he travelled to Germany and Austria. He went through archives of photographs of important SS officers, anyone high up in the Nazi party. He interviewed anyone he could persuade to talk to him, which, as you can imagine, was no easy task. People were desperate to forget the collective madness that Hitler and his kind had unleashed. No-one wanted to see painful, old sores or private shames exposed. But, eventually, he was able to discover that the Klimt from his grandfather's dining room had ended up in the home of a high-ranking official in Berlin.'

'Did he manage to get it back?' Anna was experiencing a distinct fellow feeling for David Fischer's doggedly persistent father.

He shook his head.

'The house took a direct hit during an air raid. The official and his family were killed. The house and everything in it was burned down to ash. There's no way the painting could have survived.'

'Your father must have been terribly disappointed,' Isadora said.

'My father was a very patient and, despite his life experiences, an extremely optimistic man,' he told her. 'He refused to give up.'

Patient, optimistic and totally driven, Anna thought, remembering her own grief-fuelled investigations.

Fischer drained the last of his tea before he said, 'eventually my father found that first photo I just showed you of the SS officer. There was a date-stamp on the back and my father immediately realized that this date didn't make sense. The photo had been taken a year or more before Michael Kirchmann was executed, when the Thoma landscape was supposedly safely stashed away in his secret basement, yet here it was hanging in the quarters of a notable SS officer.'

He met their eyes and nodded. 'As you can imagine, my father was disturbed by this discovery. He didn't want to entertain these unpleasant suspicions of Michael Kirchmann, the righteous gentile, but what else was he to think?'

The cat wandered back, settled herself in the middle of a shaft of sunlight and began to wash one velvety, toffee-coloured paw.

Fischer went on to explain how his father had made strenuous efforts to contact those few surviving members of the Jewish community in Vienna, who had also entrusted their artworks to this man. Thanks to them, he could compile an extensive list of the treasures that had been given into Michael Kirchmann's safe-keeping. From these same survivors, David's father learned that paintings and items of jewellery entrusted to Kirchmann had been seen displayed in Nazi homes and, in the case of jewels, openly worn by officers' wives.

Anna felt numb. *Could this terrible story be true?*

'And have you ever spoken to Thomas Kirchmann about these accusations against his father?' Isadora asked.

'I've never been allowed close enough to him to have a proper conversation. Anyone questioning the authorised version of this

story – that Michael Kirchmann was a selfless preserver of art
– comes up against this glass wall of disbelief.'
 Anna swallowed. 'Everything you've said is shocking, but you
still haven't explained how my father is implicated in all this.'
 Fischer shot her a look of dismay that hardened into suspicion,
making her wish she hadn't spoken, just when he was on the verge
of trusting her.
 'I'm getting there, I promise,' he said stiffly. Still obviously wary,
he explained that, during his researches, his father had occasionally
come across what he believed to be cryptic references to the stolen
Vermeer.
 'For instance, "Dutch Gold",' Fischer said. 'Another one was
"ESIG", the initial letters of the painting's title in Dutch. *Een Studie
in Goud*. To my father these were like Hansel and Gretel's trail of
white pebbles; signs that the painting had not been lost, that it still
existed out there somewhere in the woods.'
 Involved in his story, Fischer gave Anna a fleeting smile as if
he'd forgotten his moment of anger. 'This erratic trail of pebbles
also led him to think that, at some point, the painting had been
taken out of Europe.'
 The cat rolled on to her side and began to purr to herself, a
loud, husky sound like an old-fashioned dialling tone.
 'In April 1945, as I'm sure you know, Russian troops encircled
Berlin,' Fischer continued. 'Those in command of the Russian
units knew, of course, of the activities of the Kunstschutz, as did
the American and British allies. In the middle of the chaos and
confusion at the end of the war, the Soviets, British and Americans
loaded their trucks with any stolen treasures they happened to
stumble across and took them back home.'
 'You think your painting could have ended up in the US or
Russia?' Isadora sounded astonished.
 Fischer nodded. 'My father was absolutely certain it ended up
in Russia, for a time. One of his sources intimated that, after
passing from hand to hand, the Vermeer had ended up in Moscow,
in the private residence of some extremely high-ranking communist
official. You know a little about the Cold War?'
 Anna avoided looking at Isadora whose Cold War experiences
had cost her more than one friend, as well as almost costing her life.
 'A little,' Isadora said drily.

'So you know that, during the 50s and 60s communications, between east and west were not exactly welcomed on either side. It was almost impossible for anyone in the west to find out what was going on behind the so-called Iron Curtain. But my father went on patiently searching, until one day he was contacted by a Russian émigré, a man who was formerly involved in intelligence. He told my father that a disgraced official had defected from Soviet Russia in the 60s and the Vermeer he was seeking had been used as payment for his safe passage to the west.'

'You mean, like a bribe?' Anna was cynical enough not to be surprised that asylum could be bought in such a way.

Fischer gave her an ironic smile.

'My father's source told him that certain British agents routinely demanded payment in valuable artworks to help high-placed Soviet citizens make their escape.'

Isadora went very still and Anna guessed she was thinking of one particular British agent, Matthew Tallis.

'The Russian advised my father to give up his search before he got himself into serious trouble. He said he should just accept that his family's paintings had disappeared. "You've survived the unthinkable," he told him. "You have a wife and child, a life. Millions were not so lucky."'

'And did your father stop?' Anna asked.

Fischer sighed. 'I don't know if he would have stopped, if he hadn't had the stroke. Though he survived into his eighties, he was never the same. Oh, his mind was undimmed to the end, but all his old optimism deserted him. It almost broke my mother's heart that, after all his efforts, he died with the mystery still unsolved.'

'But you continued his search,' Isadora said softly.

'I'll be honest with you, to begin with it was quite half-hearted,' Fischer said. 'And so it wasn't surprising that my feeble efforts always resulted in the same dead end. Until—'

'The porter,' Anna said.

He nodded. 'Porters who work at auction houses often become extremely knowledgeable about the art world. Lionel Rosser was one of those porters. Someone must have told him about this unhinged character forcing his way into London auction houses and ranting about his imaginary Vermeer, and he must have asked around about me. He wrote to me saying he had some information that might interest me. We met in a café in Soho and he told me the story which I think you read on my website?'

'About seeing a painting in my grandfather's office and my grandfather throwing him out.' Anna only dimly remembered her paternal grandfather. She remembered being afraid of his voice, but could not have said, as a small child, just why it had frightened her so badly.

'It was the woodland landscape,' Fischer said. 'The Hans Thoma.' Anna stared at him. 'Oh,' she said faintly. She realized she was digging her nails into her palms.

'Do you see why I had to tell you the whole story?' Fischer stood up and went over to the galley kitchen, coming back with a bottle of mineral water and three glasses.

He filled their glasses and Anna drank thirstily. She was in a daze.

'That was my defining moment,' Fischer admitted. 'That was when I finally threw myself into my father's search. Before, I'd been doing it out of a vague sense of filial responsibility. But from then on it became like – my *ancestral* task. My family, my *people*, had been robbed, cheated and lied to and I was determined to get to the bottom of it. I am still determined.'

Outside there was a thunderous crash, as if someone had hurled a metal bedstead down into the street. The cat shot awake. Ears flat, she stared about her in terror.

'It's just scaffolding,' Fischer told her soothingly. He scooped her up and carried her to the sofa, where she struggled out of his arms and on to the sofa back, her eyes still wild.

'I tried several times to get your grandfather to admit his involvement,' he said. 'But he made it oh-so-icily clear that he thought I was deranged. When he retired and your father took over the auction house, for a time I thought . . .'

Anna drew a sharp breath, 'Dad listened to you?'

Fischer nodded. 'At first. Then, seemingly overnight, his attitude changed. He froze me out. Just didn't want to know.' The memory obviously saddened him.

Anna felt a pang of dismay. *Had this painful reversal come about because Ralph Scott-Neville had put money into Hempels? Had that given Dominic's father some sinister hold over Julian?*

She saw Fischer push his hands distractedly through his hair. He seemed to have lost his thread.

'And then you met Lili Rossetti,' Isadora prompted.

'Yes. We met at a party, a fund-raiser for the Wennekes Institute, ironic really. Neither of us were party people. Lili had come for work reasons. I, of course, was there in my well-practised role of *The Ancient Mariner*, buttonholing anyone who'd stand still long enough to listen.' He gave them a painful smile.

'And you buttonholed Lili?' Isadora said.

'She'd already heard of me, though I hate to think what exactly she'd heard. But instead of giving me a wide swerve, she sought me out.' He shook his head smiling. 'She actually asked me about the painting and how my father had described it. She even took out a little notebook and jotted down the colours and measurements.'

'She took you seriously?' Anna said.

'Lili was a good listener. There are some people who seem born to fight injustice. Lili was like that. She said my story made her angry.'

He'd admired Lili Rossetti, Anna thought. She had sensed something genuine in David Fischer, enough to make her ignore mocking comments about the Rasputin of Reading.

'We arranged that she'd come to my shop, so I could show her the photographs I've just shown you. Lili went off saying she'd do her best.' Fischer reached up to pet the cat, who was now tranquilly washing one of her front paws. 'To be honest, I didn't think she'd get anywhere. But it meant a lot that she was prepared to try. Yes, it meant a great deal.'

There was a world of loneliness in that sentence, Anna thought. A need to be seen, to be believed, to be accepted, however strange.

'Did she ever find anything, do you know?' Anna asked, her tone as neutral as she could manage.

Again, Fischer raked his hands through his hair.

'I believe she did.'

'You don't know for sure?' Isadora said.

He swallowed. 'A couple of weeks before she was murdered, Lili sent me an email that absolutely astounded me. You know, when you have searched without success for so long and then . . .'

Anna found she'd stopped breathing.

'What did she say?' She almost whispered.

'She said she'd seen it. She'd seen my grandfather's Vermeer with her own eyes.'

EIGHT

'So what can you see out of your window?' Anna was sitting on the floor of her living room, sorting through slippery piles of old photos. She'd put Jake on speaker phone.

'Darlin', my room doesn't have a window,' he said in a tone of such patient resignation that she should have instantly smelled a rat. Was the international security firm Jake worked for really that strapped for cash?

'However,' he said, suddenly gleeful as a small boy, 'I *do* have French doors on to a balcony! Hold up, I'll open them. If you listen hard you might hear cow bells.'

'You pig,' she said, half annoyed at being so completely taken in.

In Anna's sitting room, the original, Georgian shutters were still closed against the street. She hadn't thought to open them that morning and it was too late to bother now. She'd switched on a lamp beside the old, rosewood chest, it doubled as a coffee table and was where she kept her family photos. That morning she had dragged them all out: the neat leather-bound albums religiously compiled by her mother and then the bulging manila envelopes containing photographs that her mother had felt unable to destroy, but had never made it into the official annals of Hopkins family life. She'd just settled down with the contents of the first envelope, when Jake had phoned from Geneva.

Jake had the best timing, Anna thought. In the days when she was routinely moving from one rented flat (dreadful dives most of them) and drifting from one town to another, she'd religiously packed, unpacked and repacked her family photos alongside all her other belongings. Yet she could never bring herself to actually look at them. After she'd returned to Oxford, she had sacrificed a few to her cupboard but that was purely to help focus her search. This was something else. This was opening herself to images and sensations that she'd buried for over sixteen years. To have Jake's voice, his steady presence available, even on the end of a phone eased some of her dread.

'Ok, I'm outside now,' he said in what would have been a conspiratorial David Attenborough whisper, if David Attenborough had grown up in the American South. 'No cowbells, but I can see the sun setting over Lake Geneva which is quite a sight. If I crane over the edge of this fancy wrought-iron railing, I can just make out a little, white motor boat moored directly below. I'm thinking I might sneak off at first light to play at being Huck Finn and damn their induction session! Hang on, someone's at the door.'

Anna picked up an album, flipped to the front page and saw herself on her seventh birthday, wearing an unflattering party dress. She decided to concentrate on pictures which hadn't made the final cut. There was the possibility they'd hold more surprises.

She could hear the faint, familiar chords of Van Morrison's 'Moondance', coming from the top floor flat; her lodger Dana's break-up music. Tomorrow, Dana would emerge deathly pale in sunglasses and drop a couple of empty bottles in the recycling, before driving off to the Sir John Radcliffe where she worked in orthopaedics.

'It was room service,' Jake said, back from answering his door. 'Do you mind if I eat and talk? I am starving.'

'So long as you don't mind if I sort photographs and talk.'

Anna picked up a fading, colour photo of a long-ago family picnic. She suppressed a little huff of laughter. Her mother (she knew it was her mother, her father never took the photos), had been trying to get all her children suitably posed on the same picnic blanket. Anna, the bossy big sister, held a bewildered, three-year old Dan in such a vice-like grip that it looked as if she was marching him off to jail. Will was just a blur of chubby baby legs and feet, as he crawled rapidly out of shot. Her little sister Lottie hadn't yet been born. Anna put the photo to one side and began leafing through the others, as she filled Jake in on her visit to Dog-eared Adventures.

'Fischer came right out and accused your father of being party to some kind of shady cover-up? That can't have been fun.'

'Not really.' She'd found a photo of Dan on his first day at the Dragon School, grinning with mixed pride and trepidation. 'The more I think about it,' she said, bringing her mind back to David Fischer, 'the more I can't really blame him. Getting back his grandfather's Vermeer has become like his sacred task.'

'And you know what that's like?'

'Exactly. And he does have persuasive evidence.' She explained about the photographs and the porter, Lionel Rosser's sighting of the Hans Thoma painting, which had hung in the Fischer family's apartment in Vienna.

'I took Bonnie out for a long walk over the University Parks this afternoon,' Anna said, 'to try to clear my head and I was thinking, even if Michael Kirchmann did make a profit from these artworks, that doesn't mean he set out to cheat those poor people. Maybe he couldn't see any other way to protect his own loved ones?' Anna knew that if, by some divine miracle, she could have her family back alive and well, she'd do anything at all to keep them that way.

'How do we know what we'd do, you know, if we were faced the same circumstances?'

'We don't,' Jake said with feeling. He'd served in Iraq and Afghanistan, seen human beings behave in ways she didn't want to imagine. 'Are you applying the same thinking to your dad?' he asked.

'I'm trying,' she said. 'Though it's hard to reconcile the Julian I knew with the person David Fischer described. I think I shouldn't leap to judge him without knowing what really happened.'

'If my schedule wasn't so tight, I'd love to help you out, dig around on your behalf.' Jake rarely complained about his life, which was currently a relentless round of hotel rooms, meetings and conferences. He focused on the upside, for instance that his current lifestyle allowed him and Anna to spend precious time together.

'Thank you,' she said. 'But the truth is, I could do some digging around for myself, only I'm scared of ending up like the female version of that mad Spanish knight, charging at windmills and then I'll never get to the bottom of what happened to my family.' Hearing herself say these words out loud, Anna was startled. She hadn't known she felt this way.

'OK,' Jake said. 'Let's think this through a minute. First, I believe we already agreed there are no coincidences?'

'Yes, but—'

'Second,' he said firmly, 'I refer you to the principle, informally known as the Cosmic Ripple Effect.'

She laughed. 'You've been spending too much time with Tansy.'

'To give you just one example, darlin',' Jake's intonation was noticeably more southern, a sign he was utterly serious. 'The day I found Bonnie guarding that little boy's body, I could not have imagined the ripples that would spread out from the simple act of rescuing her. I was just someone who'd seen too much killing, evening up the score by saving one small, flea-bitten life. But, honey, it's turned out to be *so* much bigger than that.'

Anna had picked up a photo but could not have told you of what or of whom, because of the sudden blur of tears.

'Third,' Jake went on, sounding slightly husky with emotion himself, 'I once saw this card on the wall of a Buddhist café, I forget where, it said "The obstacle is the path". What if this is your path, Anna? Not a side-trip or an obstacle you need to dig up or fight or swerve around. What if it's leading you right where you need to be, the way saving Bonnie led me to you?'

Anna had to stop to blow her nose. 'Thank you,' she said, unsteadily.

'Having made you cry, I am now callously starting to eat my main course,' Jake said.

'Yeah, you brute,' she said, managing a laugh. 'You enjoy every selfish mouthful.'

She blinked away the last of her tears and the photograph in her hand wobbled back into focus. Another birthday party, Will's second. It had a double, no, a triple exposure, so that he seemed to be three ecstatic, little boys holding three brightly-coloured, Fisher Price trains. She leafed through photos: one of herself in the egg and spoon race at Sports Day, Dan in his first cricket whites, Anna and Tim at the Freemantle family's Halloween party, bobbing for apples.

Upstairs Dana had got tired of 'Moondance' and was playing 'All Things Must Pass', by George Harrison.

From the corner of her eye, Anna noticed Bonnie joyously toss a bone-shaped treat into the air. She'd sneaked it upstairs when Anna wasn't looking, then got carried away by the excitement of ownership and started tossing it and catching it again with an audible snap, sometimes giving it an occasional, possessive lick. Anna described this for Jake's entertainment, then took the next photo from the pile. Instead of another school sports day or Nativity play, she found herself looking at a picture of her parents, Julia and Julian, both wearing enormous 1980s sunglasses, against a backdrop of snowy mountains; the only photograph she'd found of the two of them so far, something that seemed, if not sinister, at least slightly concerning. She flipped it over and saw that her mother had written on the reverse; *Innsbruck 1988.*

I believe we both agree that there are no coincidences.

1988. The year that her grandfather, Charles Hopkins, had finally been forced, through ill-health, to take a back seat in the family auction house and her father, at the age of thirty-five, had assumed the responsibility for running Hempels. And at some point, for reasons unknown, he had taken her mother to Innsbruck . . .

'Jake, I've got to go,' Anna said urgently. 'I just need to quickly ask my grandfather something.'

She grabbed her car keys, called Bonnie and hurried out with her into the balmy May evening.

When she walked in, she found her grandfather peacefully listening to a concert on Radio Three. As usual, he was delighted to see her and Bonnie. Anna's White Shepherd immediately sat at his feet, eyes bright, hoping for further treats. Anna sat down, then almost immediately stood up, too jittery to obey the normal niceties.

'I've been going through old photos,' she said abruptly, 'and I needed to check with you about something.' She handed him the photo. George Ottaway put on his glasses and studied the picture in silence.

'Do you remember Mum and Dad going to Innsbruck?' she asked. 'I'd have been about five years old, so it would have been before Dan was born.'

Her grandfather was still looking at the photo.

'I remember they went abroad, yes,' he said. 'It was their sixth wedding anniversary. They'd missed out on their honeymoon because of problems with the auction house. You came to stay with us for two weeks and they had a belated honeymoon travelling around Europe. I think Innsbruck was one of the places they stayed.'

'My parents went off and left a five-year-old child for two weeks?' Anna was incredulous.

'Darling, you didn't miss them at *all!*' he said with a chuckle. 'The only time you cried was when they turned up to take you home and then you had the most spectacular tantrum. Julian was most put out!'

He's ninety years old, she reminded herself. *He grew up in a different time.* It would not occur to George Ottaway that a five-year old's 'spectacular tantrum' could have anything to do with her distress at being abandoned by her parents.

He handed back the photo.

'This has upset you, hasn't it?' He sounded baffled.

Anna hadn't known she was going to ask him, until she heard herself say, 'Grandpa, have you ever heard anyone mention a Vermeer painting called A Study in Gold?'

She saw a flicker of reaction, so quickly veiled that she immediately doubted she'd seen it at all.

'No, never.'

Her grandfather sounded uncharacteristically gruff. He quickly reached down to stroke Bonnie, with a suddenly tremulous hand.

It was the first time she'd suspected her grandfather of lying to her. There had been so many lies already and now her grandfather, her faithful guiding star, was adding to these sticky layers of untruth. Her sense of betrayal was so acute that she very nearly walked out.

The moment passed. She made them both a pot of tea, and they talked, too politely, about other things for half an hour or so.

Driving back, catching the alert gleam of Bonnie's dark eyes in her mirror, Anna kept remembering how her grandfather's hand shook, as he gruffly dismissed her question and that look in his eyes; an old man's plea not to question his version of reality, which had made it impossible to challenge him. The memory was like an ache in her chest.

She had to go back to Hempels. She had to persuade Thomas Kirchmann or Alexei to talk to her. David Fischer had enough evidence to warrant further investigation into his claims. So why was everyone hell-bent on denying it?

Next morning, Anna was sitting at a pavement table outside a café in South Kensington, until it was time for the auction house to open. She sipped her mediocre coffee, ate an almond croissant and, in between, she exchanged texts with Tansy, who was already at work in her gallery but not noticeably rushed off her feet. Isadora had already filled Tansy in on the events of the previous day, so

Anna told her about the photo she'd found of her parents coincidentally holidaying in Innsbruck.

Is that in Switzerland?

Tansy's geography was famously vague, Anna typed her reply. **Austria.**

Where they have cakes like in Pfeffers?

And schnitzel with noodles and whiskers on kittens.

Ha-ha, how very Julie Andrews.

Seconds later Anna received a texted emoji of hands folded in prayer. **Can we go on a road trip? Just you and me? I'm so overdue for an adventure.**

How would Liam feel about that?

Don't care! Tansy flashed back. **Liam's doing my nut!** A lurid scream emoji followed.

Anna couldn't help smiling, it was so Tansy, but she was also concerned for her friend. What had gone wrong between her and Liam? She dabbed up the last crumbs of her croissant and stood up.

I can do this. I can.

This time, when she arrived at Hempels, Anna found Ms Carmody, the receptionist, at her desk in the foyer.

'Mr Kirchmann is out of his office,' she said. 'And Mr Lenkov said he'll be late in today. But Ms Jinks is available if you'd like to talk to her?'

Anna's heart sank. Why hadn't she phoned ahead? Leaving aside the PA's off-putting super efficiency, Alice had to be seven or eight years younger than Anna at least, so it was unlikely she could shed any light on her father's connection with David Fischer. But Anna could hardly back out now and agreed to talk to Ms Jinks.

Alice soon appeared, wearing another of her expensive little shifts. This one was the colour of ripe damsons, a kind of twilight purple. Her long hair was done up in a silky French plait to show off her swingy gold earrings.

'How funny, I was just thinking about you and here you are!' she said, smiling. 'Let's go up to my office and have a proper natter.'

When she stepped out of the lift on to the second floor, Anna experienced the same disorientation she'd felt on her earlier visit.

Everything seemed so light, spacious and *ordered*. In her father's time, the second floor had been divided between an open-plan jumble, where Hempels' consultants competed for desks and telephones and a scruffy little accounts office.

'Heavens.' A tiny furrow appeared in Alice's forehead, as Anna described the original set-up. 'That does sound chaotic!'

'It was totally chaotic,' Anna agreed. *And gloomy and grubby*, she thought. But as a small child, she'd found it exciting too, a place where she might stumble on long-forgotten treasures.

Alice's office was a bright, white-painted cubicle, with a view over an adjacent hotel.

'Coffee?' she said. 'It's quite good coffee, though Herr Kirchmann pretends to disagree.' She laughed. She was noticeably more human today and much less like the perfect android PA. Perhaps with her boss away, she felt entitled to an hour off from her tireless smoothing, managing and filtering of Herr Kirchmann's world.

Anna took a seat and waited while Alice fetched their coffee. It came in proper china mugs, not plastic cups and was as good as she'd promised. Alice perched on the edge of her desk, one foot swinging slightly in its suede ballet slipper, which was the exact golden-brown colour of demerara sugar. She looked barely old enough to leave school, let alone hold down such a high-powered job.

'I was genuinely thinking about you, you know,' Alice said earnestly. 'That wasn't just some PA ploy to win your confidence!'

Anna laughed. 'Ok, I believe you.' She felt herself relax a little. 'What were you thinking though?'

'Oh, just how alike we are in some ways,' Alice said. 'I mean, your family's connection with Hempels goes back generations and so does mine.' She saw Anna's surprise. 'It's true! We're Hempels twins!'

'Oh, wow, I didn't know,' Anna said. 'Did you used to come here as a child?' She had a charming image of herself and Alice, two solitary little girls occupying different time-lines, separately exploring Hempels' ramshackle palace of treasures and gazing up wide-eyed at the same stuffed giraffe.

'No,' Alice said, dispelling this fantasy. 'I never saw inside. My granddad was old school. Work was work and women and children just got in the way.' She sketched an impatient little wave. 'But my grandad and his dad – and I'm almost sure *his* dad before that – absolutely lived and breathed Hempels and so I feel like this auction house is kind of in my blood. My grandfather worked closely with your father *and* your grandfather. You see? Official confirmation that we're twins!' She sipped from her cup, looking at Anna over the rim. 'Isn't that a funny little coincidence?'

'It is strange,' Anna agreed. 'Did you always want to work here, even as a child?'

'God no! I was going to be an actress or – I don't know – a rock star. I was headed for big fame! I couldn't see how messing about with a lot of fusty old antiques would get me anywhere I wanted to be. I was an extremely shallow little girl, I'm afraid,' she added with disarming frankness.

'Weren't we all?' Anna said.

'However, life has a way of changing us,' Alice said. 'And, as you see, here I am! I like to think that Lionel would be proud of me if he could see me now!'

Anna set her mug down very carefully on the corner of Alice's desk.

'Lionel was your grandfather? Lionel Rosser who worked here as a porter?'

She felt a distinct chill enter the little office.

'He might have started off as a porter,' Alice almost snapped, 'but he was an art expert in his own right by the time your father took over. He wasn't just lugging heavy furniture about.'

'I honestly didn't mean to imply that,' Anna said quickly. 'I know that porters in auction houses often become incredibly knowledgeable. It's more that I recently heard your grandfather's name mentioned in connection with something that's been giving me some sleepless nights. That's really why I'm here.'

'I see.' Alice's voice still had an edge. 'I'm sorry you've been having sleepless nights, but I can't see where my grandfather comes in.'

'I heard a rumour that, at one time, Lionel was concerned Hempels might be dealing in stolen art.' Anna tried to make her voice sound neutral. 'Had you ever heard anything like that?'

'Of *course*, I knew about that!' Alice flashed back. 'The world of London auction houses is so incestuous; it was inevitable that it would filter back. But it isn't something I exactly enjoy talking about.' She shifted her gaze slightly so that she could look out of the window, though there was nothing to see but row upon row of more windows, all with their blinds firmly pulled down. Anna heard Alice take a breath.

'I'm sorry,' she said. 'It upsets me to think about it even now.'

'No, I'm sorry,' Anna said. 'I'm sorry I upset you.'

Alice gave her a wan smile.

'Everyone understands about dementia now, don't they? My mother still blames herself for not realising. Denial, I suppose? It's a frightening thing to see someone you loved and looked up to gradually losing their mind.'

Anna had that sickening sensation of almost missing a step. 'You mean he—'

'He started making wild accusations against everybody,' Alice said. 'Not just against your poor grandfather, but my parents, his oldest and dearest friends. It was mortifying. He started forgetting to shave and change his clothes. He'd bring back some rusty junk he'd found in someone's garage and insist it was going to make all our fortunes. Just awful.' Alice passed her hand across her face. 'And so I wouldn't give too much credence to that sad little story if I were you,' she added crisply, sounding more like her PA self. 'Herr Kirchmann and his partners were brilliant though once we'd got a diagnosis. They were so generous to Lionel in his final years.'

I am a useless detective, Anna thought miserably. She absolutely hated having to keep asking these questions that nobody wanted to answer and not knowing how much of what they told her was the truth. She forced herself to plough on.

'You have to know though, that your grandfather wasn't the only person to make these allegations and similar accusations have been made against Herr Kirchmann's fa—'

'Yes, yes,' Alice interrupted impatiently. 'I know all about that. You're talking about David Fischer.'

'Yes, I talked to him just recently,' Anna said, bracing herself for another angry response.

'David Fischer is a classic attention-seeker,' Alice said. 'We get them coming through our door all the time. It's like something's wrong with their wiring. They're sad and lonely and so desperate to give their lives meaning that they concoct some grandiose little fairy-tale.'

'But he's got evidence to support his claims,' Anna pointed out.

Alice frowned. 'Well, you know, even if that's true—'

'It is,' Anna insisted. 'I've seen it.' *And so did Lili Rossetti*, she thought.

'Then obviously I have to believe that you've seen *something*,' Alice said coolly. 'Nevertheless, I'd take Herr Kirchmann's father's word over David Fischer's any time.'

Anna heard a faint movement and saw Alexei Lenkov in the doorway. She wondered how long he'd been listening.

He said quietly, 'every family has their secrets, Anna, but that doesn't mean every man and his dog has the right to go rummaging through them, whatever the tabloids would have us believe.' His tone was gentle, but she knew she'd been reproved.

'A word of advice,' he added in the same gentle tone. 'Don't buy into Fischer's florid fairy-tale as Alice so rightly calls it. Your father was a wonderful and upright man. He always, in all situations, tried his best and that's all you need to know.'

Alexei and Alice were both giving her sympathetic smiles, but Anna had a definite sense of them closing ranks.

Feeling bruised and humiliated, she hurried down the street, heading for the Tube and home and Bonnie. Alexei's words stuck with her: *he always, in all situations, tried his best and that's all you need to know*. But what if her dad's best hadn't been enough?

The obstacle is the path. But she still felt that the more she tried to find out about Julian Hopkins, the further away and more unknowable he became, like an endlessly receding figure in a dream. *The trouble is, I hardly knew him,* she thought. Hempels had taken so much of her father's time and energy when she was growing up and he'd been murdered before she could reach adulthood, when they might have attempted a different kind of relationship. All Anna had of him were impressions, like a dandelion's floating seeds, nothing solid she could hold on to, nothing that added up to a real person.

I need to talk to someone who knew him, she thought suddenly. Someone who knew Julian Hopkins before he was a husband, before he was a father.

Anna only knew one person who fitted that description and she hadn't spoken to him for more than half her lifetime. She took out her phone.

'It's Anna,' she said, when her brother picked up.

'I was just going to call you,' he said. 'Lack of sleep is obviously affecting my brain cells, it's only just occurred to me it might be useful to check out the guest list, you know, for the VE night ball? See who bought tickets? It keeps niggling at me; why was Lili Rossetti even there?'

'You're right,' she agreed. 'Why was she?'

'Anyway, enough of that, what's up? Why are you calling?'

Anna felt a sudden terrifying surge of adrenalin as she said, 'Is your dad still teaching at UCL?'

NINE

Half-way through their lunch, Anna was still sneaking glances at her biological father, for the sheer pleasure of discovering him all over again, still sitting opposite her at their table for two in this busy Turkish café in Bloomsbury.

When Chris Freemantle had walked up to her table, she'd caught her breath. How could she not have suspected? How could *everybody* not have suspected? Her father's navy blue eyes were exactly like her own. Everyone had always said how much Anna looked like her mother. Tim had said it the first time he visited her flat. Perhaps everyone had hoped that if they repeated something over and over, with sufficient conviction, it would become true.

Once or twice she surprised a wondering glance from Chris, as if, like Anna, he needed to make frequent reality checks. A sixteen-year old secret had finally been outed. On the phone, Tim could hardly contain his pleasure at setting up this meeting for his father and long-lost half-sister.

It was an undeniably awkward situation, until it dawned on Anna that Chris was leaving her to dictate the pace. He wasn't trying to rush her into an intimacy he hadn't earned, playing her long-lost daddy. He seemed astonished and grateful to be here with her at all and, for the first time, with no need to pretend.

They'd been given a window table and the sun glinted on their cutlery and two glasses of pale, yellow wine that they'd hardly touched. Their waiter had brought a procession of blue-painted, pottery dishes filled with middle-eastern snacks: stuffed aubergines, tiny, spicy, lamb meatballs on skewers and a delicate salad of baby broad beans with stuffed vine leaves.

For the first few minutes, they'd tentatively filled in some of the gaps. Anna explained about coming back to Oxford to help nurse her dying grandmother and that she was now the owner of her grandparents' house. Proudly, Chris had told her that he and Jane were now grandparents, then interrupted himself to say apologetically, 'But you're back in touch with Tim. You know all this already!'

'Yes. You're a grandparent and it seems that I'm an aunt.' Anna sounded waspish, but she couldn't help it. She saw Chris register her oblique reference to her newly discovered half-brother. He speared a small meatball with his fork, went to eat it, then laid the fork and meatball aside.

'Tim said you wanted to ask me about your dad and Hempels?'

'Yes. I've—' She swallowed and started over again. 'Something's come up that's made me realize how pathetically little I knew about him and about his work, and now—'

'He's not around for you to ask,' he said gently.

She nodded, relieved. Now no-one had to tiptoe around that grim, smoking crater in her life, where her family had once been.

'Tim also mentioned that you were asking about the Scott-Nevilles.' Chris wiped his hands on his napkin. 'I'm guessing that they're somehow connected to whatever this is that's made you want to talk to me after all these years?'

'I just couldn't.' For those first years after her family's murders, Anna would have found it too excruciating to even be in the same room with any of the Freemantles. She took a breath. 'It would have been too painful, like being bereaved all over again.' She searched for any trace of bitterness in his face, but if there was any Chris kept it well-hidden. 'I wanted to talk to you, because you knew my dad the best of anybody. I think you knew him from his university days, didn't you?'

Chris sat back in his chair.

'Anna, I'll gladly tell you everything I know, but you're going to need a bit of background first. I'm afraid this is a terrible cliché, but your dad, and your mum and I met the first week we were up at Cambridge and instantly bonded like the Three Musketeers.'

'You were friends with my mum back then?' Anna couldn't keep the surprise out of her voice. She'd known that both men had been close friends since Cambridge and that her mother had read English and French at Girton College, but she'd never pictured her as their "third musketeer".

Chris shot her a humorous look that held more than a tinge of regret.

'Did you ever see a film by Francois Truffaut, called *Jules et Jim*?'

Anna frowned. 'The one where two best friends fall in love with the same girl and they all ride around on bikes together. The bikes might have been in a different film . . .' She added uncertainly.

He smilingly shook his head. 'The bikes were in the same film.'

It was slowly coming back to her. 'There was a song, catchy, bitter-sweet.'

'Jeanne Moreau sang it. So, there you have it.' Chris gave a slightly embarrassed shrug. 'Julian et Julia. Et Chris. Not such a catchy title obviously.'

Anna stared at him. 'You *both* loved my mum? I mean, from the start, you and my dad *both* loved her.'

'I believe it's what's known in teen fiction as a "love triangle".' He pulled a rueful face.

Anna took a much-needed gulp of wine. She imagined telling Tansy, 'OK, so your dad might have been a notorious gangland boss, but my parents were in a "love triangle".'

'I've since come to realize that we were also in love with being young,' Chris continued, 'in love with being up at Cambridge and with having all our lives still in front of us. My loving your mum, loving Julia, was a part of that. And, in a completely different way, I loved your dad. Loved, admired and desperately envied him.'

'You envied my dad?' she asked, astonished.

He smiled. 'I'd never met anyone like him. Oh, Julia and I talked the talk, Save the Whale, CND marches all that, but Julian . . .' Chris shook his head. 'Julian just wanted to do the right thing because it was the right thing. Unlike the rest of us, he preferred to do it behind the scenes. He never wanted recognition. If he'd been in America in the Sixties, he'd have joined the

Freedom Riders. Once, he got his arm broken by some British Fascists at a demo in Grosvenor Square.'

'*My* dad?' she said again, as if there might be some confusion about whose father they were discussing.

'Yes, your dad,' he said amused.

'But how come you all still stayed friends all those years, if you both, you know, had such a big thing for my mum?' *Not to mention she had me . . . your secret love child.*

'Well, for one thing, we were not three, angst-ridden characters in a French film,' Chris said. 'Sometimes your mum would be going out with me and other times she'd be going out with Julian, then there'd be times when she was going out with someone totally different. One term, she was studying in Paris and came back after Christmas with a rather stunning new haircut! But it became apparent, over time, that she and your dad were going to go the distance. Then, of course, I met Jane . . .'

Anna hated to admit it, but she was shocked. Possibly Chris read her expression because he said, 'I'd hate you to think it was anything sordid, because I promise you it wasn't. Ever.'

'Except that you and Julia apparently carried on, you know, *carrying on*,' she said, 'after you were both married.'

Chris nodded, not attempting to deny it.

'I know, and I'm not proud of how we behaved and nor was Julia.'

Their waiter came by, observed their intense expressions and diplomatically departed.

'The first years of marriage can be tricky for anyone, but your parents had the additional pressure of Hempels. Julian had never intended to go into the auction house. He'd had ideas of going overseas and working for an aid agency, but when it seemed that Hempels might be lost, due to your grandfather's uncertain health – and I suspect there were other factors, which your dad felt unable to share – he, well, I think he felt morally obligated to step into his father's shoes.'

He must have felt utterly trapped, Anna thought.

'Not surprisingly, this decision took its toll,' Chris said. 'Julian became very distant from your mother and was almost like a different person. Naturally, she assumed he regretted marrying her and turned to me for comfort.'

'Hold on,' Anna said angrily. 'I'm sorry, but I think that was a really crappy thing to do! Ok, these things happen. I know that. But you were both married to other people and this obviously went on for *years*!'

'I'm not justifying what we did. It was inexcusable. I'd say it was the single worst thing I've ever done, except that I could never completely regret it because—' Chris tried to smile but seemed suddenly close to tears. 'Because of you.'

'Did my dad know?' Anna had agonised over this question ever since she'd found out.

'Oh yes. As soon as Julia found out she was having you, she offered to leave, but Julian begged her to give him one more chance. He felt he'd driven her into my arms, you see. He asked her to let him take you on as his daughter.'

Anna felt a guilty pang that was no less painful for being so familiar. Right from the start her existence had caused so much pain and confusion.

'What about Jane? Was she in on this arrangement?' She heard that same waspish note to her voice, as if part of her was stuck in a state of permanent teenage resentment.

He gave her a tired smile. 'Yes. We had a terrible few months, but she forgave me. She forgave us both.'

'But you never told the boys?'

'God, no! I have no idea how Tim found out. Jane swears she didn't tell him. Although during the investigation into—' his voice faltered '—into your family's murders, we obviously had to tell the police.'

Anna thought about all those shared family holidays, Christmases and Halloweens. She remembered growing up feeling that she'd had not one but two families and she'd been right. Inevitably, there had to have been times when the cracks must have shown. Like that holiday in Pembrokeshire, when Tim and Anna surprised Chris and a tearful Julia in the kitchen of their rented farmhouse but, in the main, they had all managed to make it work.

She thought of her father effectively immolating himself to make a success of Hempels, never once alluding to the sacrifice he'd made. She thought of him begging her mother not to leave him, to let him bring up her child as his own and she wanted to weep for this lonely, fiercely principled man.

The waiter reappeared to remove the dirty dishes and offer them dessert menus.

'Just coffee thanks,' Chris said, after a questioning glance at Anna.

When they were alone again, Anna said, 'Did my father ever confide in you about problems at work?'

'He never quite spelled it out, but it was obvious he had issues with how his father was running the business,' Chris said.

'You don't know what these issues were?'

He shook his head. 'But I had the impression that Charles had, how shall I put it, rather more *flexible* morals than your dad.'

Their coffee came with four, exquisite, hand-made chocolates.

'Julian was profoundly loyal to his father,' Chris said. 'He half-worshipped, half-hated him, in that screwed-up way that people so often love the parents who have hurt them most, but he couldn't bear the thought that he might ever become like him.'

Anna had no real memories of her grandfather, Charles Hopkins, except that she'd hated his voice. If anything, it was more of an absence of memory. A black hole. A chill.

Chris took a breath. 'One night, Julian turned up at our house absolutely distraught. He'd come straight from some grand dinner at the Scott-Nevilles.'

Every nerve in Anna's body was suddenly on high alert. 'Did he tell you what had happened?'

'I'm hazy on the details,' he said apologetically. 'But I remember that some visiting Russian dignitary was present. As the night went on, and they'd all sunk a fair amount of Ralph's thirty-year-old Macallan whiskey, the Russian started making disparaging comments about blacks and Jews. Your father protested, as he would do.'

Anna could easily imagine what had followed. She'd only had a passing acquaintance with Ralph Scott-Neville, but she'd regularly witnessed Dominic turn on anyone who thwarted, bored or merely irritated him. There had also been times – times she'd rather not remember – when she had been that boring, irritating person.

'I bet the Scott-Nevilles and their cronies totally ridiculed him,' she said, swallowing.

Chris nodded. 'In that killingly polite way of old Etonians.'

Anna's phone buzzed. She glanced at the screen, saw that her caller was Isadora, and decided that she wouldn't mind waiting.

'Poor Dad, he must have felt like he was being savaged by *frightfully* civilised and well-dressed lions.' She mimicked an upper-class drawl.

'It wasn't just the Scott-Nevilles,' Chris said soberly. 'Julian's father joined in the savaging.' He shook his head. 'Can you imagine?'

The spiteful old bastard. Anna felt sickened. Her dad had been worth ten of him.

'Julian told me he honestly didn't know if he had the strength to go on.' For a moment, Chris held her eyes and Anna understood his implication; that night, Julian had come close to suicide. Whatever had been said or done at the Scott-Nevilles, which had so horrified her father, had to have been more than some vile, racist joke, if he'd felt – even for a few haunted hours – that killing himself was the only way out.

She took a breath and asked, 'did my dad ever mention anything about a stolen painting?'

Chris poured an extra splash of hot milk into his coffee. 'I'm not sure. Can you give me a bit more context?'

She filled him in about everything that had happened, from finding Lili Rossetti's body to David Fischer's wild-seeming accusations against Hempels, which Anna was now beginning to suspect might be true.

'I've been back to Hempels twice now,' she said, 'and I have this sense of being charmingly fobbed off and I don't think it's just my paranoia talking.' She gave an awkward laugh, wondering if Chris knew how close his daughter had come to the edge. Then she saw that he was waiting calmly for her to continue, so she related Thomas Kirchmann's story about his father; the righteous gentile of Innsbruck, who had hidden precious works of art from the infamous Kunstschutz and been executed by the SS for his pains.

'But David Fischer said that the paintings his family had given into Kirchmann's safe-keeping, including what he claims to be a Vermeer, had been seen – had actually been *photographed* – in the homes of prominent Nazis, at a time when they were suppos-edly safe in Michael Kirchmann's secret vault. Fischer's father believed the Vermeer had somehow made its way to Soviet Russia, where it was eventually used as a bribe to ensure a safe passage to the west, for some defecting Russian official . . . But an art-savvy porter told Fischer he thought he'd seen one of the Fischer's family's paintings in my grandfather's office at Hempels. Only, it turns out, he may have been suffering from dementia . . . And breathe, Anna,' she added with an apologetic laugh. 'Sorry, that was a bit of a long speech!'

Her phone buzzed. Isadora again. Anna switched it off. 'Somebody's lying or, at least, not telling me the whole truth,' she said, frustrated. 'I just don't know who.'

'But, most of all, you want to know if your father had let himself be a party to a particularly despicable art theft?'

She nodded unhappily, thankful that she hadn't been the one to put this distressing possibility into words.

Chris scratched gently at his chin. 'Actually, listening to you just now has jogged my memory. I do remember Julian mentioning some problematic painting. It could have been a Vermeer. Did it have the word "yellow" in the title?'

'Gold,' Anna said before she could stop herself.

'Yes! A Study in Gold? Does that sound right? I'm afraid I can't tell you much more than that. Your father started to explain, but then he immediately backtracked. He said that Julia was always telling him he got things out of proportion when he was over-tired and everything would probably seem more manageable after a good night's sleep.'

Anna felt tears prickle her eyelids. She could just imagine Julian saying that.

'You know,' Anna said, 'before Lili Rossetti was murdered, she emailed David Fischer to say she'd actually seen the painting.'

'Did she now?' Chris said.

'If her stalker-ex hadn't caught up with her, it's possible she could have produced some damning evidence against Hempels.'

'It's equally possible that she might not have,' Chris suggested very gently.

'That's true,' she admitted.

They talked of other things for a while, then Chris had to go back to UCL to give a tutorial. She could feel his reluctance to leave her.

'You know you even have my smile,' he said almost shyly.

She swallowed. 'I know.'

Chris briefly covered her hand with his own. 'You mustn't worry. I mean about blowing the whistle if you uncover anything at Hempels. You mustn't feel you're being disloyal to your dad. He'd be cheering you on, Anna, seriously, if he was here.' He shifted in his chair. 'However, I do remember Julian saying that the Scott-Nevilles were every bit as ruthless as the robber-barons they presumably descended from, so if I'm allowed to give you advice . . .'

'I already know to steer clear of that family', she told him.

If you think I'm a monster, Dominic is the devil . . . Alec Faber's words kept coming back to haunt her.

Anna returned Isadora's call as she hurried to the Tube.

'Darling, where on earth have you *been*! I've left you *dozens* of messages. I just called Liam.'

Why would Isadora need to call Liam? Anna wondered.

'Is something wrong?' Anna hastily veered off the pavement to avoid a group of Japanese tourists.

'No, but I had this thought. You'll probably think it's mad. The disgraced official that David Fischer said had to pay British agents to help them defect. I was thinking if anyone would know what was going on back then, it would be Tallis.'

After a stunned pause, Anna said, 'You're right. I do think that's mad. You can't seriously be thinking, what I think you're thinking, not after everything that man put you and your friends through.'

'But Anna, *surely*—'

'Isadora, he murdered your best friend! Not to mention you were still practically a schoolgirl when he recruited you – under false pretences – to be part of his perverse little game of spies.'

'But if we can help David right this terrible wrong?' Isadora's rich, actressy voice vibrated with emotion. 'You know they're not going to try Tallis now?' she rushed on. 'I asked Liam and he said no further action is going to be taken against him. There's no material evidence that he ever committed any crimes.'

'You're kidding,' Anna said, appalled. 'They've let him out of prison?'

'They've taken him back to the hospice. He's a sick old man, Anna. He's only got a few weeks left to live.'

'And so was Adolf Eichmann a sick old man,' Anna said, furious, 'and all those other disgusting war criminals. Do you really want to go to see this man who is a liar and a murderer and Christ knows what else?'

'Yes, I do,' Isadora said crisply. 'Don't try to talk me out of it because I've made up my mind. It's time to exorcise him from my life after all these years.'

On the Tube, rattling through the dark below the streets of London, Anna tried to imagine how Isadora would feel when she came face to face with the dying Tallis. To be honest, she couldn't imagine Tallis ever dying. He'd talk his way out of it somehow, the way he'd talked his way out of everything else.

As it turned out, Anna wasn't the only person to be concerned. Over Sunday brunch, at The Rusty Bicycle, Isadora defensively repeated her decision to visit Tallis. Tansy traded horrified glances with Anna.

After a long pause, Liam said, 'Well, I can't stop you going, Isadora, but I'd feel much happier if you'd let me come along.'

'I'll come too,' Anna said quickly, 'If that's OK?'

'Would tomorrow morning suit you both?' Liam asked. 'After you've walked the dogs?'

He arrived at Anna's on the dot of ten. She watched him surreptitiously as he drove them over to Isadora's, his elbow resting on the half-open window.

She wondered what was going on in his life. Liam had seemed relaxed and cheerful during their brunch, until Isadora had asked him when he was taking his inspector's exams, then he'd completely shut down. His withdrawal was so noticeable that Isadora and Tansy instantly began overcompensating in that way that women do, chattering and laughing, as if, they could somehow cancel out the crashing silence from Liam. But this morning Liam seemed like his normal straight-forward self. So perhaps he and Tansy had sorted it out, whatever it was?

They stopped off in Summertown to collect Isadora, who was looking unusually pale under her makeup. On the short drive to the hospice, they discussed David Fischer and his search for his grandfather's painting.

'It's one hell of a story,' Liam said, shaking his head. 'Tansy's been keeping me updated. Don't know if she said, but I've put some cautious feelers out. Not promising anything, but something might come back, you never know.' He flashed a boyish grin at Isadora. 'Got to help the dog-walking Charlie's Angels. It's how me and Tans first got together after all.'

Despite his careless tone, Anna detected real tenderness underneath. *He loves her*, she thought, *whatever's wrong, it isn't that*. 'So if there's anything you think I can do, just shout,' he said as they pulled off the Woodstock Road turning up the wooded lane that led to the Little Sisters of Mercy hospice.

When they went to announce themselves to the nun at the reception desk, Anna was startled to see Liam flash his badge. Not a major deal in the wider scheme of things, yet dismayingly out of character for the normally upright, do-everything-by-the book, Sergeant Goodhart.

A young, sweet-faced nun came to take them to Tallis's room. Like the nun at the desk, she was dressed in a sweater and skirt; the gold cross on a chain around her neck was the only outward sign of her calling. She led them along hushed corridors to the room where Isadora's former handler would spend his remaining days. The nun knocked gently at the door before she opened it.

'Some people to see Matthew,' she called softly. She hurried away, leaving the door slightly ajar, enough to give a harrowing glimpse of what was inside. Anna felt her nostrils flare at the escaping miasma of smells that no disinfectant could entirely mask. Raised up on pillows amidst a forest of wires and tubes, Matthew Tallis lay with closed eyes. His skin was blotched and yellow. A nurse leaned over him, moistening his cracked lips with a sponge.

Isadora backed away. 'I can't,' she said in a panic. 'I can't be in the same room. I thought I could but I can't.'

'Why don't you wait for us in reception?' Liam suggested calmly, 'I doubt we'll be long.' He'd known it would be like this, Anna realized. That's why he'd insisted on coming. He knew how tough it would be for Isadora to confront the man who had inflicted so much damage on her and her friends. Anna was tempted to flee with her but she squared her shoulders and followed Liam inside.

'Matthew,' the nurse said into the sick man's ear, then in a slightly louder voice, 'you have some visitors, Matthew. I'm not sure how responsive he'll be,' she said apologetically. 'Lately he tends to drift in and out. I'll just be in the next room if you need me.' She left with a rustle of crisp cotton and without closing the door, to Anna's relief.

Matthew's eyelids had lost all their lashes. They flickered twice then opened to reveal faded eyes with discoloured whites. For a moment, he couldn't seem to focus, and then, like a raptor, his cold blue gaze fastened on Anna. *He remembers me.* The thought creeped her out. Like the black box in a fatal plane crash, some part of Tallis was still mechanically recording, calibrating and calculating.

'You've come back to see me, my dear,' he said hoarsely. 'How frightfully sweet of you.' He had deteriorated shockingly since she'd seen him last. His thin, papery skin was stretched so tightly over his bones that he resembled a talking skull.

'Good morning, Sir,' Liam said. 'My name is Sergeant Liam Goodhart. I believe you've already met Ms Hopkins. She has something specific to ask you.'

Tallis's thin lips twisted into the insinuating smile that Anna remembered from her last visit.

'Oh, I *see*,' he said. 'That sounds *most* intriguing.' She heard his breath whistle in his lungs, as he struggled to talk and breathe.

'Yes,' she said coolly. 'I want to know if it was common practice to demand bribes from people trying to defect to the West?'

Tallis made a wheezy sound, somewhere between a laugh and a cough.

'Oh, dear me. I thought you were here for my charm and good looks, but you just want to *pump* me for information.' He sniggered, delighted with his double entendre.

Anna felt Liam unobtrusively squeeze her arm, reminding her that he had her back.

Tallis gave them his sly grin. 'And who is this chivalrous Sir Goodhart you've brought along for protection? He's not the same chap who came last time.'

Liam said, stony-faced, 'Can you please answer the young lady's question?' He leaned down to show Tallis his badge, sending the dying man into an alarming paroxysm of laughing and coughing.

'Oh, how *priceless*!' he wheezed. 'How absolutely bloody *priceless*!'

'Let's go,' Anna said to Liam. 'He's just wasting our time.'

To her secret revulsion, Tallis beckoned her closer. 'Defectors, you say?' he said in a hoarse whisper and she smelled his fetid breath. 'I think I did once know someone who might have been mixed up with something like that.'

This was also typical Tallis. Having toyed with them, to show who held all the power, he couldn't pass up an opportunity to show off how much he knew.

'And who might that alleged someone have been, Sir,' Liam said in a deliberately unimpressed voice.

Anna saw cold anger flare in Tallis's eyes. 'A very close colleague, my fine Sir Goodhart,' he rasped. 'His wife worked at one of the Oxford women's colleges. He helped some poncey, little official escape the Gulag. I believe my colleague may have been rewarded with some artwork or other, but that could just be folk lore.' He had to stop to cough.

How Tallis must have adored being in intelligence, Anna thought; manipulating and misdirecting from behind the scenes, availing himself of other people's secrets while he remained hidden and invulnerable at the heart of his sticky web of intrigue. Even now, with weeks or days left to live, he was addicted to that world of smoke and mirrors.

'Do you remember the name of your colleague?' she asked. 'Or maybe his wife?'

The sick man turned on her with a venomous expression. 'Do you know who you're *talking* to, young woman?' he hissed. 'I know people who could take you out in a million different ways and it wouldn't leave a mark. A jab with a poisoned umbrella. Quick shove from behind on the underground. I've got people secretly working for me in London Transport, at the BBC, in the Vatican.' His eyes held a feral glitter. Spittle dripped from his lips as his ranting descended into incoherent mumbles.

The nurse came hurrying in. 'It's the morphine,' she said in a low voice. 'He doesn't know what he's saying.'

Shaken, Anna couldn't agree. She felt as if she'd had a chilling glimpse into a toxic old man's innermost soul.

They found Isadora pacing nervously by the car. 'I'm sorry I was such a wimp.'

'No, *Jesus!*' Anna said. 'You made the right decision.'

'You did,' Liam said with feeling. 'I see a lot of this kind of thing. Victims of crimes or their families, who turn up when the case comes to trial, hoping for closure or whatever pop psychologists call it. They usually end up sick to their stomachs, poor buggers.' His phone started to emit a hectic ringtone. Pulling an apologetic face, Liam walked off a little way to take the call.

'I still feel sick to my stomach just from being in the same building,' Isadora confessed.

'He's an utterly repugnant man. Why wouldn't you feel sick?'

Isadora gave her a watery smile. 'Was it helpful though? Did he tell you anything new?'

Before she could answer, Liam came over looking sombre. 'I told you I'd put some feelers out? That was a courtesy call from the Reading police. There was a bad fire last night in the Harris Arcade.'

For a second, Anna couldn't think where he meant. Then she flashed back to the crowded little bedsit with its faded echoes of Vienna. She saw David Fischer kneeling in front of the safe. 'Experience has taught me that I can't be too careful.' And then she remembered the books piled at the sides of the stairs, like an inferno just waiting for a match.

TEN

'**Y**ou think it was *arson*?' Tansy kept her voice low out of consideration for any sensitive diners.

'I just think there were two people who were trying to find that Vermeer, and now they're both dead,' Anna said, also in an undertone, as she pulled out a chair for her friend. 'Shall we ask them to get you a towel?' she added in her normal voice. 'Maybe *two* towels? You're drenched.'

Tansy shook her head, scattering tiny droplets. 'I'll live, unlike your poor David Fischer. I'll dry myself on a table napkin when no-one's looking!' She'd materialised out of a violent rain storm like some long-legged Goddess of the Monsoon. Her dark curls, the back of her T-shirt, the hems of her jeans, even her eyelashes were wet.

Anna had managed to get them a table in Pierre Victoire, a popular French bistro in Little Clarendon Street. *Too popular,* she thought. She'd arrived, minutes before the heavens opened, to find

a party of women exuberantly celebrating a friend's fortieth. At
the table next to Anna and Tansy's, three elderly dons loudly
rehashed a recent quarrel with their dean.

Tansy hitched her chair closer to Anna's so they could hear
themselves speak.

'Did you see in the Mail they caught up with Lili's ex? He
didn't kill her, Anna. He's got witnesses who can vouch that he
was nowhere near Mortmead Hall that night. In the Mail, it said
the police were looking for "other leads". But from what Liam's
told me, there *are* no other leads. Now the ex is out of the frame,
they've got no one. You said she had some information about the
painting. Do you think—?'

'No, you daft mare, it's only just *beginning*!' a woman called
out, to enthusiastic cheers and applause. 'Forty's where all the
good stuff starts!'

'She said she'd *seen* it,' Anna said, 'She'd emailed David to
tell him and now they're both dead.'

Death by fire. Anna couldn't bear to imagine the horror: the
tiny apartment filling with toxic smoke, the bookshop below turned
into a roaring furnace, both sets of stairs ablaze. Anna hadn't really
known David or especially liked him, but she had recognised in
him a lonely kindred spirit. He was what Anna had been in danger
of becoming, she thought, if she hadn't found Tansy and Isadora,
friends she could call up and ask, 'Can we talk? Can I run this
by you? Tell me if you think this sounds crazy?'

'Thanks for coming, Tansy,' she said. 'I've been going out of
my mind the past twenty-four hours, but it's not just me, is it?
There's something suspicious about all of this?'

'I'd say so,' Tansy said. 'Liam thinks the same, with two
unexplained deaths and the only connection between them being
a painting that everyone but David and Lili swears no longer
exists.'

'A painting that everyone swears *never* existed,' Anna said.

Their waiter arrived with two bowls of minted pea risotto, which
Anna had already ordered on Tansy's recommendation.

Shrieks of laughter floated in from the street. Tansy and Anna
glanced out to see two half-drowned, female undergraduates
wheeling their bikes through the puddles. Tansy tasted her risotto
and gave an approving nod.

'This is every bit as good as I remember.' Then, in a typical Tansy segue, she said, 'Liam said you didn't get much out of Tallis?'

'Tallis was vile,' Anna said. 'You know Isadora couldn't go through with it?'

'Liam said. He said Tallis remembered a painting being used as a bribe to bring some "poncey official" to the west, but he never came right out and said it was the Vermeer, did he?'

Anna shook her head. 'Of course not. He's into mind games.'

Tansy took a couple of sips of her mineral water. 'How the hell would it have got to Russia anyway?'

Anna remembered the elusive trail of rumoured sightings and coded references, which David Fischer's father had tracked from Innsbruck to Berlin and then to Soviet Russia.

'Fischer's father believed a Russian soldier spirited it out of Germany at the end of the war,' she said. 'After that it sounds like it got passed around like an elaborate game of pass the parcel, until it came into the possession of some high-ranking official.'

And then this painting, which may or may not have been the Vermeer, had allegedly arrived in Oxford, where, coincidentally, the wife of one of Tallis's fellow agents, taught in one of the women's colleges. Oxford, city of spies, and home to the Hopkins and Scott-Neville families. The painting's journey was not a fairy-tale path, so much as an encircling maze. Anna shivered. In the Greek myth, the maze always had a monster at its heart.

'This is really doing your head in, isn't it?' Tansy said sympathetically.

'Yes, because just about everyone who knew the truth is *dead!*' Seeing one of the elderly dons raise a shaggy white eyebrow, Anna belatedly lowered her voice.

'My dad, his father, Ralph Scott-Neville, David Fischer's dad – Michael Kirchmann – and now, David and Lili. There's almost no one left to ask or no one who'll give me truthful answers,' she added thinking of her visit to her grandfather.

A waiter brought dessert menus. A young woman left the birthday party to pace between the tables, trying to hush her sobbing baby. She gave them an apologetic smile.

'Overtired,' she mouthed.

Anna didn't plan to have children; she couldn't begin to imagine how much courage it must take, to devote your every waking moment to protecting a small life. Yet, she couldn't help wondering how it would feel to devote your energies to nurturing something or someone, instead of delving around in the dark and murk, trying to uncover the kind of secrets that got your fellow humans killed.

Instead of rushing to order her pudding, Tansy began to retie her pony tail, fiddling with her hair elastic and getting it to just the right degree of tautness, before she took a decisive breath.

'I do know we're not real detectives. I know we're just like these irritating, dabbling, though obviously much younger and sexier, versions of Miss Marple.'

Anna was surprised into a laugh. '"Sexier than Miss Marple". Why thank you for that rave review, Ms Lavelle!'

'No, but listen,' Tansy said earnestly. 'We might not be real bona fide PIs, but, on the other hand, we were there, Anna, when Lili was found. David Fischer told *you* his story. In the end, he *trusted* you to do the right thing. On some level that makes them our responsibility, don't you think? David, and Lili and the painting that never was?'

Anna stared at her, stunned. Tansy had put into words exactly how she'd been feeling when she called her at the gallery. She hadn't said it, because it had seemed such a crazy thing to say. Now Tansy had stolen the words out of her mouth.

'It certainly feels like my responsibility,' she said, swallowing. 'All the more so, because David Fischer believed my father had failed him.'

'Ancestral guilt,' Tansy said with a wise nod. 'Ironic, really, because Julian wasn't really your dad.'

Anna quickly shook her head. 'He raised me. He didn't have to, but he did. He was my dad.'

Tansy was instantly remorseful. 'Sorry, that was a stupid thing to say. But let's just scroll back to the part about this being our responsibility.'

Not *yours*, Anna noticed gratefully, but *ours*.

'Jake thinks the same as you,' she said.

'Does he?' Tansy shifted in her chair. 'But just to go back to—'

'He referred me to the theory of cosmic ripples,' Anna said with a grin. 'I told him he'd been spending too much time with you!'

The baby had fallen asleep. The mother carefully lowered it

into a bucket-shaped baby carrier and when the baby continued to slumber, Tansy gave her a friendly thumbs-up before turning back to Anna.

Some people are described as having faces like 'an open book.' But Tansy's delicate features had all the transparency of an open sky, the fast-changing weather of her moods on view for anyone to see. Now her velvet brown eyes held an expression of intense urgency.

'Anna, I'm trying to say something,' she said earnestly, 'so don't keep interrupting, OK? Did you ever think that we might be approaching this from the wrong end? Suppose we could go right back to the beginning, where this whole Vermeer business kicked off?'

'Great idea,' Anna said wryly. 'If either of us had access to a time machine.'

'Not back in *time*! I meant back *geographically*, to Vienna or wherever this whole nightmare got started.'

'Innsbruck,' Anna corrected automatically, then did a mental double-take. Surely Tansy hadn't just said what Anna thought she'd said?

'Anna,' Tansy said, eyes sparkling. 'Why don't we go? You and me?'

'You're not serious?'

'I am *deadly* serious!' Tansy undermined this solemn declaration by breaking into a wide grin. 'Plus, we owe it to the dog-walking detectives, surely, to at least *once* do some detecting in another country!'

'Yeah, but—' Anna began

'No, Anna, we do! Hercule Poirot is always setting off up the Nile or travelling on the Orient Express.'

'But what about your job? What about Liam?' Anna was torn between her sense that Tansy's instincts were sound and her inbuilt dislike of being rushed into anything that wasn't her own idea.

'What about Liam?' Tansy almost snapped. 'We have our own lives, like you and Jake, as for my job . . .' She stopped and took a calming breath. 'Please, Anna,' she said in her most coaxing voice, 'let's jump on a plane and see if we have any more luck in Innsbruck. I don't deny this is partly selfish, but it feels weirdly right, doesn't it? Ok, so we might not find anything out, but Lili and David are worth two cheap flights to Austria surely?'

It did feel weirdly right, Anna had to agree, especially given that all her attempts to get some definitive answers in this country had come up against dead ends.

'That's why I came back to Oxford,' she admitted. 'I mean I came back to help nurse my grandmother, but I stayed on because it felt like I needed to reconnect with my old life or at least the place where I was living when the sky fell in on my old life. I suppose in a way this does feel a bit like that.'

Tansy clapped her hands. 'Is that a yes?'

'It's a maybe,' Anna said.

'Oh, pooh, that's just an introvert's way of saying yes!' Tansy pushed away her menu. 'I'm too excited to have pudding now, aren't you?' Before Anna could respond she said breathlessly, 'seriously, you don't have to decide this minute. But when I get a chance, I'll look up cheap flights. What do you reckon? Say leave on Thursday and back on Sunday?'

She turned to unhook her handbag from the back of her chair.

'Anna, I so need to get away. If there was something I could do that would help Liam, but he won't let me. You saw how he was when Isadora asked about his exams? I know men have to go into themselves while they figure what's wrong, but it's that much worse with Liam because of everything that happened, you know, when he was a kid.'

'He was in care, wasn't he?' Anna remembered.

Tansy nodded. 'Until Trishie and Jim became his full-time foster parents. Up till then he'd had never had anyone he could rely on.' Her eyes clouded with distress. 'So even now when something major upsets him, he kind of reverts to that time when he was all by himself. If I try to get him to talk it just makes him clam up even more. But if I'm there, Anna, I can't *help* myself. I just go wading in and make everything ten times worse.' She gave Anna a pleading look. 'So, I *really* need not to be there.'

They paid their bill and walked back up Little Clarendon Street towards St Giles. The sun had come out and steam was rising from the wet pavements. As they walked, Tansy started checking travel info on her phone.

'Anna, listen to this! The Orient Saxe-Barthelemy Express runs from Innsbruck to Paris! How cool would that be? Oops, maybe not, just seen the price!'

Anna was only half-listening. She was wondering what had prompted her father to take her mother to Innsbruck, if it was pure happenstance or if he'd gone there specifically to investigate David Fischer's claims and what, if anything, he'd found out.

'Your dad would be cheering you on,' Chris had said. She'd be walking in her father's footsteps. Following the trail of pebbles back to the source. Was that a weird thing to want to do? Thanks to her traumatic past, Anna never quite knew if she was being normal. *Friends do go on foreign holidays*, she reminded herself, though she wasn't sure how many took advantage of Expedia City Breaks to investigate a double murder.

Beside her, Tansy was still checking various Orient Express options on her phone.

'Do you think we'd get a discount for being the famous dog-walking detectives?' She waggled her eyebrows. 'Shall I give it a shot? Go on, dare me!'

'I shan't dare you to do any such thing, Tansy Lavelle! For one thing, we're *not* going on the Orient Express and for another we're not ten years old!' Anna said, laughing, and collided with someone coming out of Taylor's delicatessen.

'Sorry,' she said automatically.

A male voice said, 'Anna?'

Even before she'd turned she knew.

It appalled her that she immediately recognised his voice, that it had been stored deep in her unconscious all this time.

'Hello, Dominic,' she managed. It was like those dreams where everything had already been decided by some malicious puppeteer and there was nothing she could do but numbly play her part.

'How amazing!' he said, half laughing. 'Wow, this is just *insane*! After *all* these years!'

It confused her that he looked not just older, but taller and far more physically imposing than she remembered. His eyes, guile-less green eyes clear as sea glass, that had once turned her knees to jelly, hadn't changed. His hair was thick, blond and still fell forward boyishly over his brow.

Everything about him spoke of moneyed ease: the expensive charcoal jacket, the white shirt but no tie, the recent suntan and hand-made loafers without socks. But most of all, it was the confidence born of six hundred or more years of Scott-Neville power and privilege.

Dominic was openly looking her over now, as if checking her off against some remembered inventory.

'You haven't aged a day!' he said in a wondering tone. 'You're exactly the same!'

She wanted to howl a protest. *I'm not the same. How could I possibly be the same?* But this was something else she remembered about Dominic; how quickly she'd lost herself around him. During their arguments, her words had instantly deserted her, scattering like frightened birds. Now, sixteen years on, she stood in the middle of St Giles and everything she'd ever wanted to say to him jammed up inside her, choking her like an invisible garrotte. Worse than that, she could feel this polite English smile plastered over her face. Tansy had been keeping a diplomatic, if puzzled, distance, but Dominic suddenly seemed to intuit that she and Anna were together.

'I'm so sorry, what appalling manners!' he said, holding out his hand. 'I'm Dominic Scott-Neville.' Tansy shot Anna a startled look, but recovered sufficiently to say, 'Tansy Lavelle. Aren't you an old friend of Anna's?'

'That's right,' Dominic said. 'I've been away for a while, but I've recently moved back with my wife. What about you, Anna? Are you just visiting or . . .?'

'No, I live here.' Anna heard herself say gracelessly.

He abruptly looked at his watch, that splash of almost white blond hair falling over his brow in the way she'd once found sexy.

'Dammit, I've got to go. I'm supposed to be meeting our solicitors.' He produced a leather card holder and Anna saw Tansy's eyes widen at the Cartier monogram. Dominic handed one of his cards to Anna with a smile.

'Promise you'll call me up soon so we can do lunch!' He stooped to kiss her on both cheeks. Stricken, Anna watched him stride away, watched until the bright flaxen head disappeared into the crowds further down St Giles.

Tansy was talking to her, but Anna couldn't hear her through the roar of white noise. Numb in every cell, she reached up to rub her T-shirt sleeve against her cheeks where he'd kissed her.

If you think I'm a monster . . .

Somehow, she got home, walked Bonnie, fed her and changed her water. Then she half fell on to her kitchen sofa and found she couldn't move. After a while, Bonnie came to rest her chin on Anna's knee, her dark-rimmed eyes watchful.

I'm in shock, Anna told herself.

No, I'm angry, she realized all at once.

How ordinary he'd seemed, not at all the Shakespearian villain who had stalked through her nightmares all these years. She hated herself for being so feeble and letting him take control of their encounter. His casually issued invitation – no, a *command* – to meet for lunch and those kisses. *How dare he kiss me*! Anna scrubbed furiously at her cheeks in the way she'd done as a child, when she'd been kissed by an especially unappealing relative.

You haven't changed either, Dominic, she thought. *You're still an over-entitled, arrogant bastard*. She hadn't seen it as arrogance when she was sixteen of course. That was what had hooked her, not the money, the manor house or the aristocratic pedigree, but the effortless way he'd moved through the world, while she'd wanted to be anybody, anybody at all, except the miserable, mixed-up daughter of Julian and Julia Hopkins.

Naively, she'd hoped that if she hung around him and his friends long enough, some of it would rub off on her. In fact, the opposite was true. Once Dominic had successfully pulled her into his orbit, he'd changed, almost overnight. The fleeting interludes when he was funny and sweet were soon outnumbered by those other times when he was cold, or bored, or scathingly unkind. This was the price of admission to Dominic Scott-Neville's charmed circle, the understanding that he, and he alone, was the golden-haired boy, and the rest of them merely unsatisfactory stand-ins for his real friends, those gorgeous, ideal lovers who had yet to show up in his life

That afternoon, transfixed in front of the delicatessen, with its window display of gourmet sandwiches and designer teas, she had morphed back into that voiceless, teenage girl.

We should have all hated his guts, she thought. Instead they'd hated themselves. When Dominic had tired of Natalie and started flirting with Anna instead, she'd been thrilled. She'd been *chosen*. Even Max Strauli had been grateful to be chosen by Dominic, though so far as she knew he and Dominic never had sex.

'Stupid, *stupid*!' she said aloud, and saw her White Shepherd's eyes widen with worry. 'No, Bonnie, not you sweetie! You'd have had *far* more sense than me!' She knelt on the floor and wrapped her arms around her dog, inhaling her clean, sweet, peanut butter smell. Bonnie made the happy grumbling sounds she made whenever her humans made a fuss of her. Anna pressed her face against her dog's warm muscular flank.

'You're the best dog in the world,' she whispered. 'You always know how to make everything better.' Keeping one arm loosely around Bonnie's neck, she reached for her phone and found a little flurry of text messages.

> **So that worked out well! Chris totally over the moon after your lunch. Talk soon, Tim.**

> **Tansy said you'd bumped into DSN. Hope you're OK, darling girl?**

> **You said he was a bastard. You never said he was smoking hot!**

Jake had left a message to say he'd hoped to make it back to Oxford this weekend but now it turned out he had to go to Berlin for a couple of days. He signed off:

PS That little white motor boat is looking more attractive by the minute!

After she'd read all her messages Anna decided she could give herself a pat on the back for having survived her first encounter with Dominic Scott-Neville in God knows how many years. Now she needed to do something real, something sane. That's what Miriam, her therapist, used to say: 'Any time you feel yourself going into a downward spiral, do something real. Clean something. Cook yourself something you'll enjoy eating.'

She went to her fridge and took out: a sweet, red pepper, the remnant of a courgette, a potato, an onion and a slightly, over-the-hill carrot, found a sharp knife, a chopping board and began to chop everything into small dice for a frittata. She put a glug of olive oil in a pan and, while it was heating up, she beat some eggs in a bowl. As soon as the oil was hot, she threw in tiny cubes of potatoes and grated some pecorino cheese while the potatoes slowly started to turn crisp and golden brown.

When she heard her phone ring, she hastily moved the pan off the flame. This was the time when Jake often called if he was free. She frowned a little at the screen which showed an international number she didn't recognise. Was he in Berlin already? She snatched up the phone. 'Yes, you have reached the Park Town psych ward, how may I help you!'

'Is this Anna Hopkins' number?' The caller sounded understandably cautious, his intonation faintly Germanic. 'This is Thomas Kirchmann.'

She felt her cheeks burn with embarrassment. 'Oh, Herr Kirchmann, yes, it's Anna. I'm so sorry. I thought you were someone else.'

'I apologise for phoning so late, but I've been meaning to get in touch. Alice told me you came into the office the other day.'

So much had happened since Thomas Kirchmann had swept her off for coffee and cake in Pfeffers, that it took her a moment to reorient herself. 'And did Alice happen to mention why I came?' Anna wished she hadn't answered. She didn't have the energy for this.

'Alice didn't go into details, but I gather it was something to do with my father, my biological father in Innsbruck?'

'Yes, when I came, I was hoping to talk to you. I'd been to see David Fischer.'

She heard him sigh. 'I wondered if you would do something like that.'

'Yes, I know, you see, what it's like to be labelled as the – the crazy person. I needed to hear his side of the story.'

'And what did you find out?' Herr Kirchmann sounded almost resigned.

'I think you probably know what he had to say about your father.'

'*Ja, ja,*' he said wearily. 'I think I have a very good idea but, Anna, my dear, nobody's history is ever as black and white as we would like it to be.'

'So, it's true!' Anna felt anger blaze up.

'No. It is not, but if you had the choice of saving fifty percent of something or losing absolutely everything, wouldn't you choose to save the fifty percent? Sometimes in this imperfect world, to save a little, you must sacrifice the rest.'

It was dawning on Anna that she had the most appalling, left-sided headache; the shock of seeing Dominic, the hornets' nest of memories he'd let loose and now Thomas Kirchmann was talking in riddles.

'Why won't anyone ever give me a straight answer?' She pressed the heel of her hand hard against her forehead, praying that she still had a couple of paracetamol in her bag.

'My dear, I know you don't think so, but you are still very young,' Herr Kirchmann said in a sorrowful voice. 'One day you will learn that sometimes there *are* no straight answers.' Anna heard him murmur something in German to someone before he said, 'I'll be in London again next week. Come and see me and we can talk properly then. Alice will email you some dates.'

Closing her eyes against the pain, Anna said, 'Could you answer me just one thing? Do you happen to know the Scott-Nevilles? Because I bumped into Dominic Scott-Neville earlier today and your name came up and he said his family does a lot of business with Hempels.' The lie just jumped out, she couldn't have explained even to herself why she did it.

There was a silence so total that Thomas Kirchmann didn't seem to be breathing. When he finally replied, his voice was tight.

'No, Anna. Ralph Scott-Neville is dead, therefore we no longer do business with those people. I have to go now. *Gute Nacht.*'

And he'd gone.

Anna stared blankly at her phone, but she was seeing the coolly speculative expression in Dominic's eyes, as he looked her over like a foal he was considering buying. She saw David Fischer earnestly describing his father's long search for the missing Vermeer as his pale knobbly hands stroked and soothed his cat.

Then she saw the scene she'd only heard described, Julian arriving at Chris Freemantle's door straight from that hideous dinner at the Scott-Nevilles, not sure if he had the strength to go on living. Last of all, she saw her grandfather's face, the way he'd looked that evening when he lied; frightened and old, silently begging her to leave it alone.

'Dammit!' she said aloud. 'Dammit, dammit, *dammit!*'

First, she had to fix this headache. She went to hunt for some paracetamol found some in a drawer and swallowed two tablets with a gulp of water. *Well, Jake McCaffrey, if the obstacle is the path, I must be bang on target*, she thought. *My path consists of nothing but bloody obstacles.*

She picked up her phone and called up a number on speed dial.

'My introvert's "maybe" just became a "yes",' she said grimly. 'I'm in. Book our flights for Thursday morning.' And was deafened by Tansy's screams.

ELEVEN

Anna and Tansy boarded the early-morning flight for Munich under lowering, bruise-coloured clouds. By the time they'd taken their seats, rain was hammering on the windows. Later arrivals were hastily wiping their glasses or brushing off raindrops as they made their way up the aisles, contributing a damp fug to the air-conditioned atmosphere of the plane.

There had been a time, before she came back to Oxford, when Anna had been a regular, not to say compulsive flier. Now she couldn't remember when she'd last jumped on a plane, but everything seemed exactly how she remembered. Travellers ranging from fraught to blasé as they peered at seat numbers. An overweight businessman unapologetically trapped a woman in her seat, while he attempted to stuff his belongings into the already full overhead locker. A beautifully dressed young woman carried a see-through, plastic bag containing enough cosmetics to last Anna for several lifetimes.

Light-headed from lack of sleep, she still couldn't believe they were really here, that they were really doing this. She'd dropped Bonnie off at Isadora's the night before and when she'd admitted that Geraldine, Isadora's ditzy art historian friend, still hadn't been in touch, Isadora had immediately called her up despite the lateness of the hour. In a tone that curdled Anna's blood, so who knew what effect it had on the hapless Geraldine, Isadora had scathingly swept her apologies aside.

'Of *course* your life is hectic, darling! *Pre-schoolers* live hectic lives these days. But my friend is leaving for Innsbruck at first *light* and it's a matter of life and *death*!' Ending the call, she'd said darkly, 'That should do the trick!'

It did. Anna had come home to find that Geraldine had emailed her the details of an Innsbruck lawyer, who was an expert in art restitution. Anna had sent him a late-night email apologising for the short notice and asking if they could meet. After that she'd stayed up late, looking at the lawyer's website on his restitution work, then made the mistake of looking at a sidebar showing images of wartime Innsbruck.

What are we doing? She thought suddenly, *just setting off into the blue like schoolgirls in a 1950s adventure story.* What were she and Tansy even expecting to find? A helpful clue left on a hotel pillow? A trail of pebbles leading to the evildoer's house?

She felt Tansy touch her arm. Apparently untroubled by dark thoughts, she was bubbling over with excitement.

'I don't mind now that we've got that hour's stopover in Munich, because, you know, *two* countries in one day! This is the start of the new me – Tansy Lavelle, international traveller!'

Anna couldn't help smiling. 'Oh-oh,' she teased, 'there'll be no stopping you now!'

Her phone gave a peremptory ping. Maybe Geraldine's lawyer friend had replied to her email? Maybe he'd tell them something that might point them in the right direction; Anna needed something, *anything*, which would make this trip less pathetically random. But the message was from Herr Kirchmann letting her know that he was in London next week and would be free on Wednesday afternoon, if she'd like to come in and talk.

'I apologise for the abrupt end to our call. I didn't mean to make light of your very real concerns. When it comes to such serious matters, I think it is better to talk face-to-face when there is less likelihood of misunderstanding.'

Anna could see the cabin crew working their way up the aisle securing lockers, checking seatbelts and table-trays. Since she still harboured a secret dread that her mobile would be the one rogue electronic device, which would fatally disrupt the plane's guidance system, she composed a very hasty reply.

'Thank you for holding out the olive branch. I'm actually on my way to Innsbruck to check out David Fischer's claim about my dad.'

She hoped Thomas Kirchmann wouldn't see her decision to go to Innsbruck as an insult to the memory of the father he seemed to regard almost as a holy martyr. With half an eye on an approaching air steward, she signed off, 'I'd be happy to meet you on Wednesday. Let me know what time suits you.' Anna switched off her phone.

Announcements came over the intercom, first in German then English; the doors were closed and the plane began to taxi slowly towards the runway.

Most of the passengers had gratefully settled down in their seats to catch up on their sleep. Others (*morning people, damn them,*) chatted to their companions. Tansy leaned in to Anna, looking distinctly freaked.

'Almost everyone's talking German,' she hissed.

Anna just nodded, unsure what the problem was.

'I've started teaching myself German online, but I only know sorry, thank you and where is the post office? I can't say anything useful.'

'Everybody in Innsbruck will speak English,' Anna reassured her. 'Pretty much anywhere you go nowadays there'll be someone who understands English. Even in China and Cambodia, people were desperate to try out their language skills on me.'

'That's so humbling,' Tansy said, ashamed.

'I did have one quite major misunderstanding in China,' Anna said, 'when I ended up eating the extremely private parts of a donkey.'

Tansy gave a little shriek. 'You didn't!'

'No, I did! Once it arrived there was no going back! It would have caused the worst kind of offence.'

Tansy looked at Anna with new respect.

'You went to China and Cambodia all by yourself, weren't you scared?'

'Not until that moment, no!' It was hard to explain to someone as sociable as Tansy that for half her lifetime, Anna had found a safety in solitude that she never experienced with her fellow humans. In the not-too-distant past, she'd have sawed off her own arm rather than share a hotel room, as she and Tansy were doing on this trip to save money.

The plane was picking up speed. The heavy rain was a steel-grey curtain making it impossible to see out. The plane began its final thundering approach down the runway, before launching them impossibly into the air. At this moment of no-return, Anna felt a rush of euphoria. She had surrendered herself to those fickle gods she didn't believe in, trusting they'd deliver her and Tansy safely to their destination.

She turned to smile at Tansy and saw that her friend's skin, normally a delicate amber-gold, was suddenly ashen.

'You know how I said I wanted adventures?' she said in a small voice. 'I've just remembered that I'm a tiny bit scared of flying!'

Anna gave her hand a squeeze. 'Don't be scared. Look, now we're up above the clouds. It's magic! And when we come down again, there'll be cake!'

It was early afternoon when they eventually touched down in Innsbruck. A twenty-minute taxi ride took them to the Altstadt, the Old Town, where they were staying.

'Let's dump our stuff and go straight out to lunch,' Tansy said as they pulled up outside their hotel. 'I've already seen about a dozen gorgeous, little cafés!'

Their small, family-run hotel was on a narrow street of mostly medieval buildings, but looked to have been built around three hundred years later.

The brisk, grey-haired lady on the desk wore a black dress with a white, hand-crocheted collar, giving her a look of a grandmother in an old Austrian portrait. She spoke fluent English just as Anna had promised. An expressionless teenage boy took them up in the lift – the old-fashioned kind in a brass cage – and he unlocked the door of a spacious twin-bedded room, then vanished without a word, before they could decide if they should tip him for his trouble.

Tansy admired their snow-white bed linen and exclaimed over the strangely shaped German pillows and quilts. Then she flung open the shutters and gave a shriek of delight at the panoramic view of mountains rising up above the higgledy-piggledy medieval skyline of the old town.

'Did we *die* on that plane?' she demanded. 'Because this is like my idea of heaven. I don't think I have ever – *ever* – breathed air this pure!'

'Not in Oxford, that's for sure!' said Anna.

Tansy stretched out her arms and went twirling around their room.

'I totally understand, now, why Maria thought the hills were alive with the sound of music!'

They washed and tidied themselves then went down to reception. When they stepped out of the lift they saw the teenage boy waiting glumly beside a pile of baggage, ready to show three new guests up to their rooms.

'That boy does not love his work,' Tansy whispered into Anna's ear. At the reception desk, the lady with the crocheted collar had been replaced by a friendly, ruddy-faced man in a striped waistcoat.

'Someone left a message for you.' He consulted a notepad. 'Herr Muller regrets that he is out of town, but his colleague Frau Brunner will meet with you instead.' He smiled as he added 'He says she will wait for you at 6.45, at the beer garden at Schwartzes Roessl – that is "the Black Horse" in English,' he explained.

Anna thanked him. 'We're just going to find somewhere to have lunch. Is there anywhere you'd recommend?'

He laughed. 'Oh, there are so many superb cafes in walking distance, but do you like sachertorte?'

'Yes!' Anna and Tansy said simultaneously.

'Then you should try Café Leopold. It is close to the Golden Roof, a very famous Innsbruck landmark.'

'You see,' Tansy said gleefully as they left the hotel. 'Now we're here everything's working out!'

Half an hour later, they were seated at one of Café Leopold's outdoor tables, eating something called Tiroler Bauerngroestl, in which tiny fried potatoes mingled with savoury cubes of pork and onion and everything was topped off with a fried egg. According to Tansy's guidebook, this hearty dish was especially beloved of Tyrolean mountaineers. For a while, they ate in companionable silence.

It was warm and sunny. Music floated from a nearby church. Early music was played on medieval instruments; a crystalline melody that perfectly suited the peaceful medieval square. Her eyes kept being drawn to the mountains that encircled the city like a snow-rimmed bowl. Like the air, the Alpine light had a purity you could almost touch or taste. Just at that moment, Oxford and England seemed very far away.

'Would it be *really* immature,' Tansy asked wistfully, when their sachertorte arrived, 'if I had cake for breakfast, lunch and dinner until we leave? I mean, this *is* like, *once* in a lifetime.'

'Hey, what goes on in Innsbruck, stays in Innsbruck!' Anna told her.

Tourists were shopping for souvenirs at a nearby stall selling cuckoo clocks and teddy bears in alpine climbing gear. Anna saw Tansy casting glances towards another group of obvious tourists forming around a short fair-haired man in medieval costume. Holding an ornate staff, he had an actor's presence, which his lack of inches did nothing to diminish.

'Shall we check out some of the must-sees in your guide-book?' Anna suggested. 'Later we can try out a different café, with different cake!'

Tansy watched as another two tourists joined the little group.

'Guided tours probably aren't your thing, are they?' She sounded wistful. 'It's just that Liam says, you should never pass up a chance to gather useful intel.' It was the first time that Liam's name had been mentioned since they'd left Oxford and Anna suspected it had only escaped now under extreme pressure.

No, tours weren't Anna's thing. Like sharing a room, it was something she didn't do. Until now, apparently. She signalled to the waiter for their bill.

'I agree with Liam,' she told her friend. 'Let's do it.'

'Seriously!' Tansy's face lit up. 'It's just, you know, since we're here . . .'

'Absolutely,' Anna said putting all possible conviction into her voice.

They tagged on to the tour, as the guide began to explain that the Golden Roof was, disappointingly, not made of solid gold, but from 2,738 gold-plated, copper tiles. The roof had been designed to shelter a kind of royal box, to afford the Hapsburg Emperor Maximilian a birds-eye view of the tournaments in the square below.

Anna admired the Golden Eagle hotel, where Napoleon had once stayed and some other hotel where the poet Goethe had holed up on his way to Italy. She followed the others down a medieval arcade, past leaded windows filled with dark, rich, glazed breads, smoked meats, sausage and exquisite patisserie. They wandered around the Court Church and dutifully inspected Maximilian's tomb, then Anna caught a glimpse of a smiling, old man, who was with another tour group and was guiltily reminded of the rift with her grandfather.

As they continued along Marie Theresien Strasse, Anna was still thinking about her grandfather. She'd told him that she and Tansy were going away for a city break, not mentioning which city. She disliked herself for keeping this information from him and didn't fully understand why she had.

'And this is Saint Anna's column,' the guide said. Surprised to hear her own name Anna was jolted back to the present. She looked up to see a landmark that seemed oddly familiar.

'In fact, the statue on top is of St Mary,' the guide explained, 'but it was dedicated on St Anne's day and so we call it Saint Anna's column.'

Anna felt a thrill of recognition. *This is where they stood.* This was where her parents had posed for an unknown photographer on their long-delayed honeymoon. In real life, the column, an unremarkable brown in the photograph, was made of a similar polished red marble to Maximilian's tomb.

She suddenly knew why they'd wanted the photo. They had stood on this exact spot and thought: we must take a picture to show Anna that there's an Austrian landmark which shares her name. Here in this city they had thought of her. She felt ridiculously moved.

They retraced their steps back along Marie Theresien Strasse into another shadowy medieval arcade. Anna breathed in the distilled fragrances of ground coffee and caramelised sugar, as their guide delivered his spiel on fourteenth-century signage, before leading them out into a hushed little cul-de-sac. The narrow houses painted in pale primrose, dull rose and pistachio, seemed taller in such a confined space. A ring-tailed dove walked about on the sun-warmed cobbles, untroubled by their presence. The only sound was the splashing of a fountain. They had halted outside what Anna took to be an exclusive jewellery shop.

Wondering why they were here, she glanced around for a street sign and felt her heart miss a beat. Kerzenstaendergasse. Candlestick Lane. She remembered Herr Kirchmann's words: 'My father had a gallery in Kerzenstaendergasse.'

She tried to catch Tansy's eye but her friend's attention was focussed on the guide as he said soberly, 'I have brought you to a place that you will rarely see mentioned in guide-books. In the nineteen-thirties and forties, this building was an art gallery belonging to a very brave man. His name was Michael Kirchmann.'

Anna heard Tansy's soft intake of breath. *A trail of pebbles*, Anna thought. Without trying, they had come back to the place where it had begun.

She let the guide's words flow over her as he related the same events Thomas Kirchmann had described to Anna that day in Pfeffers. She pictured towering pyres of burning canvases as the Kunstschutz disposed of artworks the Fuhrer had designated as 'degenerate'. She saw the cattle truck arriving under cover of night outside the apartment block, where David Fischer's father had lived as a little boy, then abruptly resurfaced to hear a horrified American woman exclaim, 'Gunned down in this darling little street? How *awful*!'

'As you see there is now a small fountain to honour his memory,' the guide said. 'If you don't read German, the words on the plaque say only, "Michael Kirchmann, a hero of Innsbruck."'

'Well, he was *definitely* one of the good guys, like Schindler,' another American woman said.

Everyone seemed moved by what they'd heard. *No wonder*, Anna thought. Thomas Kirchmann's father had died, not just to help Jews but to protect the noble cause of Art itself. Standing in this peaceful courtyard, where Michael Kirchmann's blood had been spilled over the cobbles, Anna longed to believe in this story of selfless courage. *Except*, she thought, *that would make David Fischer's version a lie . . .*

Back at their hotel, they rested their sore feet and then took turns to shower, before going out to meet Frau Brunner.

They set out through the silky, golden light of early evening and quickly found the beer garden. As they waited at the entrance, Anna saw a fair-haired woman walking slowly towards them, using a stick for support.

She smiled and called out, 'I think one of you must be Anna?'

Anna laughed in surprise. 'Yes! I'm not even going to ask how you could tell we were English! This is my friend Tansy. You must be Frau Brunner?'

'Clara, please. Let us first find a table. Fortunately, it is early so there is still plenty of choice.'

A waiter came to take their order.

'Shall I order beer for you?' Clara asked them. 'And pretzels? They are so good here.' She leaned her silver-topped cane against the table. For the first time, Anna saw that Clara's blonde hair was thickly threaded with grey. She was probably Isadora's age, but dressed more conservatively in a high-necked blouse, tweed jacket and skirt.

'So,' Clara said, 'to get down to business. I understand you have questions about the restitution of stolen artworks?' She smiled at their expressions. 'You are surprised to find me so blunt! But that is why you are here? You did not come to Innsbruck solely for a holiday?'

'We actually came for both,' Tansy said.

'But the artworks part is the main reason,' said Anna. Their beer arrived with the promised plate of pretzels. When the waiter had left Anna asked, 'how did you become involved with restitution?'

'In my former life I was an art historian,' Clara said. 'These days I am what you might describe as a family archivist. Nowadays, I prefer to do this only part-time, but I like to help Heinrich with this important work when I can.'

'Heinrich is Herr Muller?' Anna said. 'The lawyer?'

'Yes and very knowledgeable in this field. But I will try my best to answer any questions you may have.'

Anna broke off a glossy piece of pretzel. 'I'm guessing it must be quite a complex process to reunite claimants with their stolen artworks?'

'It is *incredibly* complex,' Clara said. 'Imagine, Anna, that – against all odds – you have survived the Holocaust. You have had every-thing stripped from you, everything that you thought you were: your profession, your home, your loved ones and finally the last little shreds of your humanity. Then, when the war is over and you try to reclaim that which is rightfully yours, you find that the Kunstschutz have sold your most precious possessions for profit or stored them away in some secret vault for future insurance. For these survivors, it is tragedy heaped on yet more tragedy.'

Clara took a sip of her beer. 'Even when lost paintings are successfully located, legitimate claimants find themselves having to compete with museums and galleries or super rich collectors. It's likely that they no longer have receipts or any written proof of ownership, assuming they ever had those in the first place. A painting might have been an old heirloom handed down through the generations, originally gifted by the artist to the family. He may have eventually become one of those artists who is nowadays revered as a genius, but back then he was just some rascal with gambling debts, who offered to paint his landlord a flattering portrait in lieu of rent!' She laughed. 'I am exaggerating of course, but you get the idea?'

'It sounds like a nightmare task,' Tansy said.

'It is.' Clara leaned forward and the flame of their tea-light bent very slightly in its glass holder. 'But it is a task that is *right*. Our work is about what is *owed* to these people, these survivors and their children and grandchildren.' She regarded them with her clear blue gaze. 'You understand that I am not referring only to money? We talk about "sentimental value" and it sounds so trivial, but what can be more important than the human heart? It is wrong that people should be profiting from such suffering. To my mind, it is the equivalent of blood diamonds.' She stopped. 'I'm sorry. I did not mean to make a speech. But we *have* to care where these paintings come from. It's our moral responsibility.'

Above them the mountains were gradually veiling themselves in violet shadows. Somewhere far off a dog barked, the sound carrying in the stillness.

'That's actually why I'm here.' At that moment, Anna felt almost as if her parents were listening, as if she'd waited her whole life to speak these words in this place. 'I have a – a particular concern that a very valuable painting, stolen during the war, may have passed through the hands of someone in my family. I'm worried that they might not have done the right thing.' She took a sip of her beer. 'I'm sorry. That sounded really incoherent.'

Clara shook her head. 'Not at all. I understand perfectly and I wish I could say this was unusual. After the war, all these wonderful paintings, drawings and engravings began to appear from out of the woodwork.' Her forehead puckered. 'Is that the correct expression? It was impossible for anyone to know how legitimate these sellers were. After all anyone could claim that something belonged to them or their old great-granny.' She gave them a fleeting smile. 'The first months after the war had ended were what you might term a free-for-all. Former Nazis, the Soviets, professional art thieves and opportunists of all political shades were all fighting for their share of the loot, before the window of opportunity slammed shut and law and order was restored. Again, I am over-simplifying, but yes, what you describe could have happened and we know that it did happen.'

'I don't care if it isn't unusual!' Anna was suddenly scalded with shame. 'It's unbearable, knowing that someone I was close to, someone I – I *loved*, might be involved in such a disgusting heinous thing.' Tansy touched her hand, concerned, but Anna went on talking. 'Hempels, that was my family's auction house, prides itself on being ethical and responsible, yet at some point I am afraid that it might have gone rotten.'

'*Hempels*?' Clara's blue gaze sharpened. 'I never thought,' she murmured almost to herself. 'Are you possibly related to Julian Hopkins?'

Anna stared at her, completely taken aback. 'He was my father. Did you ever meet him? He came to Innsbruck in the late eighties.'

'Your father came several times to Innsbruck,' Clara said to her surprise, 'and in between we corresponded. I was so very sorry to hear of his death.'

Anna felt her heart racing. 'Do you know – is it at all possible that these visits had anything to do with a stolen painting?'

Clara nodded. 'Julian consulted with me about several problem-atic paintings. Whenever he was concerned about the provenance of pieces that came into the auction house, he always called me or Heinrich.'

Anna could have wept with gratitude. She let this welcome news sink in before she said huskily, 'My dad was really involved in restitution – like you and Herr Muller?'

'In his quiet way.' Clara smiled and it was obvious that she remembered this diffident Englishman with affection. 'Your father was extremely anxious that no one should find out that he was helping us. Though he never said this in so many words, I sensed he was taking particular care to conceal his activities from a busi-ness partner of some kind.'

Tansy fidgeted with the thread of her Buddha bracelet. She was being careful not to intrude but Anna could hear her mentally yelling; *ask her about the Vermeer*!

Anna's mouth had gone dry. She quickly drank some of her

beer before she asked, 'have you ever heard of a Vermeer called A Study in Gold?'

She saw a change in Clara's eyes, as if an old sorrow had suddenly come close to the surface.

'*Ach*, that painting,' she said with a sigh. 'The trouble it has caused, you would think the artist himself put a curse on it.'

Tansy's eyes went wide. 'It actually *exists*?'

Anna found she'd forgotten to breathe.

'For years, your father searched to find the truth about that painting.' Clara shook her head. 'It haunted him, poor man.'

Anna felt herself go still inside. She heard Chris saying, 'Julian wanted to do the right thing because it was the right thing, but he preferred to do it behind the scenes. He never wanted recognition.' *He was still looking*, Anna thought. *He couldn't tell David Fischer, but my dad never stopped looking.* She felt her eyes sting with tears.

'But he never got anywhere,' Clara was saying. 'Until a few weeks before—' she checked herself, 'before his unfortunate death, he wrote saying that at last he had irrefutable evidence of its existence.'

Anna quickly brushed her hand across her eyes. 'Did he – did he say where it was?'

Clara shook her head. 'He didn't know, but he told me who did.' All at once, she looked old and very tired. 'I suspect you know this man, actually? He is now the new owner of Hempels.'

Anna felt as if she'd plummeted down several floors in a lift.

'Oh, dear God,' she whispered.

TWELVE

Anna woke from a fathoms-deep sleep to the distant hum and clatter of trams, and the clangour of foreign-sounding bells calling people to morning Mass. Sunlight filtered through gaps in the shutters, creating moving patterns on the walls and the white cotton of her quilt. For a moment, she lay, stunned by the fact of having slept at all and listened to the bells, imagining the sound travelling over the medieval rooftops and through the still alpine air of Innsbruck's Old Town. Then she remembered Candlestick Lane where Thomas Kirchmann's father had died in a hail of bullets; *Michael Kirchmann, a hero of Innsbruck.* And Clara Brunner's troubled blue gaze as she said: 'I think you already know him. He is the owner of Hempels now.'

Clara had left the beer garden soon afterwards, having made plans to meet a friend for supper. But even if they'd had more time to talk, Anna had been thrown into such confusion by what Clara had told her, that she couldn't begin to frame the questions she needed to ask: why her parents went to Innsbruck, for instance, and what – if anything – they'd found out? She was grateful to Clara for inviting them over for a proper Austrian breakfast, so that they could continue their conversation.

Anna heard Tansy's quilt rustle. A bare arm emerged as she consulted her phone, then she sat up, pushing her hair out of her eyes. In the dimness of their room, her dark curls stuck up in all directions.

'Are you awake?' she whispered.

'Yes. Just.'

'When did we agree to meet Clara for breakfast?'

'Around ten, but I need coffee first.'

'How long did I live with you, Anna Hopkins?' Tansy said, shaking her head. 'Of *course* you need coffee!'

When Anna emerged from the bathroom, her friend, still in her sleep shorts and camisole, was just setting down a tray, on which two steaming cups of coffee nestled beside a plate of wafer-thin almond biscuits.

'Room service,' she said, beaming. 'I love hotels! I think I could live in a hotel!'

'You're like Jake,' Anna said. 'Every time he goes somewhere new he says, "I could live here!"' She took a grateful sip of velvety continental coffee. 'I wish I could be like that, but it's like there's some invisible magnet that's always pulling me back home.'

'To Oxford?'

'It's Oxford for now, before that it was wherever I was living at the time.'

'How do you feel about – you know – what Clara told us.'

'Unbelievably relieved about my dad. Utterly confused about

everything else.' Anna looked at Tansy over the rim of her coffee cup. 'I always felt there was something Herr Kirchmann wasn't telling me, but out-and-out lying? I like to think I'd have sensed it if he was stringing me along, but my track record isn't great as you know.' She gave her friend a wan smile.

Tansy went off to shower. Anna dressed in a light sweater and jeans, then took out the small envelope she'd slipped into her travel bag before she left home and drew out three photos: The one of her, Bonnie and Jake; the badly faded snap of her parents in Innsbruck; a rare picture of herself, the one with all her siblings that she'd found when she was searching through the trunk. She sat studying their four young faces. She had never felt close to Will or Dan, but Lottie had been different. Six-year old Lottie had loved her out-of-control teenage sister passionately and against all reason, so that it was impossible not to love her back. Seeing her glowing intelligent little face, Anna felt an ache that would never fade. If she'd lived, Lottie would have been a couple of years younger than Tansy now. Who would that loving, little six-year-old have grown up to be? Anna wondered, then quickly pushed the thought away.

She felt as if she was trying to fit not just one but two, or even three, puzzles together and all the edges were obstinately refusing to match up. A half-formed thought kept nudging at the underside of her mind. Something about fathers and sons and their different legacies: Thomas Kirchmann, proud son of the hero of Innsbruck; David Fischer, who'd made his father's quest his life's work; her dad, Julian, who had dreaded growing cold and corrupt like Charles. Not to mention Ralph and Dominic Scott-Neville. But in this tangle of lives, one constant kept recurring: Hempels, her father's auction house.

A terrible suspicion had begun to dawn on Anna, too terrible to voice aloud. *What if her family had been murdered because of David Fischer's Vermeer?*

Tansy came out of the bathroom, trailing wafts of her favourite, white jasmine and mint cologne.

'You OK?'

Anna mustered her brightest smile. 'I'm fine! Let's go.'

Clara's home was just off Innstrasse, named for the river which gave Innsbruck its name. They were a few minutes early, so they walked beside the water for a time, looking up at the row of brightly-coloured houses with the mountains beyond. If Tansy noticed that Anna was unusually quiet, she was too tactful to say.

At last they made their way through narrow lanes to Clara's apartment in Museumgasse. As they turned into her street, they came to a bewildered standstill. A police car was parked up on the pavement in front of Clara's building. Clara herself was coming out of the building, limping and looking pale and shaken, escorted by two Austrian police officers. A man in a leather jacket and jeans waited by the car, arms folded and emanating stony-faced authority. Anna barely had time to take this in, before Tansy yanked her back out of sight.

'Don't let them see you!'

'What are you *doing*?' Anna hissed. 'We should go and see if Clara needs help.'

'Not a good idea,' Tansy hissed back. 'That man by the car? He was at the hotel yesterday waiting for the lift with a bunch of other people, as we were going out to lunch and later he joined our tour.'

'Are you sure?'

'One hundred percent,' Tansy said in a whisper. 'He wasn't dressed like that guy in Chicago P.D. yesterday though. He smiled at me. I thought he was a bit lechy.'

Anna risked another peek and saw someone looking so much like the tough, TV cop that she would have laughed, if she hadn't been so scared. She could hear the men talking, but their German was too fast and too colloquial for her to follow.

'I didn't think anything of it at the time,' Tansy was saying. 'It's a little tourist town. You're bound to run into the same people. But now . . .' She gave a shiver.

Then, amongst the rapid stream of German, Anna heard the man in the leather jacket say shockingly and unmistakably, 'Anna Hopkins.' She felt the tiny hairs rise on the back of her neck.

Tansy's eyes went wide with shock. 'Listen,' she whispered, 'I didn't want to say before, but that guy has got a really suspicious-shaped lump under his jacket, like a holster with a gun in it.'

'How can you possibly tell that?' Anna's heart was thudding.

Tansy gave her a look. 'I *know*, OK.'

Anna had another cautious peep. Clara was in the back of the car now, with one of the Polizei. The leather-jacketed man, who Tansy had recognised from their hotel, was in the passenger seat. The officer who was driving did a fast U-turn and an elderly woman, who had come out to walk her giant white poodle, stopped open-mouthed, as her neighbour was taken away. For an instant, Anna was equally stunned by this surreal event. Then it flooded back to her, the fear she hadn't dared to speak aloud.

'We've got to get out right now,' she told Tansy.

Tansy just nodded.

'We'll go back to grab our stuff and jump on a train.' It was only rarely that Anna got to glimpse Tansy the gangster's daughter, but this was one of those times.

'I'm feeling totally paranoid now,' Tansy confessed as they hurried back to their hotel. 'Yesterday if people were looking at us, I thought it was because we were cute. Now I'm worried they're concealing side-arms.'

'They're not looking,' Anna said, still feeling that chilling prickle on the back of her neck. 'They've got no reason to look.'

But when they walked into the little family hotel that had seemed so friendly the previous day, Anna was immediately, ridiculously self-conscious. Judging from Tansy's bright chatter, as the grand-motherly woman on the desk handed over their key, she felt the same.

'Did you feel like her eyes were following us?' Anna whispered as the door to the old-fashioned brass cage slid shut and the lift started to ascend.

'It's like everyone's been exchanged for pod people,' Tansy whispered and they giggled, slightly hysterically.

Back in their room they packed their bags at lightning speed. Not wanting to wait for the lift, or worse, risk getting into the lift with someone who might drag them off to an Austrian jail, they stole down the back stairs.

Even before they reached reception, they could hear the woman berating her teenage grandson for his permanent state of gloom. 'Dein missmutiges Gesicht erschrickt die Gaeste,' she scolded, which Anna roughly translated as 'Your miserable face is enough to frighten the guests.'

Under cover of this family quarrel, Tansy and Anna slipped out into the street and began to power-walk in the direction of the train station.

'Damn,' Anna said abruptly. 'I've still got our key.'

'We can post it back later.'

'It won't take a moment.' Anna made to turn back.

'Are you crazy?' Tansy protested. 'They'll have spares.'

A police car pulled up with a squeal of brakes. Two police officers, Anna wasn't sure if they were the same two and the man in the leather jacket, jumped out and disappeared inside the hotel.

She dropped the key in the street and they ran.

'People do run for trains,' Tansy panted. 'It's not suspicious in the least.' Anna was past caring. She just wanted to get the hell out of Innsbruck, before their unknown pursuer caught up with them.

They ran, occasionally shifting down to speed-walking, all the way to the station.

'Do you mind getting the tickets?' Anna was gasping for breath now. 'I'll call Jake. If something does go horribly wrong, we might need someone to be our advocate.'

'You swear they'll speak English.' Tansy looked anxious.

'Yes, I swear.' Anna had already pulled up Jake's number.

Tansy hovered. 'So, um, I'm getting us tickets for the next train to Vienna?'

'No! The next train out of Austria!'

'Jesus, this is scary,' Tansy said and sprinted towards the ticket office.

Anna's heart sank as Jake's phone went straight to voicemail. In her panic, her words tripped over each other.

'Jake, sorry to sound dramatic but someone's after us. Tansy saw this guy in our hotel and again on our guided tour of the Old Town, then this morning we went to meet someone. Clara Brunner, she's involved in art restitution, she knew my dad. But when we arrived at her apartment he was outside – the man, I mean – with the Polizei! And Jake, I heard the man say my name! And then they just took Clara away. We didn't want to be next, so we're at the station and we're getting the first train out of Austria.' She saw Tansy emerging from the ticket office, a lone figure in a vast space of steel and glass. 'I've got to go; I just wanted you to know.'

She hurried to meet Tansy. 'Did you get the tickets?'

'No,' she said tersely. 'There's a train to Venice but it doesn't leave for an hour and a half.'

'We can't wait that long!'

'There is one train that's leaving for Paris in twenty minutes.'

'So why didn't you get tickets?' Anna could have shaken her.

Tansy gave a despairing shrug. 'Because it'll cost us over five grand.'

'You're kidding! Is it covered in gold and jewels?'

'Almost. It's the bloody Orient Express. You have to get the tickets from a special booking office. Oh, and I embarrassed myself by saying "merci" instead of "danke".' Tansy was near to tears. 'What are we going to do?'

They stared at each other, breathing fast from running and from fright. The available credit limit on Anna's card was slightly under a grand, less than one fifth of the money they'd need for the fare. Tansy didn't even possess a credit card.

Anna had no clue what they were going to do. While they stood dithering about train tickets, the police were probably already on their way. *It's anyone who gets close to the Vermeer,* she thought. *Lili Rossetti and David Fischer, Clara.* She felt a deep trembling start inside. She mustn't think about her family now or she'd fall apart.

'Dammit,' Tansy said. She took out her phone.

'Tansy, no!' Anna was mortified. 'We can't ask Liam to bail us out.'

'I'm *not* asking Liam.' Suddenly tight-lipped, Tansy was rapidly entering numbers into her phone. She shot a look at Anna. 'There's only one person I know with that kind of money. Oh, hi Dad. Yes, fine, thanks. But my friend and I— Yes, you've met her. Frankie, listen, I need a *really* big favour. We're in Austria and we need to leave in a bit of a . . .' Still talking, she began to sprint across the station. For the first time, Anna properly registered the retro-style ticket booth, decked out in splendid blue and gold.

The one time Anna had met him, Frankie McVeigh had sworn to his daughter that he'd changed, that he'd forsaken his old life along with all his criminal associates. But if he had that kind of easy access to a spare five grand, no questions asked, this declaration seemed slightly premature. In any case, Anna doubted that he'd be able to magic them tickets at such short notice. Which was just as well since she knew she'd feel queasy about taking his money or, more likely, someone *else's* money that he'd acquired.

Then she thought of the man she'd seen leaning on the police car, with that air of cold satisfaction at a job well done. *The man who knew my name*, she thought, with a flicker of terror, and knew she and Tansy couldn't afford that kind of moral squeamishness. They had to get away.

To her surprise, she saw Tansy hurrying back towards her.

'God bless Frankie,' she said shakily.

'He got us tickets?' Anna laughed with disbelief. 'In less than five minutes, your dad got us a berth on the Orient Express?'

'I know it's wrong,' Tansy said, 'but I didn't know what else to do.'

Anna checked her watch. They had approximately fifteen minutes before departure. She gave a surreptitious glance around the station concourse. No blue-uniformed Polizei. No leather-jacketed man.

The entrance to their platform was cordoned off with plushy ropes in the same distinctive blue and gold. A sign said *The Orient Saxe-Barthelemy Express*. A self-possessed woman, wearing a modern approximation of Twenties-style livery, checked their passports and a cheerful porter – also in vintage style blue and gold livery – appeared, unhooked the ropes and picked up their bags.

'If you would just follow me, *Mademoiselles*. I will show you to your cabin,' he said. Tansy turned to Anna and breathed, 'Oh. My. God.'

Anna followed the porter on to the platform feeling as if she was dreaming. She barely had time to take in the gleaming, dark-blue, express train, with its lovingly-restored old carriages, before they were hurrying along to find their coach.

'Dad says sorry he could only get us one cabin. It's a double,' Tansy reassured her quickly. 'But I think he felt like he should have done better.'

Each coach bore the name, in gilded letters, of a figure out of classical mythology. Their coach was *Ariadne*.

'It was so last-minute,' Tansy added, as they followed the porter up the steps. 'Frankie had to pay over the odds to get us on at all.'

'He paid *more* than five grand!' By this stage, Anna was almost beyond being astonished. 'Your dad must *really* love you!'

'I guess,' Tansy admitted reluctantly. Her relationship with Frankie McVeigh was best described as 'turbulent'. 'I'll find a way to pay him back though, don't worry.'

'*We'll* find a way,' Anna said.

But by then they were inside the Orient Express and Tansy was gazing around like a child who had accidentally found her way into Hogwarts. *Saxe-Barthelemy* had recreated the perfect fantasy of a 1920s travel experience. Their version of the legendary Orient Express had Art Deco interiors, with polished walnut panelling and muted blue and gold upholstery. It smelled of excellent continental coffee and an elusive, unnameable fragrance, which somehow conjured up the ghostly perfumes of wealthy and glamorous women gone by.

'Here is your cabin, *Mademoiselles.*' The porter set down their bags. 'I hope you enjoy your time with us.'

'This is insane,' Tansy whispered. 'Can you even believe we're here?'

Anna shook her head. The subtle SB monogram was everywhere, on the soft blue and gold Art Deco sofa, the corners of the curtains. They peeped into the tiny bathroom and Tansy exclaimed over the bath essences and lotions, the fluffy robes and slippers.

'Tansy,' Anna said quietly. 'Not to spoil the moment, but for once in my life I'd feel better if we could be with other people. Until we're out of the station.'

'Good thought,' Tansy said.

The crowded bar car was pure Art Noveau, smelling of schnapps and coffee, and featuring a gleaming, baby, grand piano. Tiffany lamps, like branching blossoms, cast a blushing pink light. It was impossible to imagine anything frightening ever happening in this rose-tinted space.

But frightening things can happen anywhere, as Anna knew too well. She couldn't stop glancing at her watch. She sipped at her coffee, dimly aware of a gentle babble of different languages: Italian, French, German and Russian, as well as English. Someone said in an American accent, 'How is your headache, Countess?'

Tansy's eyes went wide. 'Countess?' she mouthed, then had to fight a fit of giggles.

'Sorry,' she whispered, 'this is *so* nuts!' She saw Anna's eyes stray back to the platform. 'They won't guess,' she said. 'This is the most outrageous escape since forever.'

We haven't escaped yet, Anna thought. It made it more frightening that they had no idea who they were escaping *from*. Clara Brunner was undeniably a good person, yet she'd been taken away like a criminal. The randomness of it, the suddenness with which disaster had struck, chilled her blood. If the Austrian Polizei burst in now, it would make no difference that they were on a luxury train.

Tansy quickly covered Anna's hand with her own.

'It's going to be OK. The train's moving. No stopping now till Paris.'

Anna watched the platform slowly sliding past, and breathed out for the first time, since Tansy had recognised the man from their hotel.

'Anna.' Tansy suddenly sounded so anxious that Anna turned from the window, alarmed.

'What?'

'What do people wear for dinner on the Orient Express?' Now the immediate danger had passed Tansy had moved on to new concerns.

'If you're worried, we can eat in our cabin,' Anna suggested.

'Are you kidding!' said Tansy. 'When they've got Michelin star restaurants!'

They decided to have lunch in the dining car, having missed out on breakfast.

'Not to mention, inadvertently running a marathon,' Tansy pointed out. Then they returned to their cabin where they settled themselves grandly on their sofa and watched the passing scenery. The train began to make its unhurried way across the Austrian alps and the celestially lovely, flower meadows, waterfalls and streams, seen from their privileged surroundings, helped to banish the shadows of their morning.

They rested, chatted and gazed their fill at the views, then went for a leisurely afternoon tea in the dining car. Tansy, being Tansy, started chatting to some passengers at the next table: two retired colonels and a world-weary literary agent, who had recently sold her agency and was, as she joked, working her way down her bucket list before she decided what to do next – the Orient Express being number one on her list.

'Of course, the original Orient Express used to go to Istanbul,' said the more elderly of the colonels, who had a moustache the colour of iron filings.

His friend poured more Lapsang into his delicate china cup.

'I believe some of the new ones still do,' he pointed out.

'But the original train would have gone to the *old* Istanbul,' the agent reminded him, piling cream on her scone. '*So* much more romantic.'

'So, what brings you two girls on the Orient Express?' asked the first colonel. 'Surely you are too young to be needing a bucket list just yet?'

Tansy and Anna traded discreet glances.

'Well,' said Tansy confidingly. 'My father bought us tickets for a surprise present. We didn't even know we were coming until this morning, did we, Anna?'

'Heavens,' said the agent, taken aback. 'What a generous father!'

'I'm very lucky,' Tansy said demurely.

'I believe we've just crossed into Germany,' said the colonel with the moustache, glancing out of the window. 'Think I'll go for a snooze till dinner.'

Anna and Tansy went back to their cabin, where they experimented with outfits and hairstyles until Tansy was satisfied they wouldn't shame themselves at dinner. Then Anna read her copy of *A Moveable Feast* until it was time to change into their modest finery.

In the dining car, candle-lit tables were set with white linen, heavy silver, fresh flowers and fabulous Lalique glasses. The menu included citrus roasted skate-wing with truffle mash, tagliatelle of wild mushrooms with a poached hen's egg and parmesan *tuile*, and a salad with wild flowers and chamomile curd.

Neither Tansy nor Anna were drinkers, but Tansy said Frankie would expect them to get the full benefit from his five thousand quid, so they took advantage of the plentiful champagne.

'*Dom Perignon*?' Tansy said in awe, when she saw the label, 'isn't that the super-posh kind?' Then, they moved on to the excellent red wine and became pleasantly tiddly.

'This is *so* perfect.' Tansy said lowering her voice. 'Travelling across Europe with total strangers. It's like we're starring in our own Agatha Christie. I still have no idea which one is the countess though, have you?'

'No, but I'm picturing Dame Maggie Smith.' Anna saw Tansy take out her phone. 'Are you taking pics for Isadora?'

She nodded. 'She'd love this so much.'

'Isadora was *born* for the Orient Express,' Anna agreed.

'These pralines are amazing,' Tansy said dreamily, moments later. 'I could eat them all day.'

She went to pour them more wine. Anna tried to cover her glass.

'No, honestly, Tansy. I'm already losing the power of speech!'

'Just a little drop,' Tansy insisted. 'I'm going to make a toast. "To Frankie,"' she said, clinking her glass against Anna's. '"For services rendered!"' The happily inebriated Americans at the next table, echoed, 'To Frankie!' and cheerfully raised their glasses.

'Pity we didn't video that for your dad,' Anna whispered as they got up to leave.

'Nah,' Tansy said, 'Frankie has a high enough opinion of himself already.'

Live jazz floated from the bar car; a woman singing with a voice like golden gravel. The bluesy sound followed them down the corridor. Through the windows, Anna saw endless, rushing forest lit only by the impervious, blue-white light of stars.

They returned to their cabin to find that their steward had folded away their sofa and made up their bunk beds with crisp white linen, under hyacinth-blue quilts, patterned with gold art deco fans.

Anna came out of the shower to see Tansy softly closing the cabin door on their steward. She turned, obviously startled to see Anna. Anna thought she looked faintly guilty. Her friend quickly held up two Aegean-blue glass bottles.

'I thought all that champagne might make us dehydrated,' she said airily, 'so I rang for extra mineral water.'

Tansy went to use the shower. Anna had just climbed into the bottom bunk, her skin smelling of Moroccan Rose shower essence, when her phone rang. It was Jake. Anna had spoken to him very briefly while they were having lunch, to let him know they were safe.

'You and Tansy are still Ok?' he asked at once.

'We're more than Ok,' she reassured him. 'We're in the lap of luxury. I'm not sure if we'll ever be able to go back to ordinary life! We get into the Gare de Lyons around 11 a.m. tomorrow.'

Jake gave his husky laugh. 'You know, darlin', sometimes it feels like I'm dating the Scarlet Pimpernel! But you're quite sure nobody followed you from Innsbruck?'

'No. And nobody has tried to push us out of the train. Sorry, you must think I was really overreacting.'

'No, Anna, I don't. You and I both know there are no coincidences.' She heard a muffled announcement coming over a tannoy. 'I'll meet you guys at Gare de Lyons tomorrow morning. You can tell me all about it then.'

She closed her eyes in relief, if Jake was with her she could cope with anything.

Tansy came back from her shower. They switched off the lamps and settled down to sleep.

'Have you decided what you're going to do, when this is all over, now you've given up your job?' Tansy asked.

'Nope,' Anna said. 'Don't laugh but I had this idea I might train as a therapist. I sent for loads of post-grad prospectuses, but so far they're still sitting on my desk.'

Her phone lit up. To her surprise, she had an email from Heinrich Muller. Anna turned her lamp back on and read his startling message.

'Oh, my God, Tansy, listen.' She read the email aloud.

My colleague Clara Brunner regrets she is no longer able to assist you in your inquiries, as she is being investigated in connection with a serious fraud. Frau Brunner and I both urge you and your friend to please take care.

Tansy sat up. 'That doesn't make sense. If it's a fraud case, why would the police be interested in us? We'd just that minute arrived in Austria.'

'I know. It's crazy.'

'But that guy knew where we were staying,' Tansy said. 'I mean, the only people who knew we were in Innsbruck were Isadora and Liam, oh plus Isadora's ditzy friend.'

'Herr Kirchmann knew,' Anna admitted. 'I emailed him on the plane.' She switched off her lamp.

Tansy shifted in her bunk.

'Do you think David Fischer was right and that story Herr Kirchmann tells everyone about his dad is a lie?'

'I honestly don't know.' This was just one of many things she'd have liked to ask Clara.

'Do you think Thomas Kirchmann believes it though?'

'He made *me* believe it,' Anna said.

Yet her father had written to Clara claiming that Kirchmann knew the whereabouts of the Vermeer. An art-lover, a hero's son, befriender of Afghani taxi drivers and Father Christmassy provider of afternoon teas . . . Was Thomas Kirchmann maybe just a bit too good to be true? Anna wondered.

'I'm supposed to be meeting him on Wednesday,' she remembered.

'You're not still going? Not after Clara?'

'Not sure. I'm still thinking about that.' Anna said.

Overtired from a day that had started with church bells in Innsbruck and was ending in a bunk on the Orient Express, via the thrilling silliness of being rescued by a notorious gangland boss, she was experiencing a sense of anti-climax, followed by her usual tedious feelings of failure and shame.

I was in Innsbruck less than 24 hours, she thought, *I had one conversation with Clara Brunner and just hours later she was taken in for questioning on some spurious charge. I'm like David Fischer's Vermeer.* 'The trouble that painting has caused, I could almost think the artist had cursed it,' Clara had said last night.

Now they were hurtling through the night at vast expense, but no nearer to solving the mystery. If Anna had been at home, these thoughts would inevitably have driven her to her murder cupboard. But she was trapped in a claustrophobic bunk bed, listening to her friend's soft breathing.

And furtive rustling, she realized.

The seductive scent of chocolate pralines unfurled in the dark. It seemed that Tansy had asked their steward for more than just mineral water.

'Tansy Lavelle,' Anna hissed. 'What do you think you're doing?'

She heard Tansy's unrepentant giggle. 'I know I'm evil, but I'll probably never have another chance to lie in bed on the Orient Express eating gorgeous chocolates again.'

'Throw me one down,' Anna said, 'and I promise not to tell.'

'Have two,' Tansy offered. 'That steward gave me loads. Plus, what happens on the Orient Express stays on the Orient Express, right?'

THIRTEEN

'Can't we just have breakfast in here?' Anna had woken with a mild hangover, and the thought of lively morning chatter made her want to barricade herself in their cabin. 'You can if you like.' Tansy called from the tiny bathroom.

Unfairly, Tansy didn't seem to be suffering any ill effects from all the free champagne. Anna reluctantly followed her to the dining car and ordered coffee, croissants and fresh fruits. The coffee helped a little. Tansy wandered away to chat with the elderly colonels. Anna watched the French countryside, with its donkeys and vineyards and sleepy, little villages rolling by, secretly counting down the minutes till she could see Jake.

'I've seen her!' Tansy was back, breathless with excitement.

Anna gave her a blank stare. 'Seen who?'

'The countess. She's – you have to see her.'

'Why?'

They were travelling more slowly now as they passed through the suburbs of Paris. Anna wanted to go back and finish her packing before they disembarked. Tansy looked astonished.

'Why do you have to see her? Because she's *amazing*! Plus, you might never ever see another real live countess!'

Anna followed her wearily to the colonels' table. Everyone exchanged polite pleasantries, then Tansy gave Anna a sharp dig in the ribs.

'That's her, two tables down, look, with the amazing hair.'

Tansy's countess was eighty years old and Anna had to admit she was a vision. Her pure white hair fell silkily past the shoulders of an exotically-patterned, buttercup-yellow garment that seemed part kimono, part dressing gown. Diamonds flashed in her ears and on her knobbly fingers. Her bony old face was alight with humour and mischief, as she read something out to her male companion from her copy of Le Parisienne, peering through the kitschiest pair of spectacles Anna had ever seen.

'I bet *she's* had a lover, or twelve,' Tansy murmured as they made their way back to their cabin. 'Don't you think she'd get on with Isadora?'

'I think she actually *is* Isadora,' Anna said. 'In an alternate reality.'

'I just thought she was like, the *Spirit* of the Orient Express,' Tansy said. 'Aren't you glad you saw her?'

Anna laughed. 'Yes, Tansy, I'm glad I saw her.'

'And you're glad you ate chocolate pralines in the dark, aren't you,' Tansy said earnestly, 'instead of lying awake telling yourself how useless you are? I bet you slept like a baby?'

Anna felt her cheeks burn. 'Am I that obviously neurotic?'

Tansy gave her a brief hug. 'No, but you're my friend and I feel stuff.' She pulled a face. 'That's one good thing I've inherited from my old man.'

Twenty minutes later, they were descending from their coach into the bustling, wonderfully ornate, Gare de Lyons. They began to make their way through the crowds. Suddenly, Anna saw him on the platform; his arms filled with dusky, antique pink roses. Jake saw her at the same moment and next minute he was hugging both her and Tansy, until Tansy squeaked, 'Eek, thorns!' and he quickly let them go.

'Did you buy up every rose in Paris?' Tansy demanded laughing.

'Hey, how often do you get to meet two, beautiful women off the Orient Express?' he said solemnly. 'You got to do it right. Sorry about the thorns though!'

Anna couldn't bear to let go of his hand, couldn't stop looking at him.

'It's so good to see you.'

'And you, darlin',' he said, 'and I am so glad you're both OK.' He looked tired, but as always utterly calm. She saw the fair glints in his hair, the here-and-gone-again smile which revealed the tiny chip in his front tooth. He smelled of clean cotton and crushed roses. He led them through the station under ornate stone arches. The noise was tremendous, the air full of echoing tannoys, departing trains, a babble of French, all ricocheting off the high glass and iron roof.

'We're getting a cab to the Gare du Nord,' he told them, raising his voice so they could hear. 'We'll go back to Oxford, then we'll sit down and try to figure out what the hell is going on.'

Next day, they all met up at Isadora's. Anna had texted their friend from the Eurostar, to let her know that she and Tansy had come back early. Isadora had replied, inviting them to bring Jake over for Sunday lunch.

'You can pick up Bonnie then. Just go back to Park Town and have some time with Jake.'

When Isadora led them through into the kitchen, Bonnie let out one of her rare excited barks and flung herself down at their feet, uttering the little moans and groans which Anna now understood to be shameless solicitations to be stroked.

'Young *lady*,' Jake teased her, as he rubbed her belly in the way she adored. 'Where is your *decorum*?'

'Bet you don't say that to Anna!' Tansy was perched in the small wickerwork chair, holding Hero on her lap. She'd been here a while, Anna thought. Isadora's books and papers had already been cleared away and the table was laid with glasses and cutlery for their lunch.

Jake looked up from Bonnie. 'Can I smell roasting chicken?'

'You can,' Isadora said, 'and I'm making an apple pie though I know you don't eat pudding, Jake.' She went back to peeling a large, Bramley apple, the shiny green skin falling in a single obedient curl before her knife. 'Tansy's been telling me about your adventures,' she shot at Anna. 'I'm *so* cross with you for going on the Orient Express without me! I've never ever been.' But Isadora had a smile in her voice so Anna knew she wasn't *seriously* cross.

Tansy's phone pinged. She glanced at her screen and looked furious.

'If Frankie refers to me as a chip off the old block one more time I'll – I'll bloody get a contract taken out on him, seriously I will!'

'Why are you a chip off the old block?' Anna asked puzzled. 'Oh, because we had to leave Austria in a hurry?'

Tansy was still scowling at her phone.

'I'm nothing like him.'

'Except for "feeling stuff",' Anna reminded her. 'Plus, you've got to admit we'd have been totally stuck without his help.'

'I know. But I don't have to *like* it,' Tansy said fiercely, then she flashed Anna a mischievous grin. 'It was brilliant fun though, wasn't it?'

'Ok,' Jake said, 'so while our lunch is cooking, how about you guys give me some help reconstructing events?' He got out a lined jotter and pen.

'Well, presumably it starts with finding poor Lili after our murder mystery weekend.' Isadora dropped a handful of apple peels into her compost bin.

'David Fischer would disagree,' Anna said. 'For him everything went back to the Vermeer.'

'This is getting to be too much of a tradition,' Tansy said abruptly. 'It's like those death dinners.'

'What on earth is a *death dinner*, darling?' Isadora went to her fridge and took out a chilled wodge of short-crust pastry wrapped in cling-film.

'When a character dies in a long-running TV series, all the actors and the crew hold a death dinner in his honour. This feels like that.'

'But nobody died this time,' Isadora objected. 'Yes, the police took Clara away, but for all you know she's already been allowed home.'

Tansy still looked mutinous, but Anna suspected she was mostly upset because of her dad.

'Let's start with Lili,' Jake said. 'We can broaden it out later.'

He began to create a simple spidergram on his pad, starting in the centre with finding Lili's body, then connecting each subsequent event from that central hub: Anna's return to her father's auction house where she'd first heard of the Vermeer; David Fischer's accusations against her father; the visit to the Wennekes Institute; finding proof that David and Lili were allies; their conversation with Fischer at Dog-Eared Adventures; photographic evidence that Jewish artworks, supposedly under Michael Kirchmann's protection, had been displayed in Nazi homes; David's death in his blazing bookshop; the visit to Tallis, who backed-up David's claim that stolen paintings had been taken as bribes to help at least one Russian defector get to the West; the Scott-Nevilles, who had apparently wielded some mysterious influence over Charles Hopkins and possibly over her father, but who Thomas Kirchmann denied doing business with.

Anna stood watching Jake's hand move across the pad, his face in profile, feeling the quiet strength coming from him. She remembered him waiting on the platform, his arms full of roses. Suppose she and Jake had never met? Suppose she'd never brought Bonnie back from the rescue shelter? How different, how barren, would her life be now? As if reading her thoughts, Jake reached up, took her hand and quickly kissed the inside of her wrist.

'What else?'

'Restitution,' she said, 'Links with the Wennekes Institute and with Hempels. Julian helped Clara with restitution. Lili worked in the same field.'

'I'm making gravy,' Isadora said rather sternly. 'Lunch is almost ready.'

Jake obediently put his pad away.

'Yes, Ma'am. Let me help bring the dishes.'

They sat around the table, eating Isadora's roast chicken, with perfect roast potatoes (crispy on the outside, soft and fluffy within) and minted carrots and peas. Tansy reminisced happily about the splendours of the Orient Express and their sighting of a real, live Countess.

'Countess of *where*, I wonder,' Isadora mused.

Everyone except Jake had apple pie, then Tansy made coffee and Jake brought out his jotter and started on a fresh page. At the top, he wrote in thick capitals. SUSPECTS.

Isadora stirred sugar into her coffee.

'Can I ask, what you intend to do with all this? Are you planning to take your suspicions to the police?'

Her voice was so sharp that Anna and Tansy stared at her.

'Because, before you take that step,' Isadora went on, 'I think we need to consider that there may be alternative explanations for absolutely everything that's happened.'

'You *seriously* think—' Tansy started. Anna thought of the stony-faced man with the Polizei. She thought of the shock and fear written on Clara's face and her own terror as they fled Innsbruck.

'Do you think we're making all this up?' Anna was as astonished as if Isadora had slapped her.

'No, darling girl, I'm *not* saying that. I just want us all to stop and *think*, instead of react. What I really want is to stop any more people getting hurt.'

'Amen to that,' Jake said. 'But—'

'For instance, it could be that Lili's murder had nothing to do with David and the Vermeer. Her husband could have paid someone to have her killed. It happens.'

'Yes,' Tansy said, 'but Isadora—'

'And the book shop fire,' Isadora continued imperturbably, as if she was deconstructing some hapless student's essay. 'You saw what a death trap it was, Anna. I very much doubt it was up to code.'

'But we *saw* Clara being taken away,' Tansy said. 'We *heard* the man say Anna's name!'

'Darling, you spoke with Clara for an hour or less. I know you liked her, but that doesn't mean she wasn't guilty of *something*! The police could have read her diary, realized she'd had a meeting with an Anna Hopkins and just wanted to . . .'

'. . . eliminate me from their inquiries?' Anna suggested icily.

'Well, yes,' Isadora said. 'It's a possibility.'

'What about Tallis?' Jake asked. 'He as good as admitted that the Vermeer had been used to bribe a British agent to assure someone's safe passage to the West.'

Isadora's face darkened. 'Tallis, as I should know, is a compulsive game player. I wouldn't trust him as far as I could *spit*.'

'But Clara *knew* about the painting.' Anna was trying to keep her temper.

'I'm not disbelieving you, Anna, please don't think that. But it seems to me that this Vermeer has almost gone into the realms of folk lore or urban legends. No-one's seen it, but everyone knows somebody's brother who has. And we all know what happens when people rush in making false allegations.'

Isadora didn't so much as glance at Anna but Anna felt exactly as if she had. Suddenly all the anger went out of her.

'Yes,' she said very quietly. 'Of course, you're right.'

'I just want to remind you that there's *always* another narrative, that we need to be cautious,' Isadora said. 'I loathe playing devil's advocate, but you have all become very precious to me and I don't want any more harm to come to you.'

Jake just listened, doodling abstractedly on his pad. Tansy shifted in her chair. She let out a sigh.

'I suppose I might have got a bit carried away, wanting an

adventure, instead of, you know, confronting my actual life like a grownup.'

Anna thought of all those unopened prospectuses on her desk. Had she also been afraid to be a proper grownup? Had she simply switched from pursuing justice for her family, to an equally obsessive search for some elusive, new, holy grail? Was this yet another of those dead-end strategies that she'd devised to protect herself from real life?

She drank the last of her coffee. Keeping her tone light, she asked Isadora, 'So have you heard any more from Valentin? Is he still badgering you to go to Prague?'

That night, Anna was curled up on the small sofa in her kitchen, a small pile of prospectuses at her feet. She had leafed through a couple, but wasn't really taking anything in. James Bay was on her stereo. Bonnie was sound asleep in her basket, snowy paws twitching as she raced through the rabbit-filled fields of her dreams. The room held a pleasant scorch of fresh ironing, as Jake finished the last of his shirts.

'I wish I didn't have to go to Israel,' he said soberly. 'Not with everything that's been happening.'

'Let's not talk about it now,' she said. 'We've only got a few hours before you leave.'

Jake came to sit beside her and Anna moved into his arms.

'Have you heard any more from your biological dad?'

'No,' she told him, resting against his chest, feeling his heart beat, 'I think he's leaving me to set the pace, but Tim said he's happy that I got back in touch.'

'You got a lot going on, darlin',' Jake said.

'You too,' she said.

'Me?' he said, 'No. A lot of conference rooms and airports, that's what I got.'

'It's getting to you, isn't it?'

'It seems to be lately,' he agreed. 'Technically, I've left the military. Technically, I'm a free agent now, yet I'm still working for the same kind of people that I've always hated. Sorry,' he added quickly. 'I'm not much fun when I'm tired.'

'I don't need you to be fun,' she said. 'Just real will do me.'

He kissed her.

'Thank you. Good to know. Remember that guy I met in Paris, who's setting up a charity? Man, he *really* loves what he does. I can't help wondering how it would feel to get up in the morning and feel genuinely useful. I was wondering if I could set up as some kind of security consultant, something where I could stay in one place, instead of living out of a suitcase.'

Anna sat up. 'If you could live anywhere else in the world, where would it be?'

Jake shook his head. 'I've been thinking about that a lot. The trouble is, I don't know if Oxford would work. And, as you know, I have someone quite special in Oxford.' He tried to smile.

'Doesn't matter,' she said fiercely. 'It doesn't matter to me where I live. Not anymore. I came back because of ghosts.' *And that's what I was turning into,* she thought. *Another ghost.* It was a chilling revelation. Ghosts couldn't change, only repeat their past actions over and over and over.

'Are you serious?' Jake looked astonished. 'You'd really—'

'Yes,' she said. 'Yes, I would. Really. Anywhere.'

Next morning, Anna got up to see Jake off to the airport, then, since there was no point trying to go back to sleep, she took Bonnie for a dawn walk over Port Meadow, where the birds were singing with that high-octane, heart-piercing intensity that she associated with English springtime. She walked for almost two hours, amongst the cow parsley and flowering hawthorn, where wild horses grazed, peacefully as they had done for centuries. She kept hearing herself say, 'Yes. Yes, I would. Anywhere.' She loved Oxford, but for the first time she imagined the possibility of leaving. She'd come back because of her grandmother, but she'd stayed, she thought, because this strangely timeless city had once been her world, a world where she still had parents and siblings, a future. Anna hadn't died that summer's night, but nor had she been truly alive. Until now.

When she got home, she made herself coffee, opened the French windows and settled down at her kitchen table with the prospectuses. She became so engrossed that she jumped in surprise when her mobile started to ring. She didn't recognise the number but she suspected it might be Thomas Kirchmann.

'Hello.'

'Anna? It's Alice Jinks. I'm here in Oxford at the train station.' Alice sounded strained, almost scared. 'I need to speak to you. It's – it's quite urgent. Is it convenient if I come to your house? I know it's terribly short notice.'

'No, it's fine,' Anna said. 'I haven't got anything planned.' She gave Alice her address, wondering what on earth could have happened.

Alice Jinks arrived on Anna's door step about twenty minutes later. Dressed in a pair of old yoga trousers, trainers and a faded Henley top, her hair scraped back from her face in a ponytail, she was hardly recognisable as Herr Kirchmann's highly-groomed PA.

'Thank *God*,' she said fervently, the instant Anna opened the door and she briefly closed her eyes. 'Thank God, you're Ok. I've been out of my mind worrying.'

'Let's go downstairs,' Anna said. 'I've just made some fresh coffee. I hope you don't mind dogs?' she added as they descended into Anna's sunny kitchen.

'No, no I like dogs,' Alice said, so distractedly that Anna doubted she'd even registered the wolf-sized, White Shepherd interestedly sniffing around her trainers.

'Sorry. I must seem a bit mad.' Taking the nearest chair Alice gave Anna a wan grin. Anna poured coffee into two of the new, midnight-blue mugs and brought them to the table. Alice wrapped her hands around hers and Anna saw that she was trembling.

'I don't know where to start.'

'It's usually best to start at the beginning,' Anna said.

Alice shook her head. 'Too complicated. We'd be here for hours if I went back that far.' She sipped shakily at her coffee. 'This is very good.' She was gazing around the room as if she'd forgotten why she'd come. 'You've got a lovely home.'

'Alice, what's wrong?' Anna asked.

'I wanted to warn you,' Alice said abruptly, 'that day when you came to the auction house looking for Herr Kirchmann. I was terrified for you but I didn't know what to do. We'd have been overheard. There's always someone listening. And Alexei . . .' she shivered.

'As you see, I am perfectly OK,' Anna said. 'But I'm interested to know why you thought I might not be.'

Alice set down her mug. 'Ok, I'm just going to come out and

say it. I have reason to believe that Alexei and Herr Kirchmann are using Hempels as some kind of front for illegal activities.' She heard Anna's sharp intake of breath. 'I know,' she said softly. 'Quite a shocker.'

'Go on,' Anna said huskily.

'It's like I'm being gas-lighted, you know? Every time I draw Alexei's attention to yet another document that doesn't make sense or some reference to a meeting – that, for whatever reason, I've been deliberately excluded from – he tells me I'm being a hysterical paranoid woman.' She gave an edgy laugh. 'Maybe I am! But, God, Anna when I think of what happened to your family, I'm terrified.'

Anna went completely still. 'What are you saying?'

'I'm saying it's all happening again!' Alice sounded anguished. 'Only this time it's me! *I'm* the one stumbling over their dark secrets, just like Julian did!' She began fumbling in her bag, scattering tissues, train tickets and an oyster card. She pulled out her phone, turning it so that Anna could see a picture.

'This is my little girl. She's two.' Alice took a shuddering breath. 'She's called Poppy. She's my life. She's *everything*, Anna. If something happened to her . . .'

Anna stared down at the picture of the solemn little girl. There was something oddly familiar about her face.

'She looks like me, doesn't she?' Alice said. 'She's certainly *nothing* like her father,' she added swiftly. 'He's not in the picture any more, I'm glad to say.'

At that moment, Anna realized that she had no idea who Alice was. *She's got a child and she thinks she's in danger.* She felt a prickle of fear.

'Do you mind closing those French doors?' Alice said abruptly. 'Not to be a hysterical, paranoid woman or anything.'

No one would be able to hear them, but Anna did as she asked.

'Alexei outright lied to me, Anna.' The angry words seemed to burst out of her. 'I *know* he knew Lili. I *know* she used to work for Hempels.' Alice gulped some of her coffee. She flashed an unreadable look at Anna. 'You shouldn't have told my boss you were going to Innsbruck. That story he tells, you know, the Kirchmann legend, "the Righteous Gentile", that's his shtick, his Open Sesame. Everyone loves it and the business comes rolling in. I thought he was going to . . . Oh, God!' She buried her face in her hands. 'This is a nightmare.'

There's always an alternative narrative, Anna told herself, fighting for calm. She didn't doubt the authenticity of Alice's terror, she could *feel* it like a coming tsunami, but nor did she want to get pulled underwater with her.

'You seriously think,' she said, as evenly as she could manage, 'that because I asked a few questions in Innsbruck, Herr Kirchmann thought it necessary to draw on his extensive funds and contacts, not just to discredit me but someone like Clara Brunner?'

Alice gave her an odd little smile. 'Wouldn't be the first time. They succeeded in convincing everyone my grandfather was senile, didn't they?'

Feeling as if she was going mad, Anna said, 'but *you* told me that story.'

'I know! Because I had to follow the party line! You saw how Alexei was listening to our conversation. Who knows how long he'd been hanging about outside?'

Anna's mobile started to ring. Alice caught sight of the number of Anna's caller.

'It's my boss!' she hissed. 'Don't answer!'

Anna ignored her and took the call. 'Good morning, Herr Kirchmann, how are you?' she asked, striving to sound normal.

Thomas Kirchmann's jolly, Father Christmassy voice came booming down the phone.

'And good morning to you, Anna! Did you have a wonderful time in Innsbruck? I hope you went up into the mountains? They're so beautiful this time of year.'

'I did have a wonderful time,' she said. 'We didn't get up into the mountains unfortunately, as we had to cut our trip short.'

'I'm sorry to hear that.' Anna couldn't tell if Herr Kirchmann was surprised. 'Are you still able to meet me for lunch on Wednesday?' Alice frantically shook her head.

'It's Ok,' Anna mouthed to her.

'Yes, that's fine,' she told him. 'Shall I come into Hempels?'

The instant Anna had ended the call, Alice jumped up from her seat.

'Have you got a *death* wish?'

'Alice, I can't just hide away from all this!' Anna told her.

'We're not in a Jason Bourne movie. There isn't going to be a sniper waiting on a rooftop!'

Alice let out a grim little laugh. 'Don't be so sure. I'm his PA, Anna. I know who Herr Kirchmann's meeting for drinks on Wednesday night.'

Anna was finding this new volatile Alice hard work. It felt too much like being trapped with her younger self, at her paranoid worst.

'Who?' she asked wearily. 'Who is he meeting?'

For the first time, Alice deliberately met her eyes.

'Dominic Scott-Neville.'

FOURTEEN

A nna rinsed and dried their coffee mugs, while she waited for Alice to finish freshening up in her bathroom. She wondered what she was supposed to think about Alice's feverish accusations against her bosses. Though Anna had her own doubts about the new guard at Hempels, she distrusted Alice's motives in bringing her troubles to Anna.

Anna was finding it hard to get a clear fix on Alice Jinks. She still had a mental image of her squashed into the back of the car between her boss and Alexei, coolly sending and monitoring Thomas Kirchmann's emails on the move, as if caring for her employer's needs was the sole reason for her existence. It wasn't like Alice had lied about being a single mother, Anna thought. She simply hadn't advertised the fact, and why should she?

Anna wondered if Alice's family helped her out, or if she was bringing up Poppy entirely alone. If so, Alice must be stretched to the limit, taking care of her demanding boss by day, then going home to her still very young child.

She heard the toilet flush but minutes went by and still Alice didn't come downstairs. She'd been unusually pale, Anna remembered, perhaps she should go up and check that Alice was Ok?

At that moment, she heard a faint creak of floorboards over her head. *Her study.*

Fear and fury sent Anna flying up the stairs. Alarmed, her White Shepherd came dashing after her, paws skidding on polished wood.

The study door stood open. Inside, Alice quickly stepped back from the armoire. She turned to Anna, smiling, seeming utterly composed, not at all as if she'd just been caught snooping around someone's home.

'Do you have any idea how valuable this cupboard is?' She asked in a reproving tone.

'What the *hell* are you doing in here?' Anna could hardly breathe for rage. 'That door was *closed*.' Bonnie had come to sit beside her; Anna could feel her quivering, every canine atom on high alert.

For an instant, there was absolutely no-one at home behind Alice's eyes. Anna could almost feel her swiftly recalculating. Then she held out her hands in an imploring gesture and, for the first time, Anna noticed her nails, bitten down to the quick.

'Anna, I'm so, *so* sorry! I simply didn't think. I'm permanently terrified. I'm all over the place. And your home is so beautiful. Everything here is so perfect. And I couldn't help wanting . . .' Her eyes filled with tears.

'I don't want to be rude,' Anna interrupted, fighting to keep control. 'But I think you should go.'

'You don't believe anything I've told you, do you?' Alice said, tearfully. 'You think it's all a pack of lies.'

'I didn't say I disbelieved you,' Anna said. 'But you need to go now.'

She closed her study door, made Alice wait in the hall while she fetched her bag, then showed her to the door.

At the bottom of the steps Alice turned around. 'I was up all night with my little girl. I didn't have to come here, Anna. I came to warn you. You have no idea what you're getting into. Don't trust anybody.'

'Including you?' Anna said.

'You must make up your own mind about that,' Alice said coolly. For a moment, Anna saw the aloof, unflappable PA. 'I was trying to be your friend,' she added. 'To look out for you, because of us both being Hempels girls. I'm leaving now, but please, Anna, watch your back. I see you've got a burglar alarm? Then I'd advise you to use it.'

She took out her phone, as if dismissing Anna from her thoughts.

'Yes, can I have a taxi? Right away please.' Anna watched her walk to the end of the crescent, still talking on her phone. She looked ridiculously young and defenceless. Anna closed the door, activated her alarm and realized she was shaking.

No, she didn't trust Alice Jinks. Not now. While Alice's fear was viscerally real, her explanation of corrupt goings-on at Hempels struck Anna as far too convenient. Alice had her own agenda. Anna only wished she knew what that was.

If this was a movie, the villain, whoever he or she was, would be accompanied by an ominous soundtrack. But all Anna had to go on were her own instincts and they'd almost got her killed. Twice.

She made herself more coffee, forcing herself to concentrate on each part of the familiar process, as she fought the almost overwhelming compulsion to check on her murder cupboard. Like the nosy girl in a Brothers Grimm fairy tale, Alice had found her way unerringly to the one part of Anna's home that was out of bounds and the violation had shaken Anna to her core. She heard Alice's chilly little voice saying, 'I see you've got a burglar alarm? Well, I'd advise you to use it.' Had that been a warning or a veiled threat?

Anna took her coffee up to her sitting room, followed by an obviously concerned Bonnie and saw Jake's jotter pad, where he'd left it on her book shelves. She sat staring blindly at his spider gram, but could only see Alice coolly stepping back from the monstrous cupboard with its ugly secrets.

She made herself picture Jake waiting at the Gare de Lyons, with his arms full of roses and how he had said: 'We'll go home and we'll try to figure out what the hell is going on.' She saw him in Isadora's kitchen, his pen moving swiftly over the jotter she was holding in her hands, his absorbed expression. Gradually her whirling thoughts calmed and the names, places and events recorded in Jake's surprisingly readable handwriting appeared out of the blur. She studied them for a few moments to remind herself of the order of events, then she turned to the page where Jake had written SUSPECTS and been interrupted by Isadora's announcement that she was making gravy.

Anna frowned as it dawned on her that her current list of suspects was unlikely to fill an entire sheet of paper. In fact, she could only think of two names that belonged under Jake's heading: Thomas Kirchmann and Dominic Scott-Neville.

Next morning, Anna drove to Abingdon where her brother lived with his family. Isadora, Anna's usual go-to-dog-minder had been asked to give a lecture at Somerville, Isadora's old college. Not wanting to leave Bonnie by herself for another long day, Anna had asked Tim if he'd mind taking her.

She turned off the A34 and eventually found the turning into the modern estate, where Tim lived with his family. She parked in Anjali's space and let Bonnie out of the back. She thought she could hear Loki, Anjali's Bengal, yowling from inside the house, but it could have been the baby.

Tim opened the door, unshaven and crumpled in a sweatshirt and jeans, holding his four-month-old daughter in his arms. The baby's enviably long, dark eyelashes were still gemmed with unfallen tears. After lengthy discussion, he and Anjali had named her Edith Rose; Edie for short. 'We intend to call all our daughters after Edwardian housemaids,' Tim had joked. Edie gave Anna a delighted if teary smile.

'Hey, she recognises you,' Tim said. 'Come in and try to close your eyes to the chaos. Sorry about Loki. He's trying to guilt-trip me into letting him outdoors.'

In the sitting room, the coffee table was strewn with bibs, crumpled tissues and Edie's half-finished bottle. A paperback copy of *How to Calm your Baby* had been left face-down on Tim's laptop. Loki, whip-thin and moody as a supermodel, glared down at them from the top of the book shelves with marigold yellow eyes and let out another heart-rending yowl.

'I've just got time for a cup of coffee,' Anna said. 'I'll take little Mademoiselle here.' She took Edie from her brother and the baby immediately grabbed hold of a strand of Anna's hair.

'Oh, she is getting really strong.' Edie let out a triumphant shriek. 'And *loud*!' Anna's little niece had Anjali's jet black hair, with occasional glints of mahogany. She smelled of soap flakes and baby shampoo.

'Listen Edie,' Anna confided, knowing that Tim could hear, 'I'm going to make you a promise. When you're thirteen and awash with hormones and teenage angst, I shall take you to one side and I shall frankly and faithfully answer all your questions, Ok?'

'Ha!' Tim called from the kitchen. 'The bare minute Edie turns thirteen I'm going to lock her up in a high tower. No frank talk needed!'

Bonnie came and sat by Anna's knee. Edie let out another delighted shriek and reached out with little starfish hands to this thrilling new creature.

Tim came back with their coffee. He gently took Edie from Anna's arms and strapped her in her baby-seat.

'If we're in luck she might fall asleep and we can talk.' The baby's dark brows knitted in protest. She drew a breath, turned brick red and let out a roar that made Loki's ears go flat.

'Or not,' Tim said philosophically.

Bonnie padded over to the baby, sniffing her over with soft whiffling sounds, as if she was trying to identify the source of her distress. Edie stopped yelling and gave a startled chuckle. Entranced by her new playmate, she began to coo and babble to the dog.

'Lie down,' Anna told Bonnie, thinking that Tim might not like her getting so close to his tiny baby. Bonnie obeyed but made sure to stay where the baby could see her, her brown eyes super-alert.

'She's guarding Edie,' Anna realized, amazed. 'It's like she's picked the most defenceless person in the room.'

With another blood-curdling yowl, Loki swiped a pile of books off his shelf. They crashed to the floor, taking more books with them on their way down, narrowly avoiding Tim.

'I'm not sure Bonnie got that right,' he said plaintively.

Eventually, Edie's eyelids fluttered closed, briefly reopened and then finally closed in sleep.

Anna had already told Tim about her and Tansy's trip to, and premature departure from, Innsbruck.

'So now you're going into the lion's den?' Tim whispered, to avoid waking Edie. 'You're actually going to have lunch with the guy who might have set the police on you?'

'Because I need to know if he *was* that guy,' Anna whispered back. 'Did you have any joy with the guest list?'

Tim shook his head. 'It only told me who had registered for the murder mystery weekend. If you wanted to go to the ball you could simply print off e-tickets.'

'Damn,' Anna said. 'And you can't trace who bought the e-tickets?'

Tim shook his head. 'I don't have the resources police or private eyes have at their disposal. I'm afraid I've pretty much reached a dead end.'

'Oh, well,' Anna said, disappointed. 'Thanks for trying.'

'There's one very faint possibility. Anjali's company had a professional photographer in, to cover the ball. I'll forward you the photos when I get a chance. The police have been through them and didn't find anything but you might have more luck. I wish we could somehow access Lili's emails and phone records, but we can't.'

Anna glanced at her watch and quickly drained her coffee.

'I've got to go. Thanks so much for having Bonnie.'

Tim indicated the peacefully sleeping baby. 'Anna, she's been awake since five. I should be thanking you.'

On the drive to London, Anna caught herself singing along to the radio. She was on the way to a potentially frightening meeting, yet she felt almost euphoric, though nothing at all noteworthy had happened. She had dropped off her dog at her brother's, cuddled her little niece and had coffee. People did those things every day. It was just that Anna had never been one of them, until now.

I could have been though, that's the stupid thing, she thought, with a pang. Chris and Jane had tried to stay in touch. They'd written and phoned and sent her little gifts.

Anna had a sudden flashback to the funeral. Jane breaking down in the middle of reading a Robert Frost poem; Chris swiftly taking her place, reading the last two stanzas in a shaking voice as he gripped the lectern, his knuckles blue-white. Chris must have been beside himself with grief for his friend and for the mother of his child, a child who had never been allowed to know that he was her real father. Yet somehow he had made his way through to the end of the poem, as Jane continued to weep inconsolable sobs.

Until today Anna had never once thought how they must have felt. *I was only sixteen,* she thought, quickly staving off the inevitable wave of guilt. *My world had imploded. I was a mess.*

But she'd survived and the beauty of it was that the Freemantles were still here – they hadn't gone anywhere. *I'll go and see them both*, she promised herself. *When this is all over.*

An hour and a half later, Anna was in South Kensington having managed to park her car. She made her way to Hempels, suddenly nervous, wondering which Herr Kirchmann she was going to meet, the Father Christmassy idealist or the cunning Euro-criminal as described by Alice Jinks?

But when she announced herself to Mrs Carmody the receptionist, it was not Herr Kirchmann who appeared to welcome her, but Alexei Lenkov.

'Anna, how lovely to see you again,' he said warmly. 'Thomas sends his apologies and has asked me to look after you until he's free to join us.' He gave her an apologetic smile. 'I'm afraid his new PA is still learning the ropes and he's running late.' He gently steered Anna towards the lifts. 'Fortnum and Masons have delivered an extremely nice lunch to our conference room in your honour.' he told her. 'Usually we make do with sandwiches from Pret!'

New PA? Anna felt a flicker of dismay. 'What happened to Alice?'

Alexei's jaw tightened. 'I'm afraid we had to ask Ms Jinks to leave.'

She'd been fired. When? Anna had been trying not to let Alice's lurid warnings sweep her off into the realms of paranoia, but now she wondered if Alexei was really taking her upstairs to give her lunch, or if she'd end up drugged and bundled into the boot of a car. She followed him warily out of the lift, completely thrown by this turn of events.

'But Alice seemed so . . .' *Perfect*, she thought. 'Outstandingly good at her job,' she said out loud.

Alexei made an exasperated sound. 'To begin with she was exemplary, I agree. But recently her conduct was not what we would expect of an employee at Hempels.' His normally open and friendly face was suddenly closed off. 'Alice was in a position of trust and she violated that trust.'

Alexei stopped in front of a door marked Conference Room. He opened the door, ushering her into an oak-panelled room that looked like something out of a stately home. The table had been laid with a miniature buffet, slivers of quiche, slices of game pie, Scotch eggs and other savoury morsels, alongside bowls of fresh salads. It was like a feast provided by benevolent fairies. They surely wouldn't bother feeding her Fortnum and Masons quiche, only to later bundle her into the boot of someone's car?

'Alice's behaviour had become increasingly inappropriate,' Alexei said sounding genuinely upset. 'She even – if you can believe this – insulted one of our best clients!'

Anna felt a new twinge of doubt. Alice had behaved oddly, to say the least, when she'd visited Anna's flat. But she was surely far too controlled to publicly lose her temper? Was she being deliberately discredited, as Alice believed her grandfather Lionel had been? Or had she cracked under some unbearable new pressure? 'She's called Poppy. She's my life. She's everything.' Anna heard her distraught voice and felt again the tidal wave of Alice's terror. 'I'm saying it's all happening again! Only this time it's me! I'm the one stumbling over their dark secrets, just like Julian.'

It was odd though that Alice hadn't thought to mention that she'd been fired. Was that the real reason she'd turned up at Anna's in such a state? Anna belatedly noticed that Alexei had pulled out a chair for her, before seating himself opposite. Behind him tall, Georgian windows looked out over London's rooftops and spires. The sky was a hazy grey, with that faint yellow cast of pollution.

Alexei took a breath. 'I'm sorry, Anna, I have been most unprofessional. It has been an unusually difficult week, but I should not have spoken of Alice in the way I did. There are extenuating circumstances, I know. She is bringing up a little girl on her own. That can't be easy.'

They had almost finished eating when the door opened and Thomas Kirchmann came in, obviously stressed.

'Anna, Anna, *entschuldigen sie bitte*. This is not at all how I imagined our special lunch, but Alexei has been looking after you?'

'Yes, thank you,' she said.

Alexei pushed back his chair and smiled at Anna. 'I hope you enjoy the rest of your meal. Please excuse me, but I must get back to work.'

Herr Kirchmann took the seat that Alexei had just vacated, inspected the remains of Fortnum's savoury platter with a critical eye and eventually helped himself to salad, quiche and a tiny jewelled slice of game pie.

'You have eaten enough?' he asked Anna.

'Yes, it was lovely, thank you,' she said.

They exchanged polite pleasantries as Herr Kirchmann ate. Then he dabbed his mouth with a napkin.

'So, Anna. You and I need to do some straight talking.' He leaned back in his chair.

'I didn't lie to you about my father,' he said. 'He did hide valuables for Jews. But as so often happens, someone found out. A man called Stefan Schneider; he was a local council official, who had apparently thrown in his lot with the Nazis. In reality, he was an opportunist.' He gave Anna a tight nod. 'They exist in all countries, these men, but given certain conditions they flourish.'

'Certain conditions like war.' Anna took a sip of her water.

'War, chaos, civil unrest. Schneider saw an opportunity to earn favours with senior Nazi officials and he offered my father a bargain. In return for being allowed to cherry-pick certain artworks for his own profit, he would generously allow all the rest to remain hidden until the war was over. My father very reluctantly accepted. He felt he had no choice. He had to save what he could. The man's scheme was eventually discovered and both Schneider and my father were executed.' Herr Kirchmann pushed away his plate. 'Would you like coffee? I need coffee. And I believe there are petits fours. Would you like to try them?'

He went over to an antique sideboard, poured coffee into two fine china mugs, brought them back with the plate of petits fours and returned to his seat. 'So,' he said. 'I have given you my straight answer, Anna. And I want to reassure you that I am not hiding any more horrible secrets from you. I admired your father very much and I wish only to be your friend.'

Anna tried not to hear Alice's voice echoing his word: 'I just want to be your friend, to look out for you.'

Anna watched his face as she said, 'Clara Brunner told me that you knew the whereabouts of David Fischer's Vermeer.'

Herr Kirchmann sighed. 'I once knew its whereabouts and I have even seen it.'

Anna felt her hair rising on her scalp. 'You *saw* it? Where?'

'You must understand that even Alexei knows nothing of this, so I must ask you to keep this strictly between ourselves.'

Anna heard herself say, 'Of course,' though she could hardly breathe.

'It was before I took over Hempels. One day, at a meeting in the library on the Scott-Neville estate, I saw it – on the wall! Can you *imagine*, Anna? This – this unknown treasure! Because it *is* a treasure – just *hanging* there.' Thomas Kirchmann's tone was almost hushed.

'Did you say something to someone?'

'Of course! I asked Ralph Scott-Neville outright if it was a Vermeer.'

'What did he say?'

'Nothing,' Kirchmann said in a disgusted tone. 'He just smiled like a crocodile. I could see I wasn't going to get anything out of him, so I went to ask your grandfather, Charles, but he insisted that I was mistaken, that there could not possibly be any unattributed Vermeers, as he put it, "running around in the wild". He said, "you'll be telling me next you've seen a unicorn, old chap."' Kirchmann mimicked Charles Hopkins's chilly patrician tones. 'And then one day, Julian came to see me. He had heard of my father's work during the Nazi occupation. And that's when I learned the provenance of the Vermeer I had seen in the Scott-Nevilles' library. I did my best to describe this painting to your father. Julian thought it sounded suspiciously like the painting David Fischer called A Study in Gold and which he insisted had been given to my father for safe-keeping. Let me tell you, Anna, that night I could not lie still in my bed for worrying. I paced and paced. I was sick to my stomach that such a thing had happened.'

'Did you ever go back for a closer look?' Anna asked.

'Not immediately, unfortunately,' Kirchmann said soberly. 'I became ill.' He briefly touched his chest. 'My heart. When I came out of hospital, it was to find that the world had changed for the worse. Your father and all your lovely family—' He stopped abruptly, shaking his head. 'But as soon as I had recovered, I went back as I had promised. I felt I owed it to Julian.'

Kirchmann went on to describe how he had paid them an unexpected visit, on a day when he knew that Ralph Scott-Neville had an appointment elsewhere, using the pretext that he had left his cigarette case behind.

'I had been a heavy smoker before my illness,' he explained apologetically. 'But when I walked into the library, I was shocked to see that the painting was no longer hanging on the wall.'

'No,' Anna said. 'Oh, *no*.'

Thomas Kirchmann thumped the table making their glasses ring. 'Anna, yes, that was *exactly* my reaction! I had had that one elusive glimpse, very like the mythical unicorn, and now – gone! Then, as I was making my way back from the library, I almost collided with Ralph Scott-Neville's son, Dominic. He was extremely drunk. He kept repeating that his father was a monster and that he was terrified he was becoming a monster just like him.'

Despite herself, Anna had almost begun to trust this old man's version of events but now he'd lost her. She shook her head.

'I'm sorry, Herr Kirchmann, but I knew Dominic—' *Far too well.* '—and I know that he would *never* express those kinds of sentiments to anyone, no matter how drunk.'

He gave her a sad smile. 'I can only assure you that it happened and that Dominic went on to tell me what had happened to him, on the night your family died so tragically.'

Anna felt herself turn cold. 'What?' she demanded. 'What did he say had happened?'

'He had to be rushed to hospital,' Kirchmann said very quietly. 'He had overdosed on heroin. When I asked him about it, Dominic couldn't seem to remember if he had done it by accident or if he had genuinely wanted to die.'

Anna felt as if her known world had just gone up in flames. She had never believed Dominic's story about where he was that night, no matter how many witnesses his father had produced. Though her mind instantly repudiated Herr Kirchmann's explanation, it made a certain terrible sense. Ralph Scott-Neville would have felt compelled to supply Dominic with a socially acceptable alibi. He would have bullied and bribed, doing everything in his power to conceal the truth, that his son and heir was, in fact, a common junkie.

'You never suspected?' Thomas Kirchmann said.

Anna shook her head, not yet trusting herself to speak.

'I told Dominic I was seeing you today and he said he would very much like to meet you. I've arranged to meet him at the Mandarin Oriental later, if you'd like to join us?'

'I think,' she started, huskily, then cleared her throat. 'Yes, I think perhaps I would.'

Anna flashed back to the morning in the park, when she had asked Isadora: 'Do you ever really know anybody?' Well, she had obviously not known Dominic at all. As a teenager, she had admired him, desired him even. Then later, she had demonised him, but none of these projections was the real Dominic. She took a breath.

'Herr Kirchmann, I think you should know what happened to us in Innsbruck. I don't want to seem like I'm pointing my finger, but apart from close friends, you were the only person I'd told where we were.'

He shook his head, perplexed. 'Forgive me, Anna, but I have absolutely no idea what you are talking about.'

Anna gave him an edited version of their experiences: their conversation with Clara Brunner and her subsequent arrest, in which the unknown man Tansy had seen at their hotel and on their guided tour, appeared to be implicated. When she reached the part about them fleeing on the Orient Express, Herr Kirchmann was open-mouthed.

'I knew nothing about this,' he told her, appalled. 'Did you seriously believe I might be involved?'

Anna spread her hands. 'Honestly, Herr Kirchmann? We didn't know!'

'This is most upsetting,' he murmured. 'I must find out what has happened to Frau Brunner. I do not know her personally, but naturally I know of her excellent work.' He passed his hand over his face. 'Anna I am going to tell you something else now in strictest confidence. Things have not felt right at Hempels recently. Both Alexei and I are doing our best to get to the root of it. I think what happened to you in Innsbruck may be connected to this same problem. That's all I can say at present. But you have my word that we will get to the bottom of it somehow. Now will you come with me to meet Dominic? I have my car here today.'

But Anna said she'd meet him there.

She parked a few streets over from the Mandarin Oriental, walked the short distance to the hotel and found her way to the bar. She immediately spotted Dominic talking to Herr Kirchmann and felt a flicker of fear. She wasn't even sure why she was here. She had nothing whatsoever to say to him.

As if he'd felt her come in, Dominic glanced around and their eyes met across the bar. He smiled, such a painfully uncertain smile that Anna felt a confused rush of shock and pity. If Bonnie was here there was no doubt in Anna's mind that she would have instantly sniffed out Dominic Scott-Neville as the most defenceless human in the bar.

Was she only noticing his vulnerability now because of what Herr Kirchmann had told her? Or had it always been there and the adolescent Anna had simply been too wrapped up in her own emotions to see? Taking a deep breath, she walked forward to meet him.

FIFTEEN

The sun was setting as Anna drove back up the M40, scrawling streaks and swirls of improbable colours across the sky, heightening her sense that at some point she'd crossed into a parallel world. Four plus hours of intense talk had left her exhausted yet completely wired.

In the dim lights of the strange bar they'd moved on to from the Mandarin Oriental, Dominic's face had been a silvery blur, his eyes graphite, his voice low and raw with hurt: *I've done terrible shameful things.* Knowing that her face must be similarly leached of all familiarity by the eerie purplish lighting, Anna had felt as if she and Dominic had been exchanged for wiser, yet oddly impersonal, avatars of themselves. Her sense that none of this was quite real, but somehow occurring outside the normal laws of physics, had made the intensity of their encounter easier to bear. Until now . . .

Anna switched on her car radio, nervously flicking between music stations but could only hear Dominic's voice, urgent, imploring: *But I swear to you, Anna, I would never . . .* She'd seen a sign. She was sure she'd seen a sign. Motorway Services 10 miles. She must have passed it without realising or she'd have surely reached it by now? Dominic's right hand tightly imprisoning his left wrist as he talked and talked: *Terrible shameful things.* When he stopped to gulp his mineral water, she saw pressure marks printed on his flesh: *Shameful things.*

She opened the window. Needing air. Needing something, any-thing, real. She could smell diesel fumes, scorched rubber and a shocking, sweet whiff of wild honeysuckle: *But I swear to you, Anna, I would never, I have never . . .*

Anna saw the exit for Services at last and almost wept with relief. Being with Dominic after so many years, covering too much ground, too fast, too intensely in too short a time, had suddenly overwhelmed her; she wasn't safe to drive: *I swear to you, Anna, I would never . . .*

She signalled, changed lanes, signalled again, turned off the motorway and found her way to the vast car park, doing everything as slowly and deliberately as if her old driving instructor was sitting beside her. She locked her car and walked unsteadily towards the stark, white lights of the service station, feeling as if she was floating, scarcely tethered to the earth.

Inside the single-storey building, fighting the urge to flee back to her car, she was assailed by confusing signage, fast food smells and the babble of strangers in transit. Eventually she spotted the familiar, Starbucks logo and somehow made her way to the counter, where she found herself queuing behind some young women, who were obviously returning from a hen party. With their elaborate hairdos slipping undone and gold and silver eye make-up running, they resembled exhausted mermaids bewildered at finding themselves washed ashore. Anna ordered a large coffee and, dimly conscious of her plummeting blood sugar, a piece of lemon drizzle cake. Feeling like a ghost trying to pass unconvincingly among the living, she found a table, numbly unwrapped the square of dry sponge cake: *I swear to you, Anna . . .*

A large Punjabi family had spread themselves over three tables at the Burger King concession opposite. An elderly Punjabi woman, wearing colours as improbably vivid as the sunset, distributed shocking pink and lime green sweets to a flock of dark-eyed, silk-clad little children.

I've done terrible things, shameful things but I swear to you, Anna, I would never, I have never killed another . . .

Glancing down, Anna was puzzled to see that she'd taken out her phone. Grief sliced through her as she realized who she'd wanted to call. It was the first time in sixteen years, if you discounted her weeks in the psych ward, that she'd even momentarily forgotten that her father was dead. The jolt of loss was chilling and final. Nothing and no one could ever make this better, except her diffident, painfully private dad, but Anna would never see, touch or talk to him again. She had thrown herself into a whirlwind of activity, jumping on planes, trains, changing countries, but Julian, Julia and Anna's brothers and little sister were still dead. Anna still didn't know why they'd been murdered or if it had anything at all to do with her father's auction house or David Fischer's Vermeer. All she knew was that she was no longer entitled to hate Dominic Scott-Neville. Hunching over her table, she desperately swallowed down sobs, waiting for the shockwave to pass. Dominic's words replayed in her mind: *When I got to Argentina I wrote you all these mad letters, Anna. I wanted to tell you how sorry, how bloody sorry . . .*

Three of the little Punjabi children raced past shrieking, high on their own excitement and too much sugar. One little girl, a tiny princess in gold earrings and sequinned green silk pyjamas, tripped, fell sprawling and began to howl. Her father, a tall bearded Sikh, calmly went to her and swept her up in his arms. Anna had to clench her jaws against the pain. The yearning to be small again, to feel her own father's arms around her again, was intolerable.

What do I do now, Dad? She asked her dead father. *What the hell do I do now?* For sixteen plus years she'd had an enemy. A mission. A spar to cling to in the wreckage. A reason to keep living, to keep on hating. Sitting up at night trawling the net. Living for the next google alert. She'd told herself it was the drive to know, find answers and get justice for her parents and her siblings. But deep down she'd always been chasing the shadowy figure of Dominic Scott-Neville. *A ghost chasing another ghost*, she thought. That, essentially, had been her life until she'd got Bonnie.

Oh, God – Bonnie! Anna was guiltily startled back to her responsibilities. She couldn't believe she'd forgotten to call Tim! She quickly sent a text.

Not just a bad sister but a terrible dog owner. So sorry, on my way to you now.

Tim's reply popped up moments later.

**Anna, post Edie, (the child who never sleeps) I can
guarantee that one of us is ALWAYS awake. Bonnie has
been a star. She reminds me of our old dog Rook, do you
remember him?**

Tim had apparently forgotten that she'd never known Rook
when he was old and presumably slightly less bonkers. But Anna
was surprised to discover fond memories of him as a mischievous
puppy, a glossy, black, working cocker crossed with equally hyper-
active Border collie. One day on the shore at Dunwich, Rook had
rashly sampled seawater and gone racing up the pebble beach to
some dismayed picnickers, where he had gulped down a small
child's orange squash in his desperation to rid himself of the taste.
Anna's brother – Dan – who, like Anna, had secretly longed for
a dog of his own, had said: 'I don't see why they were so mad. I
thought it was *really* smart of him!'

Anna's phone pinged. A follow-up text from Tim.

You Ok?

She sent him a smiley face. The disturbing feeling of being out
of her body was beginning to ebb away.

A small gang of boys and girls, Anna thought they were maybe
aged seventeen or eighteen, came to take over a nearby table. The
boys impossibly rosy-cheeked with floppy public school fringes,
the girls repeatedly tossing back their silky hair like so many
moorland ponies; and every single one of them secretly starring
in their own private movie, Anna diagnosed ruefully. Just like her
and Natalie and Max and Dom. They'd acted so confident, thought
themselves so outrageously decadent. But they'd just been babies,
clueless little babies.

'God, I'm so sorry, Anna.'

Those were the first words Dominic said to her, after Thomas
Kirchmann had tactfully remembered another engagement and left
them alone together.

Inwardly panicking, unsure what exactly he was apologising
for, since it was unlikely that he was confessing to murder, Anna
had said in a strained voice, 'Why are you sorry?'

'For not getting in touch after what happened to your family,' he explained. 'Not to mention acting like a prat outside Taylors. But how do you apologise in the street to someone you haven't seen for what feels like a hundred years? I just went to my default position which, thanks to my patrician upbringing, is banal, public school dick.'

Anna had startled herself by saying drily, 'well, that's certainly true,' and he'd laughed. Then he'd said, 'would you mind if we went somewhere else? Somewhere we can talk?'

They'd walked through the streets until they found the strange bar which, like the magic toy shop in a children's story, Anna suspected she might never be able to find if she ever tried to return. And there, in the violet twilight, clamping his own wrist in a vice-like grip, Dominic had begun to talk: about his near-fatal overdose, about being bundled on to a plane by his father barely two weeks later and how, in his self-loathing, he had continued to court death. At his lowest ebb, he'd been picked up by the police in some nameless Argentinian town, been thrown in jail and later bailed out by his uncle and aunt on the condition he went into rehab.

'In Argentina?' she'd said, surprised.

He'd shaken his head. 'Some fancy clinic in New York State. Snow everywhere. When I got off the plane, I thought I'd die of cold.' He gave a short laugh. 'Not to mention heroin withdrawal.'

'But you got clean?'

'Eventually. Thanks to Ghislaine.' Dominic had told her. 'She saw something in me apparently.' He gave a self-deprecating laugh. 'Whatever it was, it had to be buried pretty deep!'

Ghislaine, former super-model and New York socialite, Anna remembered, who was now Dominic's wife.

'Where did you meet?' Anna had expected him to name some glitzy location frequented by celebs.

He'd explained patiently, 'I thought I'd told you – in rehab. Ghislaine was on her way out, having successfully completed the programme. I was on my way in, but secretly plotting to go over the wall and shoot up the first chance I got. She told me to call her as soon as I was well again and she'd come to fetch me. I didn't believe – I didn't *dare* to believe – she meant it. But in the end, I did call her and she really came.' Shaking his head in apparent wonderment, Dominic had added casually, 'I say Ghislaine saved me, but I should give God some credit for giving me a solid gold reason to get through the nightmare of rehab.'

Anna stared at him. 'God?' She'd thought she'd misheard.

He'd laughed. 'Didn't I mention the finding God part? Oh, if you *knew* how hard I fought it, Anna! It was almost comical. If, you know, it wasn't my life that was on the line! You see I *knew* how to self-destruct! I'd been doing it since I was twelve, but getting well, now *that* terrified me!'

'Why do you say it was God?' She'd asked. 'And not – I don't know – some other healthier part of you?' Lulled by the smoky violet intimacy of the bar, by her sense that she and Dominic were not their normal daylight selves, Anna had forgotten that no one in their group had ever challenged Dominic's version of events. She belatedly braced herself for the inevitable retaliation.

But he'd just shrugged. 'Because, at that time, any part of me I could access would have immediately let me off the hook. God, on the other hand, asked me to do ten uncomfortable, sometimes frankly impossible, things a day and still does.'

'So, would you say He was worth it, I mean, ultimately?' Anna was the last person to kick away a drowning person's life raft, but she couldn't quite hide her scepticism.

He'd laughed. 'You mean do I think I'll get my heavenly reward? Anna, I don't even care! Because God – or whatever you want to call a power greater than ourselves – showed me that I didn't have to turn into a newer but equally disgusting version of my father. I was free to become my own person.'

'Does Ghislaine feel like you?' She really meant was; *has Ghislaine been born again*?

'She does. We've both been given so much and, for our different reasons, our reaction was to piss it all away. Now we want to give something back. We've bought this monstrosity of a country house which we're planning to turn into a women's refuge.' Dominic had left a long pause before he'd added quietly, 'you see neither my mother or my grandmother ever had anywhere to go.'

Before they'd left the bar, before its twilight spell could wear off and she lost her courage, Anna had told Dominic, 'a few months ago, on New Year's Eve, a man killed himself. He tried to take me with him. He told me he was . . . somehow connected to your family.'

If you think I'm a monster, Dominic is the devil.

Dominic had steadily returned her gaze. 'I think you're talking about Alec Faber?'

'Yes.'

He'd nodded soberly. 'His brother was one of my godfathers. Alec was the black sheep of the Faber family. Did brilliantly at Oxford, but then lost his job at the Foreign Office; I never knew why. My dad always said he was a failed gambler, failure being the ultimate sin in my father's eyes, next to getting caught. Alec's family had disowned him. His fiancé had broken off their engagement. Years later my father and I were in London – I would have been in my early teens – and we passed Alec sitting on a bit of old blanket, with his dog on a piece of string.' At this point, Dominic had interrupted his story. 'I need to give you a bit of background. In the usual way, my father barely noticed me. But, once a month, we had this surreal father-son ritual, where he'd take me to London and we'd have an excruciatingly uncomfortable dinner at his club, where he'd interrogate me about my many failings. I suspect that my mother had asked him to make more of an effort with me and this was his bizarre solution. I was desperate to impress him, Anna, and at that age the only way I could think of was to be just like him. So, like I said, we saw Alec on the other side of the road, and my father reminded me that this was someone who'd got a first at Oxford and had once been a member of my dad's club. "This is what happens to weaklings and failures. It will happen to you too, Dominic, if you don't buckle down to your studies." Then I did something unthinkable.

'I interrupted my dad. I said, "I'd like to talk to him." My father was appalled. Why bother with this piece of human detritus? But I told him, "I know what I'm doing, Dad." We crossed the road and I was almost sick with excitement. I introduced myself to Alec and told him we were going to have dinner at his old club. If he could get hold of a tie somewhere, tidy himself up, he could join us as our guest. "We can feed you up, maybe help you out." He must have been half insane with hunger, poor guy, because he glanced at my dad who hadn't said a word, didn't even acknowledge him, and I could actually *see* Alec's desperation overruling his common sense. Maybe I was different to my dad and the other Scott-Nevilles? Maybe his luck had changed at last? I told him what time he should come and we walked away. My dad started to protest. "People like Alec are weak, they're vermin." "I *know* that, Dad!" I told him. "And after tonight, so will Alec, trust me!" And I saw my father's eyes light up, as if he was thinking that maybe I wasn't such a waste of space after all?

'So, that evening, my dad and I are sitting at our usual table when the maître d' comes over to tell me that the person I'd warned him about had showed up and was asking to see us. I said grandly, "Show him in."

'I could see that Alec had made a pitiful attempt to tidy himself up. He'd managed to acquire a tie and combed the tangles out of his hair, though he was still smelly and unshaven. He gave me a pathetically grateful smile, went to pull out a chair and, quick as a flash, I said, "you didn't *seriously* think we'd invited you to dine at our club?" As you can imagine, the dining room suddenly went deathly silent as everyone watched this little drama play out. I said, "What I *meant* was, if you go around to the bins at the back, I'm sure you'd find the kitchen staff quite charitable."'

When Dominic reached this part of his story, he'd forced himself to look Anna in the eye. 'Then I saw Alec's humiliated face and almost threw up with shame. I've done some shabby things in my life, but that moment will stay with me until I die.'

Anna hadn't known what to say. It was a horrible story and she absolutely believed it had happened exactly the way Dominic said.

'Oh, it gets worse,' Dominic told her. 'Some of the diners started to snigger. Alec went stumbling from the dining room, knocking into a waiter on his way out and sending a tray of drinks flying. Then my father did something unprecedented. "Nicely done, my boy!" he said, with real pride. "Well done! Never show weakness!" And he slapped me on the back.'

After that final humiliation, Alec Faber had clearly been left with nothing to cling to but thoughts of revenge. Even as he'd prepared to plunge to his death, he'd felt compelled to pass on that last drop of poison. *If you think I'm a monster* . . . and because it had fitted her narrative, her version of Dominic Scott-Neville, Anna had swallowed the lie.

She drove back to Abingdon, with Bob Marley turned down low, still trying to process her thoughts about her evening.

Did she believe Dominic had found God? Anna didn't really think that was any of her concern. To quote Isadora Salzman, quoting John Lennon; 'Whatever gets you through the night.' Did she believe Dominic was genuinely trying to make amends for past mistakes?

Yes, she thought. *Yes, I do.*

But despite all these revelations, she was no nearer to knowing who had killed Lili Rossetti or if David Fischer had been murdered. She no longer believed that Thomas Kirchmann was involved, but suspected that neither he nor Alexei Lenkov had told her what was really going on at the auction house. 'Things have not felt right at Hempels.' He'd said. 'Alexei and I are doing our best to get to the root of it.' Alexei's explanation for firing Alice Jinks didn't ring true. Though Alice had arrived on her doorstep in – for Alice – a dishevelled state and in obvious distress, there had been a distinct element of performance. Like Anna, Alice Jinks was first and foremost a survivor, but she was also a strategist. Anna simply couldn't imagine the cool, calculating Alice stepping out of her perfectly polished role as Kirchmann's PA so far as to start insulting clients unless, Anna thought, she felt spectacularly threatened in some way.

Shivering with tiredness, Anna turned into Tim's badly-lit estate, peering at street names and wondering irritably why they'd all been given the names of ridiculously obscure wild flowers, when she thought of something else to add to her catalogue of failures. She had never asked either Kirchmann or Alexei Lenkov what had really happened to Alice's grandfather, Lionel Rosser.

Next morning, Anna was awake at 5.30 a.m. To Bonnie's delight, she immediately sat up and went downstairs in her PJs to make herself a pot of tea. The feeling she'd had last night with Dominic that normal reality had been suspended, of being under some mysterious yet kindly dispensation, an alternate, more complete version of herself, still lingered.

When she'd arrived at Tim's, Anjali had been upstairs giving Edie her last bottle of the day. She'd briefly come down in a pretty, cotton kimono, to say hi, holding her sleepy baby in her arms, before disappearing off to bed. Anna had intended to leave then, but she and Tim had both found a mysterious second wind. They'd stayed up reminiscing for almost two hours, about

Rook, their childhoods and her brothers. She'd given him a shortened version of her conversation with Dominic. Second wind or not, Anna had been aware that underneath they were both exhausted, to the point that they'd become slightly giggly and trippy, but it had felt – to both of them, Anna thought – that this opportunity to recapture their old easy dynamic, was too precious to waste.

The thought made Anna smile to herself, as she poured tea into her midnight-blue mug. She looked out through her open French doors into the garden, where Bonnie was nosing about in the silver-grey light of dawn. The early-morning air felt cool and fresh.

Initially, her conversation with Dominic had left Anna feeling that she'd been scattered into a million tiny drifting pieces, her very last certainty stripped away. But today she felt, she felt . . . on the cusp of something new, a new way of being in the world. *It's time*, she thought. *I can do it. I think I can really do it now.* She hurried out into the garden to find Bonnie.

'I need company,' she told her.

Still holding her mug of tea, Anna ran upstairs to her study, her bare feet leaving damp prints on the polished wood. Bonnie bounded after her, catching her excitement.

She opened the door and hesitated. For a moment, the room was haunted by the memory of Alice Jinks: 'I was trying to be your friend. To look out for you, because of us both being Hempels girls.' Anna set down her cup, took the key from the desk drawer, unlocked the double doors of her armoire and recoiled as if she'd come up against an electric fence.

Chaos. Madness. Not her own private, far superior version of a police investigation room. Just a cupboard crammed with agony that had nowhere else to go. She forced herself to walk into that appalling force-field, until she was close enough to see every photograph, every word on every news clipping, police report or witness statement, all held together with a cat's cradle of criss-crossed tapes. Thick black scribbles added whenever traumatic memories overwhelmed her:

Where ARE You? Will Somebody PLEASE just BELIEVE me? I KNOW you're out there!!!

The words scrawled across fuzzy photos of Dominic and her subsequent boyfriend, Max Strauli.

Anna's eyes stung with pity for her broken younger self. How ill she'd been. How lost. *Not any more*, she thought.

She grabbed her waste paper bin, desperate to be rid of this evidence of the futile years of pain. She reached up to rip out the floor-plan of the room, where her little sister, Lottie, had been butchered in her bed.

But as she went to touch the brittle and yellowed paper, her hand jerked back, it seemed, of its own volition. It would be like a betrayal, like giving up ever knowing what had happened to her family that night.

Her heart still thumping with unused adrenalin, Anna closed the cupboard doors, relocked them and left the room followed by a puzzled Bonnie.

'I'm not ready,' Anna said aloud at the top of the stairs, and had to fight back tears. 'I don't know if I'll ever be ready.'

That afternoon, Anna went to meet Isadora and Tansy at the Randolph, where Isadora had booked them a table for high tea.

'It'll be an opportunity to catch up on everything that's been happening,' she'd added, when she'd phoned Anna to remind her.

Anna arrived to find her friends already seated in front of a glorious teatime spread in the hotel's opulent drawing-room. Taking in the crystal chandeliers and gilt-framed paintings, Anna said, 'I can see luxury is getting to be a habit for the dog-walking detectives!'

Tansy patted one of the squashy, russet-upholstered chairs so Anna could sit down.

'I was just telling Isadora that I'm suffering from serious dog envy,' she said earnestly. 'I'm not a real dog-walking detective now am I? Though Buster was only borrowed and, to be honest,' she added, 'I wouldn't actually *choose* him for my doggie soulmate.'

'What kind of dog would you choose?' Isadora asked.

'A rascally mutt,' Tansy said at once. 'With a slipping down sock and an eye patch.'

'Sounds like a cross between Just William and Captain Hook,' Isadora commented.

'You could go to a rescue shelter,' Anna suggested. 'You never know. You might find rascally, little William waiting for you?'

Tansy shook her head. 'Maybe one day, when things feel more settled.' She quickly changed the subject. 'Isadora says you talked to Dominic.'

'We talked for hours,' Anna said.

'So, we can conclude she didn't hate him,' Isadora said drily. She helped herself to a miniature smoked salmon sandwich.

'This is lovely of you,' Anna gestured at the tea table with its array of sandwiches, scones, tiny cakes and tartlets.

'Well, when I initially booked this, it was to compensate me and Tansy for missing out on coffee and cake at Pfeffers,' Isadora explained.

'Oh, no, now I feel terrible,' Tansy said. 'Because I don't think we can ever compensate you for missing out on the Orient Express!'

'You can't!' Isadora said crisply, but her eyes held a teasing glint. 'Here's the thing – I'm about to do something that I almost never do.' She flashed them another of her playful smiles. 'I was wrong. Not for playing devil's advocate but for not trusting your instincts. And now we've all forgiven each other,' she added swiftly, 'let's get down to business! Thomas Kirchmann has convinced Anna – and me – that he was in no way involved with the stolen Vermeer. So where does that leave us? Assuming Lili and David were both murdered because of their connection with this painting, who could have done it? Who had a motive?'

Tansy was spreading clotted cream on her scone. 'My money is on the bad Russian,' she said cheerfully.

'Bad Russian?' Anna said.

'Alexei, isn't that his name? The man who always remembers to buy strudel for his wife.'

Isadora laughed. 'Not the "bad Russian" trope, darling, that's been done to death!'

Tansy bit into her scone and closed her eyes with pleasure.

'I'd love to know what happened to the Vermeer after Kirchmann saw it in the Scott-Neville's library,' Isadora mused.

'Yes, well,' Anna said, thinking about her own life and her own mysteries. 'It's possible we'll never know. Not for sure.'

Isadora shot her a searching look, seeming to understand that Anna wasn't just talking about the Vermeer. 'And could you live with that, darling?'

'You don't always get a choice,' Anna said quietly. She'd become aware of her mobile vibrating inside her bag. She took it out and said, surprised, 'It's Dominic. If you don't mind, I'm going to take this.' She took her phone into the hotel lobby with its view over the Ashmolean. 'Dominic?'

'Sorry, Anna, this is going to be a big information dump.' Today Dominic sounded like a clipped, public schoolboy to the point of self-parody. It's his default setting, she remembered, when he was under stress.

'What's happened?' she asked.

'Kirchmann told me you'd asked him about a Vermeer?'

'That's right, but—'

'Sorry to interrupt,' he said, 'but the police are on their way to take me in for questioning about Lili's murder. My solicitor is here. In fact, he's standing right beside me hissing at me to hurry up. Don't worry,' he said, before Anna could react. 'I didn't kill her. I even have an alibi. It's something to do with emails I supposedly sent to her. It's all rather confused. But there's some stuff I need to tell you as a matter of urgency.' He took a breath. 'I – knew about A Study in Gold, Ok? In fact, as part of my belated attempt to atone for centuries of the Scott-Nevilles' wrongs, I tried to reunite David Fischer with his Vermeer.'

Anna was clutching her phone so tightly against her ear by this time that her fingers had gone slightly numb.

'I should have told you last night, but I thought . . . to be honest I didn't know how you'd react. I know you had your – not entirely unfounded – concerns about me and my family, but it was the first time we'd talked in over a decade and I didn't want that to muddy the waters, if that makes sense?'

Anna knew exactly why he'd think that and it made her feel completely torn. She could feel all her old Pavlovian suspicions kicking in. *He knew about the painting. What else did he know?* She was like an amputee, she thought, plagued by unreal sensations in a phantom limb.

She forced herself to focus on Dominic's voice explaining how he and Lili had come to meet at a fund-raiser at the National Gallery. In passing, she'd mentioned that she was working on art restitution. He'd liked and trusted Lili, and suddenly felt guided.

'I realize that makes me sound like a religious nut, Anna, but that's what happened,' he confided.

'You knew where it was?'

'I knew exactly where it was. After Kirchmann spotted the Vermeer in our library, my father hid it behind an amateur, not to say terrible, watercolour painting of our folly painted by my mother.'

Anna vaguely remembered the Scott-Nevilles' folly, a Victorian take on a timeless romantic ruin.

'My old man was a perverse bastard, as you know, and the idea of this lost masterpiece hanging on his wall, for all intense and purposes in plain sight, really got his juices going. But then, when he knew he was dying, he wrote to me revealing the truth, like he'd perpetrated some wonderful practical joke. He signed off with his usual wit and charm, saying he was having it auctioned off and that as his touchy-feely Christian son, I wouldn't see a penny from it.

'Sure enough, when I came back with Ghislaine to take over the estate, something even my father couldn't prevent, my mother's watercolour was no longer on the wall. I told Lili all this. The last time I heard from her she was lit up with excitement. She said she'd been called in by Hempels to advise on a completely unrelated painting and, as she was passing someone's office, the door opened and she saw what she believed might be my mother's watercolour hanging on the wall. I don't know what happened after that, but my gut-feeling is that Lili was so angry about how David Fischer had been treated that she went back later and attempted to retrieve it.'

'Dominic, you absolutely have to tell this to the police!' Anna said.

He gave a short laugh. 'I did! It turns out that babbling about stolen Vermeers and Nazi gold is a sure-fire way of getting yourself evicted from a police station.' Anna heard agitated voices in the background. 'I've got to go, but as soon as I'm done, I'll call you, Ok?'

'Yes, please. And Dominic, good luck. I'm so sorry you've got to go through this.'

She went back to the tea-room, where Isadora and Tansy were chatting quietly as they started in on the cakes.

'You could go back to college, darling,' Isadora was saying. 'You are *so* smart and you're still so young. You could do anything you like, even in these strangely blighting times.'

Anna resumed her seat and quickly drained her tea cup.

'Are you Ok?' Isadora asked her. 'You've gone awfully pale.'

'I'm a bit shocked,' Anna said. 'The police want to question Dominic about Lili's murder. There are some incriminating emails, or something. He wasn't very clear.'

'Has he got an alibi?' Tansy said.

Anna gave a tight nod. 'But even so.'

'How worrying,' Isadora said, 'but I am going to pour us all some more tea and I hope you will help us dispose of some of these divine little cakes?'

'I'm sure I can manage that!' Anna said, trying to smile.

She drove home, but instead of getting out of her car, Anna sat staring at her phone. She'd braved Herr Kirchmann and survived a life-changing conversation with her nemesis Dominic Scott-Neville, so why was she still avoiding talking to her grandfather? She hadn't been to visit him since her trip to Innsbruck. They'd spoken on the phone, stilted exchanges that left her feeling wrong-footed and oddly guilty.

Call him again, before you lose your nerve, she thought. *Ask him what's wrong.*

He answered on the third ring.

'Hello Grandpa. How are you?' she said.

'I'm fine, darling, how are you?' Her grandfather sounded tired and, to her dismay, slightly wary.

She'd done this to him, Anna thought with a pang. It was up to her to put it right. She drew a breath. 'Things haven't been right between us, not since I asked if my dad had ever talked to you about a Vermeer. It's my fault, for not saying something earlier but I can't bear to go on pretending nothing's changed, when it has.'

He didn't immediately respond; she could just hear him breathing on the end of the phone.

'I hate us not being friends,' she went on, 'and I know really that you'd never lie to me, but I have this feeling that I'm not getting the whole story from you.'

'I'm so sorry, I just couldn't!' he burst out. She heard his voice break. 'I was so ashamed. If I'd listened to your father, if I'd taken him seriously when he came to ask my advice about that painting then . . . I know it's stupid, but all these years I couldn't help thinking, he might still—' he let out a wrenching sob. 'Your father might still be alive. They might *all* be alive.'

'Oh, Grandpa, *don't*. Please don't be upset.' Anna felt her eyes filling in sympathy.

'Rationally, I know that might not be why he died. But we'd only talked such a short while before it happened. Julian needed someone to turn to and I let him down. I was no better than that loathsome snob Charles. You must know I'd never deliberately hurt you, Anna. I love you far too much for that.'

'I love you too,' she told him tearfully.

Her grandfather hadn't lied. He was not hiding a dark secret. He'd been evasive because he'd felt desperately guilty; something she might have recognised sooner, Anna thought, ashamed, if she hadn't been caught up in her own dramas. They talked until they were both feeling calmer, then she said, 'I'll come over at the weekend. We'll go out to lunch somewhere nice and we can have a proper talk.'

Back in her kitchen with no one to distract her from her thoughts, Anna was flooded with fresh anxiety for Dominic. She knew how it felt to come under suspicion. After her family's murders the police had subjected Anna to lengthy questioning about her and Max's dodgier associates. They hadn't suspected her of direct involvement with her family's deaths, but for a time they'd seemed to believe she could lead them to the killers. *The bad daughter*, Anna thought. *The mad, bad daughter.*

Inevitably, her thoughts circled back to her own toxic legacy. Forget family baggage, Anna had an entire armoire. She imagined herself dragging it with her into the future. Setting off with Jake to make a fresh start; *Oh, I'll be bringing my murder cupboard with me, if that's Ok?*

She remembered her evening with Tim. The sweet childhood memories they'd shared. Those were the images she wanted to hold on to, not the bloody horror she'd stumbled over that terrifying, summer's night.

'That's it!' she told Bonnie. 'I'm getting rid of it right now! You can be my witness.'

Anna ran upstairs, Bonnie following eagerly at her heels. She threw open the door and plugged in her shredder, weirdly elated. She was finally going to be free. She unlocked the armoire, flung back the double doors and made a wild grab for the nearest piece of paper.

And found herself physically unable to let it go.

Anna let out a scream of frustration and rage. She kicked her waste bin, sending it hurtling across the study, crashing into her running machine with a metallic bong.

Bonnie stared at her in alarm. She sidled up to Anna, tail drooping, doing her anxious grin. Anna dropped to her haunches, instantly contrite.

'I'm not mad with you, you lovely dog. I'm mad with *me*. What is *wrong* with me!' Bonnie regarded her owner for a moment as if she was wondering how best to handle this new crisis, then she very firmly and deliberately pressed her forehead against Anna's, remaining in that mutually uncomfortable position without moving a muscle, until Anna reluctantly let out a rueful giggle.

'Ok, Wonder Dog! I'm cured. You can stop my therapy now!'

Anna and her dog went back down to the kitchen. She found Bonnie one of her favourite crunchy treats and made herself a pot of Doctor Chillout's tea, with lavender and camomile. She had bought it for just such a mental health emergency, but it turned out to be so foul that she made herself a cup of strong coffee instead. She needed to eat, she thought, but she couldn't face cooking, plus her fridge was almost empty. Maybe she'd order a takeout?

Her phone lit up. Jake had sent her a text.

I thought we could take George out to lunch this weekend?

Anna shook her head amazed. She texted back.

Ever thought of setting up as a mind-reader?

She heard a *ping* from her laptop. Anjali had sent her links to the photos taken by High Table's photographer at the VE Night ball. To Anna's dismay there were over 200. She decided the photos could wait until she'd ordered and eaten her takeout.

By the time she'd eaten and stashed her plate in the dishwasher, she could hear a steady rain falling outside. She opened her laptop and began working her way through the photos. She had no serious hopes she'd find anything since the police had already been through them. As she clicked on photo after photo, Anna found herself feeling almost nostalgic for their murder mystery weekend. Looking at these slickly professional photos she could see why they'd all, herself included, gradually fallen under Anjali's 1940s spell. The clothes, the hairstyles, the hectic VE Night atmosphere came across as utterly authentic. Anna recognised the man in the kilt, importuning some unknown female. A beautiful shot of Isadora, waltzing with her air-force pilot could have been a still from a 1940s movie. There was a breath-taking photo of several, wildly jitterbugging couples, who must have come with one of the re-enactment groups. As she continued to trawl through group photos, Anna was surprised to spot herself with Tansy and Isadora, looking unexpectedly glamorous in her evening dress and almost relaxed! She scribbled down the serial number thinking she might get copies for herself and her friends.

Then some nagging awareness that Anna couldn't quite explain, made her go back to the photo of the jitterbugging dancers. This time she took special note of the gilt-framed mirror just off to the side, where the photographer had captured a passing reflection.

Anna zoomed in closer and her mouth was suddenly as dry as cotton wool. Even magnified, the reflected figure, a shadowy profile, was indistinct. But Anna knew who it was: *I came to warn you. Don't trust anybody.*

'Alice Jinks,' she whispered and felt her heart jump, warning her of a danger she couldn't yet define.

Moments later, she heard a thunderous banging at her front door.

SIXTEEN

The repeated battering from upstairs had Bonnie out of her basket in a heartbeat. She let out a short sharp bark of alarm, ran to the bottom of the stairs then immediately ran back to Anna.

'Ok, we'll just go up and see what's going on,' Anna told her, wishing she didn't have Alice's chilly little voice on a loop: *I see you've got a burglar alarm? Then I'd advise you to use it.*

She crept up the stairs and along her hallway, with a bristling Bonnie by her side. Then she noticed her White Shepherd's tail beginning to wag in an embarrassed apology. A micro-second later, Anna heard a familiar voice calling from outside.

'I think there's something wrong with your doorbell. Let me in, I'm *soaking!*'

Anna deactivated her burglar alarm and opened the door to admit a bedraggled shivering Tansy.

'Tansy Lavelle,' Anna said, not quite recovered from her shock, 'we seriously *have* to buy you an umbrella.'

Tansy wasn't just soaked through; she looked utterly woebegone, standing dripping in Anna's hallway like the True Princess in the Princess and the Pea. She was wearing a jacket, which was evidently not waterproof or even properly buttoned up. Instead Tansy was awkwardly clutching its two edges over an odd rectangular bulge.

'I'll get towels,' Anna said. 'And tea. You need hot ginger tea.'

Tansy burst into tears.

'Tansy, what's wrong?'

'Everything!' Tansy sobbed.

Anna shepherded her friend into her bedroom, where she found her warm towels and dry clothes. 'Take off that jacket.'

'I knew things were bad with Liam. I just didn't know they were *this* bad.' Tansy took a chunky plastic file out from under her jacket, handing it to Anna with an expression of doom.

'And now I've made you an accessory or whatever,' she wailed. 'And I'm making your bedroom all wet!' She started to peel off her sopping wet jacket.

Concerned that Tansy might catch pneumonia, Anna decided to ignore the mysterious file for the time being. 'Change in my bathroom. It's got a heated towel rail.'

Tansy disappeared into the bathroom, but continued to talk through the half-open door

'Liam's got us the files.' She gave a hysterical giggle. 'For the Lili Rossetti murder case and the bookshop fire?'

'You're *kidding.*'

'I'm not. I'm deadly serious and so is Liam. He said the dog-walking detectives might have more luck solving the crimes than the police.' Tansy emerged, towelling her hair and dressed in

Anna's sweater and jeans. 'I asked him if he'd get into trouble and he said he didn't care, then he went out for a bloody *run!*'

Anna felt torn. She was desperate to see the files, but she didn't want Liam to be hauled up before his superiors.

'He's not having some kind of breakdown, is he?'

Tansy shook her head, scattering sparkling droplets. 'The opposite. Liam says he's finally come to his senses, that life in the modern police force has been driving him nuts. He says it's impossible to do his job properly, because of all the cuts and the politics. He likes his boss but even his hands are tied, Liam says.'

'It's that bad?' Anna said.

'It's way beyond bad.' Tansy wiped her eyes with the corner of her towel. 'I've told Isadora and she's coming over. I know it's late, but I thought she should see them too.'

'I wasn't likely to get much sleep anyway,' Anna said. 'I just found out something disturbing about Alice Jinks. For a moment, I thought you were her.'

'Wait till Isadora's here,' Tansy suggested. 'Then you can tell us both at the same time.'

A few minutes later, they heard the familiar alarming clanking as Isadora's decrepit Volvo pulled up outside. She'd brought her little Tibetan spaniel cross. Hero waited until her owner had arranged a piece of scarlet fleece to her satisfaction, then she lay down on it, pointedly turned her back and appeared to fall asleep.

'Hero's a little rigid in her habits,' Isadora explained apologetically.

Assuming her role of canine sentinel, Bonnie watched intently as the women laid out the contents of Liam's file on Anna's sitting room floor.

'I almost didn't bring it,' Tansy said miserably. 'I've spent half my life trying to keep on the right side of the law. But Liam said letting whoever killed Lili and David Fischer go free is the real crime.'

'You suspect Alice, don't you, Anna?' Isadora said. Anna had told her and Tansy about the shadowy reflection in the mirror.

'I don't know. All we know is that she was at Mortmead Hall that night,' Anna said.

'Creeping about like a Sloaney ninja,' Tansy commented darkly. 'Not suspicious in the least.'

It was past midnight by the time they'd read all the contents of the stolen files and everyone was bleary-eyed. No wonder Liam was frustrated, Anna thought. The police seemed no nearer finding Lili and David's killers. However, the files had yielded a couple of items of interest.

Sipping hot tea, the women discussed their findings. Officers assigned to the Lili Rossetti case had found emails Dominic had supposedly sent to Lili, arranging to meet her at Mortmead Hall. Lili had agreed to bring the painting she'd liberated from Hempels for Dominic to verify, then they would take it to David Fischer.

'But why pick Mortmead Hall as a place to meet Lili?' Isadora said. 'Dominic Scott-Neville inherited a beautiful manor house. What's his connection with that hideous Victorian relic?'

Anna thought she knew. 'Dominic told me he and Ghislaine have just bought a big country house to convert into a women's refuge.'

Isadora's eyes widened. 'You think he bought Mortmead?'

'It still seems a bit cloak-and-dagger,' Tansy objected. 'I mean, why did Lili go to all the trouble of dressing up for the ball? And why go to Mortmead Hall, just when Anjali's people were putting on their big murder mystery weekend? Why not before or after when it was empty? It doesn't make sense.'

'It does if Lili suspected someone was on to her?' Anna suggested. 'Maybe she thought she'd be safer in a crowd.'

Isadora checked Jake's jotter pad, where she'd been making notes in her near-indecipherable hand.

'It was actually Dominic who suggested he and Lili should meet at Mortmead.'

'But he didn't show up,' Tansy said.

Anna shook her head. 'When Dominic phoned he seemed baffled that anyone would consider his exchange of emails with Lili as incriminating. Obviously, he could be lying. He could have sent someone else to Mortmead to kill Lili, but I really don't think he did . . .'

They'd just found one noteworthy item in the police report of the fire at David Fischer's bookshop. Among the ashes, the police had found a partly-melted steel safe. Someone had left the door of the safe open, before the fire took hold.

'Do you think someone knew about David's photos and wanted

to destroy his paper trail for the Vermeer?' Isadora took off her glasses and rubbed her eyes.

'You guys should go home,' Anna said. 'You're both shattered.'

'Not happening,' Tansy said, smothering a yawn. 'We're not leaving you alone tonight, are we, Isadora?'

'Certainly not,' Isadora said crisply. 'The murderer is still out there and recent experience suggests that he or she is utterly ruthless.'

'What happened to "there's always an alternative narrative"? Oh, sorry I forgot,' Anna added with a grin, 'all is forgiven now!' But she couldn't help wondering what had finally convinced Isadora to change her mind. Was it Thomas Kirchmann, the plundered and partly-melted safe, or that shadowy figure in the mirror?

Isadora smilingly shook her head. 'Resign yourself to the world's oldest sleepover club, darling!'

At that moment, Anna felt gratitude beyond words. She finally understood that she could ask these women anything, reveal anything, and they would never think to judge her. She stood up.

'Can I – can I show you something?'

She didn't offer an explanation and nobody asked for one. Tansy and Isadora followed her upstairs into her study and waited expectantly, while she silently unlocked the armoire.

'Oh, if it's *decluttering* you need,' Tansy started.

But by then Anna had thrown open the doors of her cupboard of horrors. For a few moments, the only sound was the three women breathing.

Then Isadora said softly, 'Oh, my darling girl.'

'I don't want this in my life anymore.' Terror dimmed Anna's vision, so that she could scarcely see her friends' faces. She wondered if she was going to die from this ultimate exposure. 'I've tried to get rid of it,' she said, 'but I can't seem to – not on my own. Could you . . .?'

'Oh, yes, yes, of *course*.' Anna felt Isadora briefly squeeze her arm. 'Shall we do it now?'

'If – if it wouldn't be too – horrible for you,' Anna managed.

Outside a police car went wailing up the Banbury Road, the siren gradually fading.

'Now, what's the best way to proceed?' Isadora said in a musing tone. 'I take it you'll want to keep the family photos?'

'Oh, *fantastic*, you've got a shredder!' Tansy exclaimed. 'Put me on shredding duty, Anna. I love shredding. Do you want to Ok everything before it goes in?' She smiled at Anna, her normal mischievous smile, Anna saw, with no trace of pity or disgust.

'I only want my family photos,' Anna said, swallowing. 'Everything else can go.'

Tansy moved purposefully towards the cupboard. '*Wait!*' Isadora said with such authority that Tansy froze in her tracks. 'Don't start shredding until I get back!'

Isadora disappeared downstairs, coming back a few minutes later with a tray bearing three clinking glasses, each with its thin slice of lime, a bottle of Bombay Sapphire and a bottle of Fever-tree tonic. Isadora mixed their drinks with her usual expertise and handed them round.

'To the dismantling!' she announced in ringing tones, as she raised her glass. 'And to the banishing of old ghosts. Ok, darlings, we can start now!' She added in her normal voice.

Only Isadora and Tansy could turn the emptying of a murder cupboard into a party. Isadora began to peel away the intricate criss-crossing strings and tape that held the layers upon layers of yellowing papers in place. At first, Anna stood by, watching as her friends worked; Isadora carefully taking down each item, and adding it to Tansy's growing pile for shredding, except for the photographs, which she laid almost reverently on Anna's desk. After a while, Anna moved to look at them. There they were: Julian and Julia, Dan, Will, and Lottie. Cheeky, alarmingly robust little Lottie.

It was ridiculous to think that her dead family were somehow watching and that Anna was simultaneously liberating them too, by this long-delayed lifting of guilt and old grief. Yet she couldn't shake the feeling that this ritual was for them as much as for her.

When the cupboard was empty at last, they left the doors standing open and Tansy opened the window letting in the mild, rainy breeze.

Anna helped to make up her friends' beds in Tansy's old room, then said goodnight, pretending not to notice Hero curled up on Isadora's pillow. Then she took her laptop into her own room, followed by Bonnie. It occurred to her that she still hadn't heard from Dominic. Hopefully the police had allowed him to go home hours ago and he'd just forgotten to call . . .

Before she settled down to try to sleep, Anna composed a long email to Tim, updating him on recent developments including spotting Alice Jinks's reflection in the mirror.

'Will you be at home tomorrow?' she typed, realized that tomorrow was already almost two hours old and corrected it to Friday. 'If so, can I come and hang out with you and Edie?' She closed her laptop. Minutes later, her phone vibrated.

Why don't I come to you? Anjali's taking Edie to see her parents and I've got a plan that I think you'll like.

Next morning, after Isadora and Tansy had left, Anna went to brush her teeth. How many times, she thought, as she efficiently rinsed and spat, how many times had she passed her study door on her way to bed, on her way downstairs? How many times had she felt that crushing weight emanating from inside? It was only now that she realized, only now that it had gone. Her home felt so light!

She heard someone knocking at the door and ran to answer it. Tim was waiting on the step. Instead of coming in, he showed her a set of hefty old-fashioned keys.

'Look what Anjali forgot to give back.' He gave them an enticing jingle.

Anna stared at him. 'Are those the keys to Mortmead Hall?'

'Anjali found them in her car last night. I'm dropping them off at the agency, but first I thought we could have a little nose around,' he said casually.'

She laughed with surprise. 'You don't seriously think Lili might have left the painting there?'

'Stranger things have happened. All those times we tried to make it through to Narnia ought to count for something!'

She knew he was teasing yet she felt a giddy rush of excitement. 'But the police must have been all over that house?'

'Like they went through those photographs you mean?' Tim said.

Anna wasn't fooled by her brother's super-casual tone. By taking her back to where they'd found Lili's body, Tim was trying to exorcise the shadows that had settled over the murder mystery weekend, reframing it for her as another one of their old childhood adventures.

'I'd say there are two possibilities,' he said. 'If Lili thought she was taking the painting to Dominic the night of the ball, but then he didn't show up and the murderer did, the murderer could have killed her to get the painting. Or—'

'Or Lili realized she was in danger and hid the painting to keep it – and herself – safe?'

'Exactly. So, get your lovely dog and your jacket and let's go!'

Tim's vintage VW Golf was so old that it still had a tape-player. Tim took a tape from its plastic case and slotted it in the machine. He'd stuck a handwritten label on the case: Tim and Anna's Awfully Big Adventure Play List. Anna laughed.

'I know you guys never sleep, but please tell me you weren't up all night compiling this mix tape?'

'I've been compiling it for a while,' he admitted. 'With you for my big sister an adventure always seemed more or less inevitable.'

They sang along raucously to tunes they'd loved when they were young. 'Ce'st la vie' by B*Witched. The Spice Girls' 'Wannabe'. They were still belting out Shaggy's 'Oh, Carolina,' as Tim drove up the weedy expanse of gravel towards the looming, castle-like facade of Mortmead Hall. Anna's high spirits faltered. It didn't help that the weather, which had been sunny, had picked that exact moment to become depressingly overcast.

'Not surprising it took so long to sell,' Tim commented. 'It's hideous. Plus, you can see how damp it is from here. Dominic is going to have to spend a fortune to get it up to code.'

'It didn't feel damp,' Anna said, 'when we were there.'

'That's because Anjali's team brought in massive industrial dehumidifiers and fan heaters at vast expense. It's been raining buckets since then.'

And there had been crowds of people, Anna thought, and costumes and sound effects, and all kinds of theatrical ploys to distract the murder mystery participants from the essential desolation of this house. But, minus the 1940s props and the manufactured excitement, Mortmead Hall seemed to exude an eerie menace. It was something about the upstairs windows, Anna thought, which made her imagine someone looking down on them with malign intent. *Damn you, Charlotte Bronte*, she thought.

Tim looked every bit as uneasy as she felt.

'We don't have to go in,' he said, 'it was probably a stupid idea.'

'It was an excellent idea,' Anna corrected him, unbuckling her seat belt. 'If we do find the painting I shall give you full credit. Plus, we're here now and I'm not letting you chicken out on the doorstep.'

'You always were braver than me,' he said with a grin.

'Ha! Finally, you admit it!'

Leaving Bonnie in the car, with a window cracked open, they crunched up the gravel towards the house. Tim unlocked the door and Anna followed him into the hall. Inside, the house was deafeningly silent. *Dead air*, Anna thought. She could feel it pressing on her eardrums as if someone had shoved her underwater. *Not a helpful image, Anna.*

They began exploring the ground floor. In the vast drawing room the furniture had been covered with white cloths. Tim opened a wall cupboard and felt around inside. They went into the library, the billiard room and the ballroom, which looked especially depressing without its forties glamour. Tim knocked experimentally on one of the walls.

'What are you doing, Watson?' Anna said. 'Checking for secret panels?'

'Does that make you Sherlock?' Tim asked, amused.

'Was that ever in any doubt?'

They walked down the long gloomy corridor to the kitchens, their footsteps unnaturally loud in that odd, bandaged silence. Something creaked, a scarcely perceptible sound and they both spun around but of course there was nobody there.

'This is dumb,' Tim said. 'We're not going to find anything.'

'Probably not,' Anna admitted, 'but we should at least check around upstairs before we go.'

They retraced their steps to the front hall and made their way up the wide oak staircase to the echoing dormitories – with their institutional bathrooms – and the old matron's room, where Anna had slept with her friends. Finally, they went up to the attics, which were also empty, echoed eerily and smelled of damp and dust.

'This house is too big,' Tim said. 'If we knew which parts Lili passed through . . .' His voice tailed off. 'We should probably look up the chimneys at least?' He didn't sound too keen, Anna thought.

She shook her head. 'I somehow can't imagine an art restorer stuffing a precious Vermeer up a sooty chimney.'

'Even if she feared for her life?'

'Even if she feared for her life.'

'I'm going to rename our mix-tape.' Tim sounded comically dejected. 'I shall call it Tim and Anna's Lost Cause. I suggest we take Bonnie for a walk around the grounds, then I'll buy you a nice lunch somewhere to make it up to you.'

'Tim, it could have worked,' she said. 'It's this house. It kills hope!'

'It must have been a seriously creepy school.' Tim shuddered. 'Those poor kids.'

They let themselves out, leaving the oppressive atmosphere behind with mutual relief.

'Before we leave, let's go and find the maze,' Tim told her as they set off with Bonnie trotting at their heels.

'I'd forgotten the maze. Anjali put it in her brochure. It was off limits for the weekend for some reason.'

They were descending the steps passing the koi pond.

'Health and safety,' Tim said with a grin. 'Lots of drunk people running around a maze at night! A catastrophe just waiting to happen.'

Trying not to picture Lili's lifeless body floating amongst the water-plants that shared her name, Anna didn't say that the catastrophe had happened regardless. Tim led her to a solid green wall at least seven feet high formed from densely planted box.

'It's a bit overgrown but Anjali says you can still get through.'

'Get through?' Anna hoped Tim was joking. 'You don't really want us to go into the maze?'

'Yes, I do! I'll race you to the centre. It'll be fun!' Tim had apparently thrown off his disappointment at not finding the Vermeer.

Anna firmly shook her head. 'Have you never watched any horror movies? The worst thing you can do is to split up. It always goes hideously wrong.'

'What can go wrong? I told you Anjali went in with her team and they came out just fine. It's got some bizarre Brothers Grimm folly at the centre. Look, I'll call "Marco", and you call "Polo" and then we can't get lost.'

'Ok,' Anna said resigned. Tim seemed determined that they

were going to have some big sibling bonding experience. She clipped on Bonnie's lead.

'I'll be right back,' Tim told her in a villainous voice and sprinted ahead through the narrow gap between the hedges.

Anna disliked mazes. She'd never seen the fun in deliberately scaring yourself or playing at being lost, but after last night's ritual banishing she felt she should give it a try. The maze turned out to be both larger than she'd thought and more complex.

A couple of minutes elapsed before she heard Tim laughingly calling 'Marco!'

'Polo!' she yelled back, feeling slightly less lonely for hearing his voice.

'Marco!' he yelled again.

'I can't believe you're the father of a child. This is an extremely silly game!' Anna shouted. 'Also, Polo!' she added.

The evergreen bushes gave off a pungent but pleasant smell. The sun came out, turning the overgrown box tunnels a brilliant green. Anna was acquiring painful scratches from pushing in amongst the spiky densely growing twigs. The backs of her hands were covered in dirty green smudges. Bonnie trotted at her side, politely perplexed by this new experience but willing to do whatever her owner required.

Tim didn't say Marco, Anna thought suddenly.

'Marco!' she shouted.

He didn't answer.

She felt a flicker of foreboding. Stupid, because, outside of a Greek myth, what harm could come to someone in a maze?

'Tim, don't mess around!' she warned. '*Tim?*'

No answer.

'*Tim*! This is not funny! I'm going back to the car!'

'Anna. Get out!'

She heard a sharp crack. Birds flew up shrieking their alarm.

'Anna *run!*' Tim's voice was an anguished bellow.

'Oh, God,' Anna whispered. She fumbled for her phone. No reception. She began to run, not back to the car but deeper into the maze, in the direction of Tim's voice.

As she ran it seemed to Anna that she was also running through her own nightmares, flying from room to room in their old house in North Oxford, screaming out their names but always, always arriving too late. The Anna who was in the maze ran faster than she'd have thought possible and Bonnie, her fairy-tale wolf, loyally matched her pace. Old scar tissue on Anna's belly, pain-free for years, started to throb; her body was warning her not to make the same mistakes.

Panting, she pushed and shoved her way between the hedges and abruptly found herself at the centre of the maze, where someone had built a disturbing, Victorian Gothic interpretation of the witch's cottage in Hansel and Gretel. Instead of sweets and gingerbread the folly was made from wood that had rotted and sprouted lurid coloured fungi. It was both desolate and faintly obscene. The hairs along Bonnie's spine were suddenly standing up in stiff bristles. She let out a low feral growl.

'It's Ok,' Anna soothed her, knowing it was anything but Ok.

Bars had been fitted to all the windows. The door, visibly swollen from damp, stood slightly ajar. Anna grasped the doorknob. In her nightmare, she was opening the door of her little sister's bedroom. Inside she'd see Lottie's night-light casting fairy-tale shadows: a castle, a unicorn and a princess, the dim light shining on the little bed. Her little sister's body bloodied and still.

Anna's scar throbbed. Her breath caught. She threw her whole weight against the door. It grated briefly against some unseen obstacle then gave way, so that she almost fell inside. The last residue of her nightmare fled, as she saw Tim slumped against the wall, clutching his shoulder, blood pooling beside him. He frantically shook his head but she rushed to him, dropping to her knees, almost sobbing with relief. She'd got here in time. He was still alive.

The interior of the folly smelled of rot, mushrooms and dank earth. Cobwebs, furry with dirt, hung in filthy swags from the ceiling and the bars of the windows. A slight noise behind her made Anna turn, as she knelt beside her brother.

'You do have the world's *worst* timing, Anna,' Alice Jinks said coolly. She was in fact dressed like a ninja in tight black trousers, short black boots and a black hoodie. In her right hand, she grasped a gun which she was pointing straight at Anna. Under her left arm, she held a cardboard envelope wrapped in plastic. Anna was reluctant to take her eyes off the gun but she was absolutely hypnotised by the envelope. She heard Clara Brunner say: 'You'd think that painting was under a curse.'

Alice was watching Anna's face. 'Since you're here, you've obviously got it all figured out,' she said in a bored voice.

'Some of it,' Anna said. 'Hush,' she told Bonnie who was continuing to growl.

'If that dog moves any closer I'll shoot it,' Alice warned.

'She won't,' Anna promised. 'She was trained by a marine.' She couldn't vouch for what Bonnie would do if Alice tried to harm her, but it seemed smarter to keep this to herself.

'I'd been watching Lili, you see.' Alice sounded almost chatty, as if she and Anna were resuming a normal, friendly conversation. 'That night, I saw her leaving her house all done up like Greta Garbo and she was carrying this identical package. Obviously, I knew where she was going.' She laughed.

'Because you'd been emailing her as Dominic,' Anna said.

Alice gave a little huff of surprise. 'Oh, you figured that out too. You're one step ahead of the police in that case. But when I caught up with Lili by the pond, she didn't have it, so I knew she'd hidden it somewhere in Mortmead Hall. I didn't look in the folly, not then, because it's such a bloody cliché.' Alice looked contemptuous. 'Ralph Scott-Neville had kept it hidden behind his wife's painting of *their* folly for years. Or I assume that was the association? Who knows? Everyone at Hempels thought Lili Rossetti was such a genius, but seriously? I might not have an Oxbridge degree, but I had everyone at Hempels fooled for years!'

Anna stole a look at Tim who seemed on the verge of passing out. 'You certainly fooled me,' she told Alice, faking calm. 'But I don't really see how you can get away with it.'

'Very easily!' Alice seemed suddenly elated. 'The people I work for are world-class fixers. There's a plane standing by, right now, waiting to get me and my little girl out of the country. By this time tomorrow, we'll be starting a new life and Dominic Scott-Neville's golden life will be let's say – less golden!' Her expression was suddenly vicious. 'He never should have told Lili the Vermeer was hidden behind his mother's watercolour.'

'Really?' Anna said. 'You decided to destroy him just because of that?'

'Of *course,* not just because of that!' Alice looked almost offended. 'I'm not that petty.' She shot Anna a sly look. 'You won't know this, but Dominic and I have a lot in common.' She gave a cold little laugh. 'Not *too* much in common hopefully! Though you never know with Ralph.'

Anna took a moment to process this disturbing new information.

'You mean, you and Ralph Scott-Neville were—?' She remembered the photo of two-year-old Poppy and Alice's protests that she looked nothing at all like her father. Poppy didn't look like Ralph, in fact, but she did have a striking resemblance to Dominic.

'Ralph always wanted me,' Alice said flatly. 'He said there had to be something majorly wrong with me, that made him want me so badly when I was still so young.' Knowing Alice would angrily reject her pity, Anna tried hard not to react.

'Is Poppy—?'

'Poppy's one of Ralph's bastard mistakes, to borrow Ralph's charming phrase,' Alice said coolly. 'He's got them all over. It's not like my story is unique or anything.' She gave another chilly little laugh. 'Poppy's the best thing in my life; Ralph Scott-Neville was the worst. I think that's what you call a paradox.'

'You couldn't tell your family?' Anna said. This time Alice's laugh had an edge of hysteria.

'My family? They thought I was the luckiest girl alive! Ralph was like their golden goose. He had it all: money, status etc. They wanted to keep him sweet, in the hope he'd be useful later and kids like me were disposable.' For a moment, Alice seemed to be looking somewhere far away. 'That's never going to happen to Poppy,' she said. 'I'll do anything it takes to keep that little girl safe. Poppy's going to have a *chance* in life. Nothing and nobody's going to get in my way.'

'Including Dominic,' Anna said softly. *And me and Tim.*

'That was a stroke of luck, when Dominic turned up out of the blue,' Alice said. 'Hempels was auctioning Mortmead Hall and Dominic – and his stick insect wife – bought it. Naturally I made copies of the keys.'

Anna noticed her very slightly flexing her shoulders and suspected that Alice's right arm was cramping. It was an unnatural position to hold for so long. Anna was supple thanks to her martial arts, but she could feel her legs starting to seize up as she continued to crouch protectively beside Tim. Her mind was racing. She suspected that she was dealing with at least two Alices: the ambitious super-bright PA she'd met at Hempels and a deeply damaged, young woman, who appeared to be unravelling before her eyes. Reasoning with her didn't seem to be an option. Anna could make a grab for Alice's gun or pull one of her old martial arts moves, maybe knock her out. But, if she screwed-up, if the gun went off in this confined space, Tim could get shot for a second time, possibly fatally. *Or Bonnie*, she thought.

Heavy footsteps outside the folly put a stop to all thoughts of heroics.

A male voice yelled. 'Did you get it, Alice?'

'Of *course*, I got it!' Alice sang out. 'Just tidying up.'

'Yeah, we heard,' said another deeper voice. 'Well, don't take all day.'

The footsteps retreated a little way.

'What was I saying?' Alice asked Anna. 'Oh, yeah, bloody meddling Dominic and Lili! They dropped me right in it! It's lucky I'd installed a hidden camera in my office, or I'd never have known for sure who took the painting.'

'Whatever happened to the "Hempels girls"?' Anna asked her. 'And: "You and I are both in the family business, Anna"?' She wasn't trying to prick Alice's conscience. It was unlikely Alice could afford one, given her upbringing. She just needed to keep Alice talking, anything to delay that ominous 'tidying up'.

'Well, as you can see, our family businesses are rather different!' Alice gave her an amused little smirk. 'Though, once the dementia kicked in, my granddad kind of rewrote the script.' She laughed. 'He ended up thinking he was one of the good guys, even thought he should help David Fischer, bless him! Me, my dad and my uncles let him go right on believing it, when really it was Lionel who inducted me into this life you might say.' She mimicked her grandfather's voice. '"You watch these people, Alice. You watch and you listen and you learn, my girl. But you don't never let them *know* you're watching and learning, right? You learn everything there is to know about the art world, until you're able to beat them at their own game . . ."' Alice seemed to lose her thread. 'Poppy's unusually beautiful, isn't she?' she asked abruptly. Her eyes became soft. 'And sweet, just the sweetest, kindest little kid. Ralph thought Alice was beautiful at first, but there was something badly wrong with her.'

Anna was aware of Tim shifting position.

'Not a good sign when people start referring to themselves in the third person,' he muttered under his breath.

Anna didn't dare take her eyes off Alice.

'I just don't see why you had to kill Lili,' Anna said. 'What did she ever do to you?'

'Haven't you been *listening*?' Alice demanded. 'The outfit I work for, it's *massive*! My dad, my uncles and me we're just their foot soldiers. Our bosses aren't social workers, they're not forgiving. They don't hand out second chances! If you screw up, you pay the price! You and everyone you care about.' Alice stopped, took a shuddering breath, then quickly regained control. 'When Lili helped herself to that painting, she put my little girl in danger. I couldn't let her get away with that.'

'That's why you murdered her?' Alice's almost clinical breakdown of her motives left Anna reeling.

'Too *right* that's why!' Alice sounded infuriated. 'It took us *months* to set this up. Lili could have ruined everything! Luckily, everyone in the business' – she gave Anna a twisted little smile – 'everyone in *our* business, I should say, knows I always deliver. So I was able to buy myself a few weeks' grace. No thanks to Lili!' She added with venom. 'I don't think you have the slightest idea how dangerous the people I work for are.'

Anna remembered Clara Brunner limping out of her house between two expressionless Polizei; the man in the leather jacket watching with cold satisfaction.

'Oh, I think I have,' Anna said. 'You read my email to Herr Kirchmann saying we were going to Innsbruck and your *people* had us followed.'

Alice shrugged. 'What did I tell you? World-class fixers.'

'What about David Fischer?' Anna risked a lightning glance at Tim, who had turned a deathly shade of grey.

'What about him?' Alice said irritably.

'The fire. Was that you?'

Alice smiled. 'Oh, that was down to you. Remember you told me Fischer had compelling evidence in that pathetic little safe? Well, my bosses couldn't have *that* getting into the public domain, could they?'

Anna thought she might be sick. She had led Alice straight to

David. *Don't think about it now,* she told herself fiercely. *Concentrate on saving Tim.*

'It's so funny that you turned up here today,' Alice said conversationally. 'This was the first opportunity I've had to get back to Mortmead, what with waiting for the heat to die down after, you know, Lili, plus waiting for the police to pick up on our trail about Dominic. Not to mention Alexei watching me like a hawk. I knew they were on to me at Hempels, even before they fired me. It's just bad timing, like I said, that you guys happened along on the same morning.'

Anna had a sudden chilling epiphany. 'Your bosses,' she said, struggling to keep her voice even. 'Are they the same people who murdered my—'

Alice's mood darkened again in a flash. 'Oh, for pity's sake!' she almost spat. 'You and your fucking, middle-class problems, seriously! You have no clue, do you? That bloody boohoo story of yours is getting *so* stale! That had absolutely *nothing* to do with my people. Things happen, Anna! Haven't you realized that yet! Totally disgusting things happen every day. People get murdered and nobody knows why. It's a disgusting world. *Life* is disgusting and death is *never* deep and meaningful. Just get over it, why don't you!'

Anna heard returning footsteps.

'You do know time's ticking, don't you?' Someone yelled from outside.

'Almost done!' Alice called cheerfully. Either Alice's thugs were unusually nervous around firearms, or, more likely, they were nervous of Alice.

'Hey, Baz! Hold this for me, will you?' Keeping the gun trained on Anna, Alice passed the package out through the door. She gave a careless glance around the dismal, cob-webbed interior of the folly. 'I was hoping to do those battered wives a favour by burning down the whole of Mortmead Hall. Oh, well, whatever.' She gave an enigmatic shrug and backed out through the door. With some difficulty, Alice managed to force the rain-swollen door to close and then Anna heard the unmistakable sound of a key turning in the lock: *Naturally I made copies.*

Anna dropped Bonnie's lead and rushed to Tim. She tore off

her scarf and made a clumsy attempt to bind his wound. Why had she wasted all those years practising martial arts instead of learning first aid?

'Anna and Tim's awfully big adventure,' Tim tried to joke through white lips. 'Who knew it would be our last!'

'Don't be stupid. I'm not losing you now,' Anna told him fiercely. 'We're getting out of this. Alice could have shot us but, bizarrely, she didn't.' Then she smelled the sharp tang of petrol, followed by the noxious reek of scorching, chemically-treated wood, and belatedly understood Alice's enigmatic farewell: 'Oh, well, whatever.' Denied the drama of setting fire to Mortmead Hall, Alice had opted for the smaller satisfaction of burning down the folly, with Tim and Anna inside.

Anna hammered at the locked door until her knuckles were bloody, then she ran to each of the three windows in turn, tugging at the bars with all her strength, in the futile hope that she might be able to shake or prise them loose. Nothing budged. There was a sudden roar and she jumped back, as blue-green flames came leaping up at the bars.

Bonnie began to bark, an urgent, astonishingly resonant sound that escalated to full-throated, blood-curdling howling and baying, as she hurled herself at the door.

'Bonnie, stop, stop! It's no use!' Sobbing, Anna tried to pull her away, but the White Shepherd frantically redoubled her efforts, repeatedly slamming her entire 80 lbs body weight into the door, as she let out howl after howl. Such heart-breaking courage made Anna want to howl herself, as the rotten petrol-soaked building properly caught fire with a ferocious crackling and spitting. They were trapped and there was nothing they or Bonnie could do.

The inside of the folly was suddenly suffocating and airless. Woolly wisps of smoke came lazily drifting and curling in through the gaps in the badly-fitting windows and walls. Anna and Tim both started to cough. Anna heard an ominous creaking and rending as beams shifted overhead and a piece of glowing red timber came crashing to the ground.

Half-blinded by tears from the smoke, increasingly woozy from the tremendous heat and noxious fumes, Anna crawled to Tim. Wordlessly, they put their arms around each other as if they were children again. Since she couldn't save her brother, Anna desperately tried to think up something silly and jokey to say before they died. *It's supposed to be the wicked witch who ends up in the oven*, she was going to say. *Not Hansel and bloody Gretel.*

But all at once everything seemed too far away. Bonnie's strangely distant howls were joined by sudden yelling and a tremendous noise of crashing and splintering, which Anna groggily decided was a crucial roof beam finally giving way. A pair of strong arms went around her, lifting her up off the floor. She must have mumbled something about her brother because a familiar male voice said, 'we've got Tim, Anna, don't worry.'

Then she blacked out.

Much later – after Tim had been taken to hospital and Anna had been checked over by the paramedics, and given oxygen – Anna and Liam sat in his police car outside Mortmead Hall waiting for Tansy and Isadora to arrive.

Even with all the windows open, Liam's car stank overwhelmingly of bonfires. Anna had caught one horrifying glimpse of her demonic, sooty, red-eyed reflection in the driver's mirror and hastily looked away.

Liam had told her not to try to talk. Talking set her off coughing; her throat and lungs were excruciatingly raw. Anna leaned back against the headrest, her eyes closed, letting the fresh breeze cool her sore eyelids, as Liam calmly passed on all essential information via the ruse of explaining everything soothingly to Bonnie.

'What a clever dog making so much noise! Me and the guys could hear you from the road! I think that merits a big, juicy steak, don't you? I've told Jake to buy one on his way back from the airport, though he might need to give you a bath before you eat it. And thank God, Anna had the good sense to text Tansy to tell her where she was going!'

Anna's dog listened spellbound from the foot-well, her eyes raptly fixed on Liam and her nose resting on Anna's knees. She'd performed her magic trick of folding herself into a space smaller than you'd think possible for 80 lbs of White Shepherd. Like Anna, Bonnie was filthy and reeked of smoke, but the kindly medic, who'd given her a quick once-over, had said she was essentially OK.

Anna abruptly opened her eyes. 'Liam,' she croaked, 'what happened to Alice?'

'Don't trouble yourself about her.' Liam's voice was suddenly steely.

'She confessed,' Anna said. 'Just before she set fire to the folly, she admitted she'd killed David and Lili. But Liam—' she had to stop to cough. 'Alice was just a pawn in all of this. It's the people she's been working for you need to catch.'

He blew out his breath, frustrated. 'Alice's bosses are like the old, robber barons. Virtually untouchable. Protected by the very people who are supposed to be protecting us.' He shook his head. 'But the Alices of this world, the little cogs in the big machine, they're the ones that take the fall.'

Anna heard Alice say: *Kids like me were disposable.*

'I handed in my resignation this morning,' Liam added in an apparent segue. To Anna's surprise he laughed. 'Who knew I'd be going out on such a high?'

'You've caught Alice?'

Liam nodded. 'But it's not just that.' He shot her a boyish grin just as Tansy tapped on the window.

'Anna, oh, God Anna, the *state* of you.' Tansy turned furiously on Liam. 'She should be in *hospital*, Liam Goodhart. What are you *thinking*?'

'She's fine,' Liam said. 'Believe me; she wouldn't want to miss this. Quick, get in the back before my boss gets here.'

Disapproving and obviously puzzled, Isadora and Tansy reluctantly did as he said. The instant they'd closed the car doors Liam took something out of his glove compartment. 'I wanted you girls to see this before it gets whisked off to some high-security vault.'

He didn't sound like someone who'd wrecked his chances of making inspector, Anna noticed. He sounded like an excited little kid on Christmas morning.

Anna felt her heart give a wild flutter as she recognised Alice's cardboard envelope, minus its plastic wrapping.

At first glance, the flat rectangular object that Liam slid out looked like a piece of antique wooden panelling. He turned it over, went to place it in Anna's hands, saw that they were filthy and bloody, and just held it up triumphantly for her and the other women to see.

Tansy instantly craned forward. Isadora put on her glasses, then drew a sharp breath. Anna started to shake. She couldn't believe that she was safe and sound in a police car with Liam and her friends, looking at a forgotten artwork so rare and precious that two people – at least – had been murdered because of it. She and Tim had very nearly been added to the statistics.

Anna had no idea if A Study in Gold was a work of genius, she only knew that, unlike the Vermeer prints in her psych ward, it moved her in some way that she didn't know how to express.

The painting showed an everyday scene from the seventeenth century. The Dutch merchant was in his counting house; his maid sweeping in a doorway. Nothing extraordinary, Anna thought, except that Johannes Vermeer had somehow discovered how to turn paint and pigment into light. Light picked out the furred edges of the merchant's sombre robe, glinted on his orderly piles of gold, silver and copper coins, and found hidden fire in the brass weighing-scales and in the ornamental iron studs on a large, oak chest. The same soft, vivifying light bloomed across the intense, little face of the maid, as she swept the tiled floor.

Quietly, yet irresistibly, the painting drew Anna's eyes from the preoccupied merchant, past the maid sweeping in her faded blue dress, through a painted doorway where they finally came to rest at an open window, where the honey-gold light of a long-ago summer's afternoon came streaming, like a benediction from a vanished world.

EPILOGUE

Midsummer, the following year.

Anna stood in front of the long mirror. She rarely wore dresses and – even though Tansy and Isadora had been with her to help her choose it and gone into raptures as soon as she'd tried it on – she felt oddly naked and vulnerable, under the antique, rose-coloured silk. Her hand went up to touch the perfect blush rose, which Tansy had carefully fastened in her hair. Lottie would have approved of her strapless, bias-cut dress, and she'd have loved the rose. Lottie was always putting flowers in her hair. Anna had a sudden vivid memory of helping her dad lift her soundly sleeping little sister into her bed, still wearing her wilting, daisy crown.

Downstairs in her kitchen, the caterers were chatting quietly to Anjali. Anna could hear Edie's imperious little voice insisting, 'Mama, mama!' A soft buzz of talk came floating in from her garden and the first thrilling sounds of the string quartet tuning up.

Her home was a bustling hive of activity, yet this room felt perfectly still, as if it was holding its breath, as if, for just this moment, Anna stood in her own oasis of peace.

'You look lovely!' Tansy came in, did a graceful twirl, then said anxiously, 'Will I do?'

Anna had already seen Tansy's midi-length dress by Ghost, in what was described as Boudoir Pink, but seeing her now, poised and slender as a dancer, she caught her breath.

'You look so perfect,' Anna said, when she felt able to speak, 'that it makes me want to cry!'

'Don't you dare!' Tansy said sternly, 'or we'll have to redo your makeup!' She fanned herself with her hand. 'Gosh, I'm nervous! Are you nervous? I don't know why I should be nervous, it's not *my* big day! What's that saying? Twice a bridesmaid never a bride? Three times a bridesmaid? And *breathe*, Tansy!' she added laughing.

There was a discreet knock at the bedroom door.

'Are you girls decent?' Anna's grandfather asked.

'Yes, don't worry, Grandpa, it's quite safe to come in!'

'Doesn't Anna look breath-taking!' Tansy said at once.

'You both look exquisite, like two Botticelli nymphs,' he said a little shyly. He held up his tie, dangling loosely from his hand. 'I was wondering, could one of you help me with this? I seem to have lost the knack!'

'Let me,' Tansy said at once. 'You look wonderful in your suit, Mr Ottaway.'

'Thank you,' he told her. 'And your young man scrubs up well,' he added to Anna.

'You've seen Jake in his new suit?' Anna had only seen it on the hanger.

'Yes, I told him he looks very nearly as handsome as me.' Her grandfather gave her a mischievous grin.

'Oh, my God! Look at the time!' Tansy said in dismay. 'I'm supposed to be keeping everyone on schedule.'

'I'll see you out there, darling,' Anna's grandfather told her.

Tansy and Anna hurried next door to Anna's bedroom, where their friend had been closeted for the past twenty minutes.

'Hope she hasn't done a runner,' Tansy hissed. 'She was looking worryingly jittery earlier.'

'I thought she might do a runner last night,' Anna said.

'You and me both!'

In the end, she and Tansy had sat up with their friend, making endless cups of tea and sharing their more scurrilous life stories until first light.

'Keeping vigil,' Isadora had commented with a nervous laugh. 'Like the knights of old.'

Tansy knocked on the closed door and they went in without waiting for an answer.

Isadora had been looking out of the window. She swung around when she heard them come in.

'I look ridiculous!' She glared at them over her half-empty champagne glass. 'Mutton dressed up as lamb!' She plucked agitatedly at her intricately beaded, vintage dress, as if she intended to rip it off.

Anna gently turned her to face the mirror. '*Look*, Isadora. Just look at yourself. You are going to be the most beautiful bride ever.'

Isadora flung up her hand, warding off the sight of her own reflection. 'I'm too *old* to be beautiful!'

'You look stunningly beautiful, also dangerously minxy,' Tansy told her.

Anna shot her an impressed look. Isadora couldn't fail to identify with 'dangerously minxy'. For a moment, Isadora seemed reassured then she let out a despairing wail.

'I don't even know why I'm letting you girls put me through such an archaic and demeaning ritual!'

'I'll *tell* you why, Isadora Salzman,' Tansy said in a threatening voice. 'It's because you and Valentin sneaked off to the registry office without telling us! And me and Anna weren't going to let you cheat us out of a proper wedding!'

Isadora collapsed on to Anna's bed making Anna fear for the fragile little beads on her dress.

'Everything just happened so *fast*! I finally let Valentin wear me down and agree to meet him in London for a drink for old time's sake and, a fortnight later, we're *engaged*.'

'It doesn't matter if it was a fortnight or forty-eight hours,' Anna told her quietly. 'This marriage was decades in the making. You always knew Valentin was the one.'

Isadora suddenly calmed down.

'Yes, I did. You're right. I just – I suppose I'm still in shock. I'd just accepted that I'd have to go through the rest of my life alone. I was happy, perfectly happy, with my little dog and my friends, writing my book. But then I saw Valentin waiting at Paddington station and I felt – I didn't feel like a dizzy teenager again. It was more like . . .'

'Coming home,' Anna said softly.

Isadora's expression was suddenly soft. 'Yes. That's exactly what it was like.'

Tansy clapped her hands. 'Come on, you two! As the official maid of honour, I'm officially telling you guys it's time to get this show on the road!'

'You know, I'd heard of Bridezilla,' Isadora said laughing. 'But no-one warned me of her equally scary sister, Bridesmaidzilla!'

In Anna's garden, Isadora's bridegroom was waiting under a billowing, white canopy, the *chuppah*. Anna saw the woman rabbi – a friend of Isadora's, who had agreed to perform the blessing

– lay a reassuring hand on Valentin's wrist, as though she feared that he too might decide to bolt. If possible, he looked more nervous than Isadora. But as the musicians began to play and he saw his old lover walking smilingly towards him, white gardenias woven into her hair, his face lit up with love and relief.

Anna had seen a faded photo of Isadora's lost love several months before she'd met him in person. But this was an older, wiser Valentin: grizzled yet distinguished, funny, kind and every bit as complicated and passionate as his bride.

The air smelled of sun-warmed roses. Anna felt herself relax as Isadora and Valentin finally came face-to-face under the canopy, which she and Tansy had decorated with roses, delphiniums and gerberas from her garden. The simple ceremony began; the unfamiliar, Hebrew words seemed to pierce right through Anna, rhythmic and compelling as a song. Looking along the rows of guests, she picked out familiar faces: Isadora's few close friends, her son Gabriel, his wife Nicky and her unofficial granddaughter, Sabina, who had Isadora's little dog sitting, surprisingly docilely, on her knee.

Anna's grandfather was seated between Tim and Anjali and Chris and Jane, holding fifteen-month old Edie on his knee. He whispered something to her and the little girl gazed at him, round-eyed. Anna had finally risked telling him about her mother's affair with Tim's father and discovered what she should perhaps have guessed; that he'd suspected all along that Anna was not Julian's child.

'Secrets are *so* stupid!' she'd said. 'And *criminally* time-wasting. Let's promise we won't have any more secrets between us ever!'

Liam caught her eye and winked. He'd left Thames Valley Police a few weeks after arresting Alice Jinks and recovering the stolen Vermeer. After the wedding, he and Tansy were going on holiday to Vietnam, after which they planned to spend several months working their way around the world.

'We've got a lot of adventuring to fit in before we hit thirty,' he'd told Anna.

Jake was sitting at the end of a row. He looked like some aloof, handsome stranger in his Hugo Boss morning suit, until he gave her his sweet here-and-gone again smile and she felt herself irresistibly smiling back. And there, sitting alertly at Jake's feet, was the fairy-tale wolf, who had begun it all. In honour of Isadora's wedding, Jake had given Bonnie a bath and her white coat was almost too dazzling in the sun.

Though Jake was in the process of setting up on his own, as a security consultant; he'd stayed in touch with the ex-soldier who had founded a charity to rescue dogs from war zones and hoped to eventually work for them part time. In a similar spirit, Anna had begun to work as a volunteer for Dominic and Ghislaine's women's refuge, until she finally figured out what she wanted to do. The important thing was that the three of them, Anna, Jake and Bonnie, were together.

The ceremony ended with the rabbi placing the ritual glass, in its blue, cloth wrapping, on the ground, so that Valentin could crush it dramatically under his heel, which he did with great enthusiasm and satisfyingly audible, splintering sounds.

There were cries of 'Mazel tov!' Everybody clapped and cheered.

'May you both always be even happier than you are at this moment!' someone called out.

'Impossible!' Isadora called back, laughing, as Valentin pulled her into his embrace.

They were quickly surrounded by their friends and, for a few moments, Anna could hear the couple being warmly congratulated in several different languages.

But then somehow, as if these were steps in a practiced dance, Anna, Isadora and Tansy found themselves holding each other's hands as everyone else milled around them.

Isadora gazed into her friends' faces with immense affection.

'Thank you, my darling girls, for bullying me into keeping my nerve. This has been the best day, probably, of my whole life.' She lowered her voice. 'And, as you know, I've had *quite* a few best days!'

'Does Valentin know about Mick Jagger?' Tansy whispered.

'Hush!' Isadora gave one of her wicked hoots of laughter. 'I'm a married woman now, remember!'

At that moment, Sabina released Hero, who came rushing towards Isadora, barking excitedly, then Bonnie too came bounding up, but for some reason both dogs stopped before they reached their owners and, it seemed to Anna, exchanged glances as if arriving at some mutual decision.

The three women watched as the, normally impeccably behaved, White Shepherd and Isadora's famously grumpy, little, black dog, took off running, ears and tails flying, pink tongues lolling, racing in exuberant circles round the *chuppah*, between the chairs, to the bottom of the garden and back, and finally looping back around their humans in a mad figure of eight, like the physical embodiment of joy.

ACKNOWLEDGMENTS

With grateful thanks to all at Severn House Publishing for their stellar support and for taking a chance on two rookie mystery writers, to Sarah Florence for her insights into the work of Johannes Vermeer, to Trish Mallett for helping us to imagine our way around Hempels, to Jen Watkiss for local Oxford info, to Jose Wennekes for allowing us to use her name for our fictitious Wennekes Institute, to Andrea Dalton for advice on Innsbruck, especially food and cafes; and an especially big thank you to Andrea's parents, Franz and Franziska Billmeier, for kindly translating a piece of dialogue into German. And finally, thanks to John and Jai for their delicious pumpkin pie!